War is not just full-scale fighting—bullets, bodies and blood. Men and officers are compelled by circumstances to act quickly, almost instinctively, totally disregarding fear, thought or feeling.

War means crawling along muddy roads and ditches on a cold, rainy evening, the din of enemy fire, shells exploding, the knowledge that in several hours, in thirty or forty minutes, a very chancy operation is to start—crossing a wide, swirling river to dark, unfamiliar shores where the enemy is waiting.

War is also learning at the very last moment that the operation has to be called off for lack of means to carry it out. And when that happens, it also means mustering the will to win despite everything, waiting for three whole hours in a raw, murky night to see what will happen, or looking round for ways and means to overcome apparently insuperable setbacks.

That was the way war was in 1944 during

THE BATTLE OF ARNHEM

THE BATTLE OF ARNHEM

BY CORNELIS BAUER

on information supplied by
Lieutenant-Colonel Theodoor A. Boeree

ZEBRA BOOKS

KENSINGTON PUBLISHING CORP.

ZEBRA BOOKS
are published by
KENSINGTON PUBLISHING CORP.
21 East 40th Street
New York, N.Y. 10016

First published in the United States of America by Stein and Day/
  Publishers, 1967

First published in Great Britain by Hodder and Stoughton Ltd,
  1966

Originally published under the title *De Slag by Arnhem* by
  Elsevier, Amsterdam

De Slag By Arnhem Copyright © 1963 by Cornelius Bauer and
  Theordoor A. Boeree

English translation Copyright © 1966 by Hodder and Stoughton
  Ltd.

This edition published by special arrangement with Stein and Day,
  Publishers, Inc.

First Printing: November, 1979
Second Printing: April, 1980

Printed in the United State of America

FOREWORD

by LIEUTENANT-GENERAL SIR BRIAN HORROCKS, K.C.B.

During a visit to Arnhem quite soon after the last War I met Colonel Boeree who lived at Ede right on the doorstep of the Battle. Even then he had made a deep study of the operations carried out by our 1st Airborne Division, north of the Neder Rhine, and since that time he has literally lived and breathed this battle day and night. The result is a book—written by Cornelis Bauer on information he has supplied—which should be of intense interest to all who fought there and of great value to historians of the future. Here for the first time, as far as I know, is the complete story of this controversial operation told by a skilled observer who has spent the intervening years carrying out the most detailed possible research which included obtaining the personal opinions and experiences of many British and German participants.

I am particularly glad the Authors have proved conclusively that the plans for MARKET GARDEN (the code name for this battle) were not disclosed to the Germans beforehand by a Dutch traitor as was widely believed at one time. Luck always plays a big part in war and it was pure chance, not foresight on the part of the Germans, which enabled the II SS Panzer Corps to intervene in the battle so quickly.

It is rather invidious to pick out anyone for special mention when the whole of the 1st British Airborne Division and Polish Parachute Brigade fought so gallantly against overwhelming odds, but the heroes of this battle were unquestionably Colonel Frost and the 2nd Parachute Battalion plus the various small bodies of troops from other units who joined up with him—some 600 to 700 men all told. It was this force which held the north end of the Bridge at Arnhem against ever-increasing German Forces from 8 p.m. on the 17th September until dawn on the 21st September when the few survivors were overrun. They thus imposed considerable delay on the German reinforcements sent by Model to oppose the advance of 30 Corps on the River Waal, because instead of being able to use the bridge, they were forced to cross the Neder Rhine by a very inadequate ferry further to the east. Had these reserves arrived earlier I am very doubtful whether we would have succeeded in crossing the River Waal at all, in which case there would have been no evacuation of the 1st British Airborne Division. So Frost's men did not die in vain.

This book is mainly concerned with the fighting north of the Neder Rhine and does not attempt to explain why 30 Corps did not arrive sooner. It was certainly not for want of trying, I can assure you. I noted at the time 'that there was a desperate urgency about this Battle which I had rarely experienced before or since'. MARKET GARDEN was the most difficult and worrying battle I have ever fought. Firstly because of the rigidity imposed on 30 Corps by its long slender axis reaching back some 60 miles which was constantly being threatened and sometimes cut by fresh German formations, and secondly by the difficulty of advancing in face of increasing German opposition over the low-lying polderland north of Nijmegen (known as the Island) where the roads all ran along the tops of dykes with wide ditches on either side. This type of country was admirably suited to defence because advancing tanks and vehicles were inevitably silhouetted against the sky and thus fell easy victims to enemy defences concealed in the many orchards.

I have thought over this battle many times and now that I have had an opportunity of studying the German side of the picture, I blame myself for a mistake in tactics. When the Guards Armoured Division was held up just north of Nijmegen Bridge, instead of continuing to attack on a more or less direct axis towards Arnhem Bridge, I should have employed 43 Division on a much wider left hook so as to cross the Neder Rhine in the Randwijk area and thus take the German Forces operating against the Airborne Division in their perimeter at Oosterbeck, from the rear. If we had done this I believe that we could have relieved the Airborne Division earlier, but we could never under any circumstances have reached our final

6

objective on the Zuider Zee. We had made the cardinal mistake of under-estimating our enemy—a very dangerous thing to do when fighting the Germans, who are among the best soldiers in the world. Their recovery after the disaster in Normandy was little short of miraculous.

ILLUSTRATIONS

Aerial photograph taken by the RAF on 6 September 1944 [1]
The centre of Arnhem, showing the bridge over the Rhine [2]
British parachutists jumping near Arnhem [1]
Major General R. E. Urquhart [3]
Field artillery and machine-guns near the bridge over the
Waal [1]
Aerial photograph of the Polish landing zone [4]
The outskirts of Arnhem after the battle [4]
A six-pounder in action [1]
Street fighting in Oosterbeek [1]
Fighting in Oosterbeek [1]

KEY TO SOURCES

1 Imperial War Museum
2 KLM
3 Associated Press Ltd
4 Royal Air Force

ACKNOWLEDGMENTS

The authors and publishers are grateful to the following for permission to quote from copyright works: —

Cassell and Co. Ltd. for extracts from *Arnhem* by Maj. Gen. R. E. Urquhart

Wm. Collins Sons and Co. Ltd. for extracts from *A Full Life* by Lt. Gen. Sir Brian Horrocks

Curtis Brown Ltd. for extracts from *The Red Beret* by Hilary St. George Saunders

Maj. Gen. H. Essame for extracts from his *The 43rd Wessex Division at War 1944–1945*

Her Majesty's Stationery Office for extracts from *By Air to Battle: the Official Account of the British First and Sixth Airborne Divisions*

The author and the Macmillan Company of Canada Ltd. for extracts from *Escape from Arnhem* by Leo Heaps

The Commanding Officer of the Parachute Regiment for extracts from *The History of the 2nd Battalion the Parachute Regiment*

8

CONTENTS

MAPS

PREFACE

When a war is over, the fact-gatherers appear. They study their own and enemy reports, orders and returns. They are sometimes able to interrogate prisoners of war. They visit the battle-fields when silence has returned and the sun is shining. And finally all the cards in the game lie face upwards before them. Then they will discover that incorrect decisions were made, that there were failures to take timely advantage of the enemy's mistakes. Acrimonious criticism may follow. But the critic, sitting at his desk after a good night's rest and with a full stomach, may be inclined to forget something. There is a chance that, with his reports, photographs and ordnance maps before him, he may overlook the conditions in which the battle was fought. He may perhaps forget that the officers directing operations, often after days of hunger and thirst and exhausted by sleepless nights, did their staff-work in a barn, by the flickering light of a candle, and bent over a map that was possibly years out of date; that their communications often broke down, so that they had only a very vague idea of the situation on their own side and knew next to nothing of the enemy. Nevertheless, they had to take decisions and give their troops orders because any order is usually better than none, because the absence of orders leads so easily to chaos and panic.

This book is written in full awareness of these things. If a critical tone occasionally creeps in, it is due to a knowledge of facts which could not have been available to the commanders concerned in the battle of Arnhem and which only many years of painstaking post-war research work have assembled. Of great importance in this research was the assistance of British and American authorities concerned with military history, and of individual Allied soldiers, from commanders to privates, who themselves took part in the battle. Information from Dutch sources—Resistance groups and civilians—formed a valuable, even indispensable, supplement. The fact that the German commanders, too, were prepared to allow their documents, reports and personal recollections to be used, created the very rare opportunity to illuminate the great and daring airborne operation at Arnhem from both sides. This extensive co-operation, without which our book could never have been completed, also offered a unique opportunity finally to disprove a number of myths which grew up round the Arnhem fighting after the war — particularly the betrayal myth.

That is why this account differs to some extent from many books, some of them excellent, which have already been devoted to the battle of Arnhem. Previously published accounts have frequently examined the battle from the point of view of personal experience; in many cases considerable stress is placed on the later phase of the operation, the fighting at Oosterbeek. In the present work the details of the heroic struggle have been deliberately less accentuated, in order to give the clearest possible picture of the developments between 17 and 26 September 1944 which led to the failure of the operations on the north bank of the Rhine. For the same reason the names of Allied soldiers and their units, and also of individual members and groups in the Dutch Resistance movement, have sometimes been omitted. They could undoubtedly be cited with honour and deep respect but mention of their names might confuse the reader and make him lose sight of the main thread of events. It is also to prevent this that summaries are occasionally given of events previously told in more detail. What is offered here is thus an overall picture, which may perhaps be of military value (because the Allied airborne operations in 1944 were the first on a large scale to give war a new dimension — 'vertical warfare'); which attempts with the aid of documents to refute the myth that Arnhem was lost as a result of betrayal; and which depicts an event occupying a special place in the five-year history of the occupation of the Netherlands.

Lieutenant-Colonel Theodoor A. Boeree (Rtd)
Cornelis Bauer

CHAPTER ONE

FROM NORMANDY TO NEERPELT

(6 June – 10 September 1944)

I

Towards evening on 10 September 1944 units of the British Guards Armoured Division, after hard fighting, reached a bridge over the Maas-Scheldt Canal in the north of Belgium. This was the bridge at Neerpelt, on the way from Hechtel in Belgium to Valkenswaard in Holland. It was five years, to within a week, since the Second World War had broken out, just over four since Hitler's western campaign had forced the British into their boats at Dunkirk. But they had come back. Hitler's blitzkrieg had been more than adequately compensated for by the Allies' equally speedy advance. And now, late on that September afternoon, the spearhead of the advancing army of liberation was several miles from the Dutch frontier. For over four years occupied Holland had awaited this moment. Now it had come. The Guards' tanks had reached the last water barrier separating Belgium from Holland. The Germans occupying the bridge tried to get another 88 mm gun across from the southern to the northern end but were foiled by a British tank. Then came the attack: four British tanks followed by infantry. Two tanks were hit; the other two reached the bridge. The German guns at the northern end, six 88 mms, fell into British hands. A lieutenant of the Royal Engineers made the demolition charge safe. That same afternoon the German NCO in charge had said to his men: 'Those explosives must and shall be used to blow up the bridge; every man will fight to his last round.' But, as it turned out later, the Germans had not expected the British tanks so soon. They were counting on the arrival of their own tanks. And that mistaken idea had left them uncertain. They fled without exploding the charge they had placed. Now the bridge was in British hands. Beyond it lay the road to Valkenswaard, Eindhoven and the heart of occupied Holland. A few tanks manned by Guards had broken through the barrier.

But the Allied campaign was concerned with more than just liberating the Netherlands; Hitler's Third Reich had to be defeated. For General Eisenhower, Supreme Commander of the Allied invasion forces, for Field-Marshal Montgomery, commanding the 21st Army Group advancing northwards, and for General Dempsey, commanding the British Second Army that formed part of that group, the capture of the bridge at Neerpelt did not necessarily mean more than a tactical success on the road leading eventually to Berlin.

Nevertheless, the crossing of the Maas-Scheldt Canal, which for much of its length from Antwerp to Maastricht runs roughly parallel to the Belgian-Dutch border, was to prove more than an incidental success. The Guards' tanks which trundled over the bridge towards the fall of evening on that 10 September thereby created a starting-off point for an operation which would, it was hoped, put an end before the onset of winter to the struggle in the west and perhaps to the entire war. On that same day, only a few hours earlier, Montgomery had discussed the plan for that operation with Eisenhower. The meeting between the British field-marshal and his commander, the American general, had taken place at the airfield of recently liberated Brussels. Eisenhower had come in his personal aircraft from Normandy, where he had his headquarters at Granville. He had injured his knee shortly before in a forced landing and he had difficulty in walking. His conversation with Montgomery at Brussels was therefore conducted in his aircraft. It was a heated talk, in which Eisenhower felt obliged to reprove Montgomery for his acrimonious tone. Yet when Montgomery left the aeroplane he had secured Eisenhower's permission to carry out the plan—a concentrated thrust to the north, across the canals and rivers of Holland to the Zuider Zee, thus cutting off all German troops in the west of Holland, and an outflanking movement to the east round the north end of the Siegfried Line, thus setting up a direct threat to Hitler's armoury, the Ruhr. That, at any rate, was how Eisenhower envisaged the scope of Montgomery's plan. Montgomery himself was looking further ahead; for him the crossing of the Maas, the Waal and the Neder Rijn or even the occupation of the Ruhr did not constitute the final aim of the attack. Montgomery intended his offensive to be the final and decisive thrust at the heart of Germany. Eisenhower, on the other hand, saw the plan as part of an attack delivered along the entire width of the front, from the Swiss frontier to far in the north. Here, once more, was revealed the great contrast, so much discussed since then, between the two great leaders' views. On the one hand, Montgomery's speedy dagger-thrust towards the heart of a harassed and exhausted enemy, a thrust to be supported by the Allies' entire power; on the other, Eisenhower's steam-roller, which, perhaps less audaciously but possibly also at less risk, would push the enemy back along the entire front and crush him.

However ideas about the final phase of the war might differ, this was the point that had been reached only a few months after the Allied invasion had landed on the coast of Normandy. From 6 June until late July there were no spectacular advances. Then the German cordon round the Allied bridgehead was pierced, and Patton's tanks streamed through the breach. Hitler, who as Supreme Commander saw to it that his own military madness prevailed against the sober wisdom of many of his generals, tried to close the breach with a counter-attack. In doing so he gambled away a large part of the German Seventh Army and the Fifth Panzer Army at Falaise. What escaped from the threatened encirclement there scarcely deserved the name of an organised army. Within a few days even the word retreat could scarcely be applied to the chaotic flight of the German troops. The Seine, Paris, Amiens, the Belgian frontier—against practically no resistance the Americans and British raced to the east and north. The American Third and First Armies to the Vosges, the Saar, the Ardennes, and, in a northerly direction, Namur; the British Second Army to Brussels and Antwerp; the Canadian First Army, though advancing more slowly, past the still stubbornly defended Channel ports. The tanks covered dozens and dozens of miles every day; they were unstoppable. Verdun fell, Namur, Brussels, Antwerp.

The tidal wave rolling to the north had cleared a channel between the German armies. To the west of this flood-stream, along the Channel coast and the coast of Belgium the German Fifteenth Army under Von Zangen was stranded; to the east, Hausser's Seventh Army was falling back under the violence of the assault.

Between them there was nothing left, nothing that could with any chance of success be thrown up as a dam to stem the Allied flood. At the beginning of September Dempsey's Second Army found a channel clear of any appreciable obstacles in the form of German troops, a channel running from North Belgium to the Zuider Zee, to the vulnerable north-west flank of Germany itself. German civilians were already fleeing with their families to the east, urged on by *Reichskommissar* Seyss-Inquart. Dutch Nazis joined on. On Monday, 4 September, British tanks pushed through to the docks at Antwerp. In Holland the almost-panic flight reached its climax on 5 September. That day will go down, at least in Dutch history, by the very appropriate name of Mad Tuesday. Trains heading for Germany were crammed to their utmost capacity. The roads that led to the border were crowded with disordered streams of German civilians, Dutch Nazis, war profiteers and soldiers, the latter mainly ancillary troops who did not form part of the fighting forces. Even at night the movement continued— wretched convoys of overladen wood-burning cars, horses and carts hastily confiscated from the civilian population, push-carts carrying furniture and luggage. The cars sometimes drove with undimmed headlamps, and searchlights were set up at crossroads: fear of the onrushing Allied tide was greater at that moment than the fear of Allied fighter aircraft. But the chief fear was that the Dutch nation would rise. More than capture by the British, those who were now fleeing eastwards dreaded the possible revenge of a nation they had oppressed for four years, and who now had a chance to settle old scores. Both *Reichskommissar* Seyss-Inquart and *Höherer SS-und Polizeiführer* Rauter were convinced that the Dutch would revolt now the chance had come. After the war, when Rauter, then a prisoner in Holland, was questioned for the purpose of the present work, he stated that he could not understand the failure of the Dutch population to rise. A native of the Austrian province of Styria, he added: 'We Styrians would have!'

In the last two or three weeks of August 1944 and the first few days of September it certainly looked as if Germany had lost the struggle in the west for good and all. Sir Alan Brooke, Chief of the Imperial General Staff, wrote in August to General Wilson, the Allied Supreme Commander in the Middle East. In his letter he stated that the Germans were beaten on all fronts and that it was merely a question of how many weeks the enemy could continue to resist in these conditions: 'In any case I consider him incapable of holding out for another winter.' Sir Alan probably based this opinion partly on reports reaching him in London from the Continent. The chief Intelligence officer (G2) at SHAEF compiled a weekly Intelligence summary. The summary of 26 August said: 'The August battles have done it and the enemy in the West has had it. Two and a half months of bitter fighting have brought the end of the war in Europe within sight, almost within reach.' According to the report of a week later Allied Intelligence considered the German strategic situation such that no recovery was now possible. It concluded by expressing the opinion that 'organised resistance under the control of the German High Command is unlikely to continue beyond 1 December 1944'.

Although this cheerful view seemed fully justified by circumstances, some Allied officers were less confident of a speedy end to the campaign in the west. At a press conference on 20 August Eisenhower warned against premature optimism. The rapidity of the advance, he said, had stretched the Allied supply lines to such an extent that a continuation of large-scale offensives had become practically impossible, however weak the enemy resistance.

The intelligence officer of Patton's Third Army—which was advancing in the east to the Franco-German border—was also less optimistic than his counterpart at SHAEF or even his own commander Patton, who at that moment was expecting to be able to cross the German frontier within ten days. On 28 August Patton's G2 declared that the enemy, despite all his losses, was still able to form a sufficiently cohesive front and bring fresh units from Germany into the struggle: 'It must be constantly kept in mind that fundamentally the enemy is playing for time. Weather will soon be one of his most potent allies.' But these pronouncements were made at a time when the Allied armies were still not, or hardly, over the Seine. A few weeks later Verdun was in Allied hands. And Antwerp. Despite the warning voices, an advance of hundreds of miles in several days.

On the evening of 4 September, the day on which Antwerp was liberated by the British, Montgomery telegraphed Eisenhower his plan for a last decisive thrust at the heart of the German Reich. But the Field-Marshal, too, saw the disadvantage of long, vulnerable supply lines along which thousands of tons of food, ammunition, petrol and all the other things a modern army needs would have to be transported daily. So it was necessary, Montgomery argued, to stake everything on a single card, a British advance in the north. Supplies to the rest of the wide front should be cut to the minimum needed to maintain the positions already reached. Montgomery pressed for a quick decision.

Eisenhower's reply did not reach Montgomery until the morning of 7 September—yet another proof of the disadvantage of imperfect means of long-distance communication. Eisenhower's headquarters in Normandy were several hundred miles from the front. Telephone contact with Montgomery's headquarters at Brussels was impossible and radio communication equally so. And when the Allied supreme commander's reply arrived finally, it did not contain approval of Montgomery's plan. While granting the northern attack priority, Eisenhower did not consider the supply facilities, even if subordinated entirely to the advance of the British, such as to guarantee the success of a thrust to Berlin. A continuation of the offensive in a northerly direction was seen by Eisenhower as an important element in the establishment of a wide front along the entire German border. Only when this front was a fact, and only when conquest of the Scheldt estuary, and access to the port of Antwerp, gave greater assurance of rapid supply of that front (on Hitler's orders most of the French ports were still being fiercely defended by their isolated German garrisons), would the great decisive attack on Germany itself be started. This difference of views between Eisenhower and Montgomery as to when and how the *coup de grâce* should be delivered, continued to exist—even when Eisenhower flew to Brussels on 10 September to discuss the matter personally with Montgomery. But despite the gulf between their respective strategic conceptions, Montgomery was given permission to drive on to the north, over the great rivers of Holland.

To the north: to Eindhoven and Nijmegen.

And to Arnhem.

III

On that 10 September not even a week had passed since the capture of Antwerp. Yet in those few days a number of events had taken place on both sides of the front which were destined to contribute in greater or smaller measure to the final result of Montgomery's plan, now known officially by the code name MARKET GARDEN. Some of these events were important, some seemed insignificant. There were coincidences and human miscalculations. It was as if fate was selecting the cards that were to be played during the next few weeks in the course of the grim game, Operation MARKET GARDEN. The result of that game was perhaps largely to determine the subsequent duration of the war, just as it was almost certainly responsible for a winter of famine and misery in western Holland. But only examination of the cards will enable us to reconstruct the game—to venture a conclusion as to the rôle played by chance and the extent to which calculations were miscalculations.

On 4 September the tanks of the British 11th Armoured Division occupied the port of Antwerp. This tank division was part of XXX Corps, which was under the command of Lieutenant-General Sir Brian Horrocks and formed the spearhead of the British Second Army. On 3 September Horrocks had instructed the commander of the 11th Armoured Division to drive straight on to the docks and prevent the Germans from destroying the valuable harbour installations. The order was promptly carried out but—wrote Horrocks after the war—'I realise now that it was a serious mistake. My excuse is that my eyes were fixed entirely on the Rhine, and everything else seemed of subsidiary importance. It never entered my head that the Scheldt would be mined, and that we should not be able to use the port of Antwerp until the channel had been swept and the Germans cleared from the coastline on either side. Nor did I realise that the Germans would be able to evacuate a large number of the troops trapped in the coastal areas across the mouth of the Scheldt estuary from Breskens to Flushing.' Napoleon would no doubt have realised these things but Horrocks didn't. His mind was fixed on the Rhine. 'I am not suggesting that with one armoured division I could have cleared both banks of the Scheldt estuary, but I believe that I could have seriously impeded, if not stopped altogether, the evacuation of the German Fifteenth Army. As it was, the German General Schwabe succeeded in evacuating some 65,000 men belonging to eight shattered German divisions, using this route.

'If I had ordered Roberts [the Commander of the 11th Armoured Division] not to liberate Antwerp, but to by-pass the town on the east, cross the Albert Canal and advance only fifteen miles North-West towards Woensdrecht, we should have blocked the Beveland isthmus and cut the main German escape route.'

Horrocks subsequently had every reason to regret not having seen what Napoleon would undoubtedly have seen, for several weeks after this missed opportunity, when he and his xxx Corps were playing an important part in Operation MARKET GARDEN, he was to find units of the Fifteenth Army which had been evacuated across the Scheldt, among the enemy troops on his western flank. Yet another opportunity was missed on that 4 September, namely to ensure that the port of Antwerp would be put quickly into use. And Antwerp was a port which could have considerably eased the strain on the supply lines, stretching hundreds of miles from the Normandy invasion beaches to the fronts in the east of France and north of Belgium, and replaced them by shorter lines. Merely by opening up one port it would have been possible to guarantee the transport of the thousands of tons of supplies that an advancing army needs daily in order to continue advancing. Supplies—the word recurs again and again.

The Allied invasion force was comparable in one respect to a gigantic business employing over a million people. The entire factory, highly mechanised, was installed in extremely unfavourable conditions on the Continent after the invasion. It was given no time to get under way but had to start production immediately. It was expanded hour by hour with men and material from England. It also changed its site daily but the new site was never known with certainty in advance—it depended on the fortune of war. The problems involved in keeping a factory of that kind operating are almost impossible to see in their entirety. The solution of these problems for the Americans was the task of a separate organisation: *Communications Zone.* An extensive plan had, of course, been drawn up to keep the advancing armies sufficiently well supplied. But reality had rendered all calculations worthless. According to the schedule of Communications Zone, not more than twelve American divisions would have to be supplied on the Seine on D plus 90 (ninety days after the start of the invasion). Not until D plus 120 was it expected to be necessary to supply these divisions for the first offensives across the Seine. Things turned out differently. On D plus 90 sixteen divisions 150 miles beyond the Seine had to be supplied. Paris, which alone required thousands of tons of supplies daily, was liberated fifty-five days earlier than expected. By 12 September (D plus 90) the Allies had reached a position originally planned for D plus 270. Supplies were therefore bound to be seriously endangered. A shortage of transport vehicles developed. New divisions freshly arrived from England were kept twiddling their thumbs in France because all their transport had been taken from them to keep the troops at the front supplied with their day-to-day necessities. The roads leading from Normandy to the front were chock-full. Miles-long traffic jams caused considerable delays. Truck-drivers and liaison officers lost their way on these long routes through a country whose language they usually could not speak. It was impossible to respond with sufficient speed to urgent special requests from commanders in the front line, eg for ammunition of a particular calibre. The British supply line was in a better state but very stretched.

Horrocks suffered the consequences of this situation when his xxx Corps had liberated Antwerp. The corps was ordered to halt its advance. After covering a distance of 250 miles in six days they came to a standstill at a time when, as Rauter was to say after the war, the road to the north lay open. Horrocks himself wrote: 'As we now know, on 4 September, the only troops available to bar our passage north-westwards consisted of one German division, the 719th, composed mainly of elderly gentlemen who hitherto had been guarding the north coast of Holland and had never heard a shot fired in anger, plus one battalion of Dutch SS and a few Luftwaffe detachments. This meagre force was strung out on a fifty-mile front along the canal . . . I believe that if we had taken the chance and carried straight on with our advance instead of halting in Brussels the whole course of the war in Europe might have been changed. On 3 September we had still 100 miles of petrol per vehicle, and one further day's supply within reach . . . But there would have been a considerable risk in advancing further north with only these supplies and a lengthening line of communication behind us.'

To both Rauter's hindsight and Horrocks' can be applied what the latter says about his own views: 'It is easy to be wise after the event.' But, at the same time, few things are more instructive than 'post-mortems'. That, then, was the Allied balance-sheet after three months' struggle in the west. Their armies occupied positions which they had not been expected to reach until six months later. But almost all the French and Belgian ports were still in German hands. Supplies had to be brought up from improvised harbours on the invasion coasts of distant Normandy. The lines of communication were too long and too intricate to keep the entire Allied machinery turning—it threatened to come to a standstill. Just at a time when, at least in the opinion of some, Germany was ripe for the *coup de grâce*. A time which might be short, very short. Montgomery realised that a crucial stage had been reached, when a decision had to be made on his long-held theory that the entire power of the Allied military machine should be put into a single offensive. It was now or never; the chance might vanish any moment. Consultation took time and was further delayed by the faulty communications between Eisenhower's headquarters and Montgomery's. Days passed. On 10 September Eisenhower gave his assent to a version of Montgomery's plan, shorn, however, of its most ambitious aims:

the capture of Berlin and the end of the war. Leaving aside the question whether those aims could ever have been achieved, the chances of achieving even the immediate aim, a bridgehead beyond the Neder Rijn as a jumping-off point for an offensive against the Ruhr, were considerably less favourable on 10 September than one week before. Through a variety of circumstances the enemy had obtained one of the few things that could still save him: time. As we conduct our post-mortem, and examine the game the enemy played, we can see what deliberate counter-measures he took in the time that was granted him—and what apparently unimportant accidents turned to trumps in his hand.

IV

After the defeats in France the remnants of the German armies had fled before the onslaught of the Allied armies. In the west von Zangen's Fifteenth Army was caught between the North Sea on one side and the advancing British Second Army on the other. The German Seventh Army, which had fought under *General der Waffen-SS* Paul Hausser in Normandy and emerged decimated from their encirclement at Falaise, was washed like flotsam to the north-east and north, towards the Ardennes and Maastricht. What German tanks survived could—in the words of General Blumentritt, Chief of Staff to the German Commander-in-Chief West—no longer be counted in divisions. According to Blumentritt, no more than 100–120 out of 2,300 German tanks had returned across the Seine. But meanwhile Hitler had called in one of his most competent commanders: Field-Marshal Walter Model, one of the few soldiers who dared stand up to him. An ambitious and dedicated man who did not belong to the military caste but had worked his way up from infantry officer to the top rank of field-marshal by the early age of fifty-four. He was among the first to send congratulations to Hitler after the unsuccessful attempt on his life on 22 July 1944. In that same month he had brought the Russian advance on Warsaw to a standstill. Hitler called him 'the saviour of the eastern front'. On 17 August he took over command in the west from Kluge, who was suspected by Hitler, in all probability wrongly, of wishing to negotiate surrender terms with the Allies. As Commander-in-Chief in the west Model was also given command of Army Group B, the more northern of the two German army groups in the west. Since Rommel had been wounded in France about the middle of July, no successor to him as commander of Army Group B had been appointed and leadership had been temporarily assumed by the Commander-in-Chief West. Model was replaced in the latter function on 4 September by Rundstedt (who had already held the post) but retained command of Army Group B; to him fell the task of halting the Allied advance.

The situation was most critical in the north. The tanks of Horrocks' XXX Corps had covered hundreds of miles in a week. They were nearing Brussels and Antwerp. Between Antwerp and Maastricht yawned an undefended gap of nearly sixty miles across. Nothing, it appeared, could halt the British tanks in their advance. At all costs, however, Model had somehow to close that gap: any further loss of ground to the north would isolate von Zangen's Fifteenth Army in the west of Holland and also the V-bomb launching sites there, while in the east an Allied outflanking movement round the Siegfried Line and across the Rhine would constitute a fatal threat to the Ruhr and to the whole of Germany. The only division that Model had to hand at that moment was the 719th under the command of *Generalleutnant* Karl Sievers. It was also the sole remaining division of LXXXVIII Corps of *General der Infanterie* Hans Reinhard, who commanded the German Army in Holland from July 1942 to September 1944. Sievers had been stationed with the 719th Division on the Dutch coast since 1940 and during all those years his troops had never fired a shot. The division, which had been made mobile just two weeks before with horses requisitioned from the civil population, had been strengthened by the incorporation of some Luftwaffe ground staff and a battalion of Dutch SS, although the morale of the latter was not such as to contribute noticeably to the fighting strength of the division. By the time the battalion finally joined Sievers' troops no fewer than seventy men had deserted. Model instructed Reinhard to send Sievers and his troops to the Albert Canal—which runs from Antwerp via Hasselt to Maastricht—but he can scarcely have imagined that by doing so he had sealed the entire gap.

Horrocks' tanks entered Antwerp on 4 September. On that and the following day Sievers' troops arrived at the Albert Canal. Since it was not possible to defend the entire line to Maastricht with this one division, they occupied a front from Antwerp to Hasselt. Sievers placed his main force opposite Antwerp because he expected the British attack to be continued there. A logical conclusion, as Horrocks himself admits in his memoirs where he discusses his failure to realise the need to push on to Woensdrecht in order to cut off the isthmus of South Beveland and make evacuation of the German Fifteenth Army impossible. Napoleon would not have been unique in realising this, for it had obviously not escaped Sievers either. The weakness of Model's opposition to the British force was almost ludicrous. But Horrocks did not know that at the time, while Model, for his part, did not know the critical supply situation of the Allied spearheads.

On 4 September Sievers' troops began to dig themselves in on the north bank of the Albert Canal, and also on 4 September Horrocks' advance south of that canal came practically to a standstill.

The position of the Germans seemed untenable. The eastern sector of the front would collapse under the slightest Allied pressure. But Sievers got help from an unexpected quarter, *General-leutnant* Kurt Chill had suffered heavy losses with his 85th Division in France and like so many other commanders he retreated northwards with the remnants of his division, picking up scattered units of the 84th and 89th Divisions on the way. When he arrived at Turnhout in the north of Belgium on 4 September, he received orders from the German Seventh Army to take his troops to the Rhineland for rest and reinforcement. At the same time, however, news reached him that Brussels had fallen. He then decided not to carry out his orders. On his own responsibility he disposed his troops along the northern bank of the Albert Canal, occupying the stretch between Massenhoven and Kwaadmechelen. At the bridges to the east and west of Herentals he set up reception centres for small groups of German soldiers fleeing to the north; by the evening he had collected a veritable patchwork army of Wehrmacht troops, Luftwaffe ground staff, administrative troops and men from coastal defence units. A hotchpotch which the energetic

Chill ('He must have been a man of great initiative', said Horrocks) managed within several hours to weld together into a more or less cohesive whole. These units, too, he disposed along the canal. On the next day, 5 September, he got in touch with General Sievers. They arranged that Chill would defend the eastern half of the canal while Sievers would be responsible for the section from Herentals to Antwerp. On 6 September Chill placed himself at the orders of General Reinhard who confirmed the arrangements and also attached a regiment of Sievers' 719th Division to Chill, to the collection of odds and ends which came to be known as *Kampfgruppe* Chill: his own 85th Division, units of the 84th and 89th, and the catch from the reception centres.

There was yet another respect in which 4 September proved to be an important date. On that day, when the German Supreme Command to their great concern observed a wide and apparently irreparable breach in the north, Goering—who was head of the Luftwaffe—surprised the German General Staff with the announcement that he had a number of parachute battalions under training and that to these he could add a group of 10,000 men made up of aircrews and ground staff whom a shortage of petrol had left unemployed. That same afternoon *Generaloberst* Kurt Student in Berlin received orders by telephone from Hitler's headquarters to form the First Parachute Army. Student, who was in command of all German paratroop formations, had led the German air landings at Rotterdam in 1940 and the invasion of Crete in 1941. With his new parachute army, the core of which was formed by the 30,000 men Goering had been keeping in reserve, Student had to try to seal the gap in the north by establishing a defence line between Antwerp and Maastricht north of the Albert Canal, ie the line which was provisionally being held by Sievers and Chill.

On 7 September the German 176th Division under Colonel Christian Landau was transferred from the Siegfried Line near Aachen to the Albert Canal and placed under Student's orders. Landau occupied the section from Hasselt to Maastricht, so that an uninterrupted line, if not a very strong one, was held from Antwerp to Maastricht: Sievers' 719th Division from Antwerp to Herentals, *Kampfgruppe* Chill from Herentals to Hasselt, and

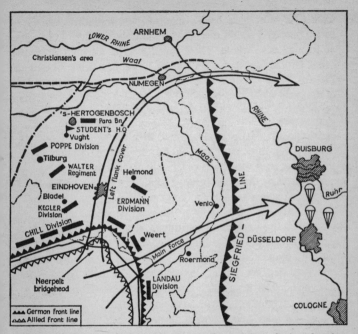

MAP I The mistaken German forecast. The German Army leaders thought that the Allies would advance from the Neerpelt bridgehead to the Ruhr by two routes: the main force via Roermond, straight on through the Siegfried Line to Düsseldorf where paratroops would be dropped 'at an as yet indefinite date', and a covering movement via Eindhoven and Nijmegen. The map shows the location of the units which had been placed under the command of General Student (Commander of the eastern sector of Model's operational area).

Landau's 176th Division from Hasselt to Maastricht (see map 1).

Meanwhile the regiments of the new German parachute army were arriving in North Brabant. Student was also given command of all garrison troops and training units of the Army and Luftwaffe in his operational area, as well as over twenty anti-aircraft batteries belonging to the German home defence forces. At the same time von Zangen was busy evacuating his Fifteenth Army across the Scheldt from Dutch Flanders to Walcheren and South Beveland. Two badly-battered and poorly-armed divisions of the troops who thus became available appeared in Brabant on 16 and 17 September: the 245th under Colonel Gerhard Kegler and the 59th under *Generalleutnant* Walter Poppe. During the weeks in which the Germans were taking measures to seal the breach in the north, a change came over the situation along the Albert Canal. After two days' standstill Horrocks had been ordered to advance with xxx Corps. General Dempsey, commander of the British Second Army of which xxx Corps was part, wished at any rate to have a bridgehead across the last two water barriers in Belgium (the Albert Canal and the Maas-Scheldt Canal) as a springboard for a new offensive. But these days' rest had lost the British a golden opportunity. The road which was practically open on 4 September was now blocked by the *Kampfgruppe* Chill. The British established a bridgehead across the Albert Canal at Beringen, but the country beyond lent itself admirably to defence. Student, realising the danger that this bridgehead constituted, sent some of his parachute regiments, now arriving at Eindhoven, straight on to the canal with orders to liquidate the bridgehead. These troops included the 6th Parachute Regiment under *Oberstleutnant* Friedrich-August Freiherr von der Heydte, a unit of hardened veterans who far surpassed a normal parachute regiment in fighting strength.

The German troops proved unable to halt the tanks of the Guards Armoured Division, who advanced slowly north of the Albert Canal. But the Germans won time. For whereas the British xxx Corps had covered a distance of 250 miles in the six days up to 4 September, the fifteen miles from the Albert Canal to the Maas-Scheldt Canal cost four days of bitter fighting. On 10 September they captured the bridge across the Mass-Scheldt Canal at Neerpelt. In the next few days the territory north of the Albert Canal was more or less cleared of German troops from another bridgehead at Geel, so that about 17 September the front ran roughly along the Maas-Scheldt Canal from Antwerp to Maastricht, with an Allied bridgehead at Neerpelt.

In his war diary, Model, who had set up his headquarters at Oosterbeek near Arnhem, states that his army commanders were informed at 8 pm on 16 September of the demarcation lines between their operational areas. *General der Flieger* Christiansen, Commander-in-Chief of the Wehrmacht in Holland, retained command north of a line running from the Brielsche Gat on the Dutch coast via Dordrecht along the Waal and the Maas to Nijmegen and thence to the German border. This by itself indicated that Model was not expecting any fighting in that area at any rate. A very mediocre soldier Christiansen—who was answerable to Model only for tactical operations but otherwise came directly under the orders of the Wehrmacht High Command in Berlin in his capacity of regional commander—would have done more harm than good as a front-line general. The terrain to the south of the line from Brielle to Nijmegen was to be the theatre of operations. Model divided it into two halves. The dividing line ran from a point east of Antwerp via Tilburg to the village of Rossum on the Waal above 's-Hertogenbosch. The territory to the west of this line (ie West Brabant and Zeeland) constituted the sector of von Zangen's Fifteenth Army. The sector to the west of the line was for the First Parachute Army, whose commander, Student, had set up his head-quarters at Vught. It is clear that Model expected the new British offensive in this sector, for the road from the front on the Maas-Scheldt Canal to the Ruhr, which was so vital for the German war effort, ran in a north-easterly direction across it.

As the war diary of Model's Army Group B shows, the Germans had already been expecting that Allied offensive throughout the first half of September. Their Intelligence were convinced that airborne troops would be used—as they had been in Sicily and the invasion of Normandy. On 6 September Model's Intelligence officer put forward the theory that large Allied air landings would take place in the area of the Siegfried Line, or north of Aachen (where the line grew thinner and thinner until it ceased altogether east of Nijmegen on the Rhine), or farther south, in the Saar (opposite Patton's American Third Army). The daily arrival of reinforcements on the eastern flank of the British Second Army strengthened the German belief that an attack on the Ruhr was imminent. On 14 September Model's Intelligence officer was so sure of it that he wrote his report—also quoted in the war diary of Army Group B—in the form of an order from Eisenhower: 'The Second British Army . . . will assemble its units at the Maas-Scheldt and Albert Canals. On its right wing it will concentrate an attack force mainly composed of armoured units, which, after forcing a Maas crossing, will launch operations to break through to the Rhenish-Westphalian Industrial Area (Ruhr) with the main effort via Roermond. To cover the northern flank, the left wing of the [Second British] Army will close to the Waal at Nijmegen, and thus create the basic conditions necessary to cut off the German forces committed in the Dutch coastal areas. In conjunction with these operations a large-scale airborne landing by the First Allied Airborne Army north of the Lippe river in the area south of Münster is planned for an as yet indefinite date.' (See map 1.)

The German reports of 15 and 16 September refer to yet more Allied activity which pointed to a new offensive; there was, for instance, the 'conspicuously active' sea and air reconnaissance by Allied naval and air forces off the western Wadden Islands. And on 15 September von Rundstedt's Intelligence officer—von Rundstedt was Commander-in-Chief of all German forces in the West—reported that 'according to reliable information the enemy urgently needs aerial photographs of the bridges over the Maas at Haelen [north of Roermond!] and of the areas south of Helmond, north of Tilburg and north-east of Dordrecht'.

All these surviving German forecasts and reports are of interest—particularly the 'Eisenhower order'—in that they show how much the Germans were in the dark about the objectives of the impending Allied offensive. The forecast of Model's Intelligence officer, the demarcation lines which Model drew for the armies under his command, and the fact that Model set up his headquarters in Oosterbeek show convincingly that fighting to the north of the Waal and the Maas was considered extremely improbable.

And that was the very area at which Montgomery's attack plans were directed.

v

As early as February 1944 voices had been raised in the US War Department demanding the use of airborne troops on a larger scale than hitherto. In the middle of August the existing allied airborne divisions—some of which had already been used in North Africa, Sicily, Italy and Normandy—were combined to form the First

Allied Airborne Army under the command of the American Lieutenant-General Lewis H. Brereton. The main force of this army consisted of three American and two British airborne divisions, together with the Polish Parachute Brigade.

Even before these forces, whose combined strength was about 50,000 men, were merged, Allied Headquarters in Europe had given serious thought to the possibilities of using airborne troops. There had, for instance, been a plan, called TRANSFIGURE, designed to prevent the Germans from escaping to the north from the threatened encirclement at Falaise. A number of variations on this plan were devised in the second week of August, but none of them was carried out. When Eisenhower finally decided on 15 August that the transport aircraft which would have been needed for this airborne operation would be used instead to fly petrol to the ground troops, TRANSFIGURE was definitely abandoned. New plans came up for discussion: airborne operations north of the Somme, in the surroundings of Amiens, at Calais, at Boulogne, north of Amiens and at Tournai. They got no farther. In many cases they were rendered superfluous by the rapid advance of the ground forces. Moreover, General Brereton came to the conclusion that the commanders of the ground armies still did not properly understand the strategic use of airborne troops. Not only was he opposed to using airborne units for operations which could equally well be carried out by advancing ground troops, but he also pointed out that an airborne army could never be in a state of readiness—and certainly not with the front so mobile as it then was—if their transport aircraft were used to supply the ground armies. If his airborne army had to be continuously able to plan and carry out operations at short notice, the indispensable transport aircraft would have to be taken off other jobs. Needless to say, this conception met with fairly considerable opposition from the commanders of the ground armies who saw in it a new threat to the already critical supply situation. A striking example of how the two views clashed is furnished by General Bradley's memoirs where he talks of LINNET I, an air-landing planned to take place at Tournai. Although bad weather was the official reason for cancelling this plan, the commander of the American 12th Army Group gives a different account. Despite the fact that Tournai was not in Bradley's sector but in that of Montgomery's 21st Army Group, Bradley ordered his First Army to take the town in a rapid advance. The action of the American ground troops made the air-landing superfluous. 'But', wrote Bradley after the war, 'although we had made good on our bluff and Ike's air drop was washed out, even our smugness could not compensate for the critical loss we had suffered in tonnage.' This was because Allied Headquarters had stopped sending supplies by air to the American First Army for six days in order to release the aircraft for LINNET I. 'That period cost us 827 tons of supplies a day,' said Bradley later.

LINNET I was followed by LINNET I I, a proposed landing in the Aachen-Maastricht area. On 5 September this plan, too, was filed. Eighteen plans were drawn up and abandoned in this way within a period of forty days.

After the fall of Antwerp on 4 September Montgomery renewed his appeal to Eisenhower to give priority to a concentrated attack in the north with the aim of delivering the last decisive blow. As part of this offensive Montgomery decided on 5 September that an air-landing with one and a half divisions would be made two days later in the Nijmegen and Arnhem areas for the purpose of occupying the river crossings. This plan was given the code name COMET.

A second obvious possibility was an attack in a north-easterly, instead of a northerly, direction. In that event the Maas would be crossed at Venlo and the Rhine at Wesel. The route though Nijmegen and Arnhem, however, had the advantage that aircraft carrying troops there would have less opposition from enemy aircraft and flak. The Ruhr was heavily defended by anti-aircraft guns. But COMET, too, was postponed from day to day. One of the reasons was the daily increasing enemy resistance. (The German 719th Division under Sievers and the *Kampfgruppe* Chill had started work on a defence line on 4 September and been joined several days later by Student's new First Parachute Army.) Partly because of this increased enemy activity General Dempsey, commander of the British Second Army, doubted whether his ground troops could advance quickly enough to relieve the airborne units in the Nijmegen and Arnhem areas. The American First Army on his right wing had their hands too full near Aachen and would be unable to support him on his right flank as he advanced to the north. When Dempsey went to Montgomery's headquarters on the morning of 10 September, he intended to propose attacking in the direction of Wesel instead of Arnhem. But Montgomery had just received a signal from London stating that the first V2 missiles, fired from western Holland, had fallen on the city on 8 September. Although Montgomery declares that it was not this message but Air Force objections to the Ruhr that led to the choice of Arnhem rather than Wesel, Dempsey considers that the chance of cutting off western Holland at Arnhem and thus neutralising the V2 launching sites had a decisive influence on Montgomery's decision. On that same afternoon Montgomery had his famous meeting with Eisenhower on Brussels airfield at which he obtained permission to force passages of the Maas, the Waal and the Neder Rijn in a combined operation using ground and airborne troops. The six-day-old plan for Operation COMET, which involved the use of one and a half battalions, was expanded into an action in which three and a half divisions would be engaged. The plan was given the name MARKET GARDEN. Eisenhower recognised the need for MARKET GARDEN but, as we have already seen, continued to regard this operation as contributing to the establishment of a broad front. He was therefore not prepared to accord MARKET GARDEN a degree of priority which would have necessitated halting other offensives (such as that of Patton's Third Army against the Saar).

After the conversation between Eisenhower and Montgomery, it soon became clear to Dempsey, who with the British Second Army was to carry out the ground operations involved in MARKET GARDEN, that the support promised by Eisenhower was not sufficient. Contact with the dropped airborne troops was to be established by Horrocks' XXX Corps after a rapid advance, in support of which VIII Corps would attack on the right flank and XII Corps on the left. A large proportion of VIII Corps' vehicles, however, had by then been diverted to carry supplies to the other rapidly advancing divisions. Deprived of its transport, the Corps was still on the Seine. On 11 September Montgomery informed Eisenhower that MARKET GARDEN could not be carried out before 23 September at the earliest. It was not possible, he signalled, to provision the Second Army for the attack and get VIII Corps from the Seine to the Maas-Scheldt Canal before that date. The very next day Eisenhower sent his chief-of-staff, General Bedell Smith, to Montgomery with the promise that 1,000 tons of supplies daily would be transported by air and road to Brussels. As every day's delay gave the Germans a further opportunity to strengthen their defences, Montgomery fixed the date of Operation MARKET GARDEN for Sunday, 17 September.

V I

And so, exactly four years from the time when Hitler's invasion of England seemed inevitable, the Allies stood at the gateway to a battered Third Reich. Under General Eisenhower's command four armies had advanced from the coast of Normandy to the east and north: two American under Bradley, and one British and one Canadian under Montgomery. The original plan that Bradley's army group should pass to the south and Montgomery's to the north of the Ardennes had been changed by Eisenhower at Montgomery's urgent request. One of the American armies, the First, was now also advancing north of the Ardennes on Montgomery's right flank. The Ruhr, industrial heart of the German war-machine, gave the northern route priority. That, too, is why the airborne army had been placed at Montgomery's disposal. But the advance had to be halted briefly for an indispensable breathing space; the tempo was too fast to be maintained. Yet the road to the north lay open and that brief, enforced rest was also to help the Germans. The competent Model, recalled by Hitler from the eastern front to avert the pending catastrophe in the west, put Student's new paratroop army into the gaping breach. Not a completely adequate measure, perhaps, but nevertheless a useful precaution. In any case, there was a steadily growing conviction at Model's headquarters that the new Allied offensive would be directed to the east, against the Ruhr. Further south, the American First Army had come to a standstill in the Siegfried Line near Aachen on their way to the Ruhr. It seemed obvious that the imminent attack by the British Second Army could be expected in the Roermond-Venlo direction; any offensive to the north, towards Nijmegen, would be to cover the flank of the main force.

But Montgomery had decided otherwise. His main force was to make for the north, for the Zuider Zee.

VII

Meanwhile, during the first fortnight of September, the remains of two German Panzer divisions were retreating unplotted over the vast European battle-ground. While the field-marshals and generals at the headquarters of both sides were carefully weighing up their chances, the mauled 9th and 10th SS Panzer Divisions, which had barely escaped total destruction in France, were fleeing to the north. Their fighting power had been reduced to a bare minimum, a large proportion of their tanks had been lost and thousands of their men had been captured. These divisions, which bore the historic names of Hohenstaufen and Frundsberg, could not be expected to play a part of any significance in the early stages of the great clash that was to decide the end of Hitler's Reich. Decimated, they moved back amidst the chaos of the fleeing German armies: on 1 September in Valenciennes, on the 2nd in Mons, on the 4th in Sittard and on the 7th in Arnhem. There, beyond the Rhine, the Waal and the Maas, out of the fighting zone, they were to re-form and reorganise. After the hell of Falaise, a breather in Gelderland.

The Frundsberg Division was stationed east of the Yssel in the area known as the Achterhoek.

The Hohenstaufen Division was scattered in small units over the Veluwe to the north of Arnhem.

Aerial photograph taken by the **RAF** on 6 September 1944 (eleven days before the start of the air-landings). Top right, the bridge over the Rhine.

CHAPTER TWO

THE MYSTERY OF THE
HOHENSTAUFEN DIVISION

(10–17 September 1944)

I

'This is a tale you will tell your grandchildren!' General Hor-rocks, the commander of the British XXX Corps was standing in the cinema of the small Belgian mining town of Leopoldsburg before a crowded audience of officers of his corps. Behind Horrocks, on the cinema screen, hung a large map of the area from North Bel-gium to the Zuider Zee. A line of march was marked in red on that map: from Belgium northwards to Eindhoven, Nijmegen and Arnhem. There was a red ellipse between Arnhem and Apeldoorn and another between Apeldoorn and Nunspeet. Areas near Eind-hoven, Nijmegen and Arnhem were ringed in a different colour. General Horrocks had a pointer in his hand. 'This', he said, 'is a tale you will tell your grandchildren,' adding almost immediately, 'and mighty bored they'll be.' His audience laughed.

It was 11 am on Saturday, 16 September 1944. The orders for GARDEN, the ground part of Operation MARKET GARDEN, were being distributed. After Montgomery had decided that the plan would be carried out on 17 September, feverish activity had started up in various headquarters, both on the Continent and in London. A large number of problems of the most varied sorts had to be solved. As its name suggests, the plan consisted of two parts. Operation GARDEN meant a thrust by the Second British Army from the bridgehead at Neerpelt on the Belgian frontier to Nuns-peet on the Zuider Zee. It was calculated that, unless unexpectedly heavy resistance was met, the Zuider Zee would be reached in four or five days. All German troops *west* of the line of advance would thus be cut off from their supplies from home and compelled to surrender, while the ports of Amsterdam, Rotterdam and Antwerp could be opened up and used instead of Cherbourg, now so far from the front. *East* of the line of advance a bridgehead could be formed for the Allied advance into Germany.

The road from Neerpelt to Nunspeet, however, crossed various small rivers and canals in North Brabant and further to the north the Waal, the Maas and the Rhine. It was necessary to capture the bridges over all these rivers and canals quickly and therefore by surprise. This task was reserved for airborne troops still in England. That was Operation MARKET.

A decision about MARKET GARDEN had been taken on 10 September. It was to start on 17 September.

There was a considerable difference between the preparations for MARKET and those for GARDEN. All the airborne troops were stationed in England, practically sealed off from the outside world, and planning of the airborne operation could therefore start on the evening of 10 September. But the Second Army, on Belgian territory and so close to the enemy lines, had to be much more careful. The plan had to remain a secret until the very last moment. That was why Horrocks, the commander of xxx Corps which formed the spearhead of the Second Army, did not summon the commanding officers concerned to the cinema at Leopoldsburg until 16 September. The check at the entrance to the building was very strict. Even the highest in rank were not allowed through the cordon of military police until their identity documents had been checked. Horrocks, who himself had already been told on 11 September to get ready for the advance on the Zuider Zee, gave his divisional commanders and their staff officers the details of the plan on that 16 September in Leopoldsburg. The Guards Armoured Division were to open the attack from the bridgehead across the Maas-Scheldt Canal at Neerpelt which had already been gained on 10 September in a surprise attack by the Guards. From that bridgehead the route ran over the Dutch frontier to Valkenswaard and Eindhoven, where contact would be made with the American 101st Airborne Division who had been dropped north of the town, and thence via Son, Veghel, Uden and Grave to Nijmegen, where it was hoped that the US 82nd Airborne Division would meanwhile have captured the bridges over the Maas and the Waal undamaged. The route then continued to Arnhem, where the British 1st Airborne Division and the Polish Parachute Brigade would be firmly holding the bridge over the Rhine, and from Arnhem it bent to the west round Apeldoorn, reaching the Zuider Zee near Nunspeet. There, in the area between Apeldoorn and Nunspeet, the Guards would cut western Holland's connections with the north. The Guards would be immediately followed by the 43rd Wessex Division, who would occupy a line from Apeldoorn to the British Airborne Division's bridgehead at Arnhem. After passing through Arnhem some units of the Wessex Division would also cross the Yssel and establish a bridgehead on the eastern bank of the river.

This division was to include the Dutch Irene Brigade, which had been assigned the special task of liberating Apeldoorn. At a conference which he held with his officers on 16 September after Horrocks' speech, the commander of the Wessex Division, Major-General G. Ivor Thomas, announced that after liberating Apeldoorn the Irene Brigade would give the signal for the people of Holland to rise.

If the Germans had blown up the bridges over the Rhine, Waal and Maas before they could be occupied by the airborne divisions, the Wessex Division had also to try to force crossings over these rivers. There was even a fantastic suggestion that in pursuance of this instruction a number of Rhine barges might possibly be captured and used to carry a whole brigade down the Waal and the Rhine to Arnhem.

But even without this nautical variation the plan was already audacious enough. It involved a march of about sixty miles to the furthest (British) airborne division at Arnhem. Could this division maintain a foothold in the midst of enemy-held territory until they were relieved by xxx Corps? According to the time-table the Guards would reach Eindhoven eight hours after the start of the attack, Nijmegen about noon of the next day and Arnhem about noon on the day after that. The American 101st Airborne Division would thus be isolated for about half a day, the American 82nd at Nijmegen a whole day, and the British 1st at Arnhem as long as two whole days. For xxx Corps this meant that during the first stage of the attack they had to force a long and very narrow corridor straight across Brabant and that there would be little time to worry about cover for their flanks. It was, of course, for the latter purpose that xii Corps was to go over to the attack on their left wing and viii Corps on their right, but various circumstances (such as the very difficult terrain) were to keep the rate of advance of these troops considerably slower than that of xxx Corps. But the long, thin life-line which Horrocks and his troops had to extend from Allied-occupied territory to the three airborne divisions would—it was clear in advance—be at first in serious danger of being cut temporarily by a German attack. Yet the possibility of German counter-attacks was not the only threat. The speed of advance would be seriously reduced if the bridges on the route were blown up. Adequate preparation for even this eventuality called for 9,000 men and 2,300 vehicles loaded with material. Traffic control, too, was an entire problem in itself. For much of the way to Arnhem there would be only a single road, along which the Corps' 20,000 vehicles—tanks, lorries and jeeps—would have to be routed. Complicated and strict organisation was essential to ensure that this road would not be rendered useless by collisions and traffic jams within the first few hours of the attack.

II

Operation MARKET—comprising all the airborne actions involved in MARKET GARDEN—was at least as complicated as GARDEN in its planning. Never in history had an airborne operation been undertaken on such a scale, and in several respects it was to remain unsurpassed in the further course of the Second World War. For the first time in Allied military history a large-scale airborne attack was to be accompanied not by an invasion from the sea, but by an advance by ground troops.

At 6 pm on 10 September—several hours after Montgomery had received permission from Eisenhower to carry out this plan—the first talks started at Allied Airborne Army headquarters at

Sunnyhill Park in England. Among those present were the commander of that army, the American General Brereton, and the commander of the British First Airborne Corps, Lieutenant-General F. A. M. ('Boy') Browning, who was also Brereton's deputy. General Browning had returned that afternoon from a visit to Montgomery's headquarters in Belgium, where he had been informed of the decision Eisenhower and Montgomery had just reached concerning Operation MARKET GARDEN.

The following troops were available for the operation: the British 1st Airborne Division under the command of Major-General R. E. Urquhart, the American 82nd Airborne Division under Major-General James Gavin, the American 101st Airborne Division under Major-General Maxwell Taylor, and the Polish 1st Independent Parachute Brigade commanded by Major-General Stanislaw Sosabowski. A fourth division, the 52nd (Lowland), would be held in reserve in England until such times as they could be brought across to the Arnhem area by transport aircraft, although the British 1st Airborne Division would first have to prepare landing strips for them. The orders of these troops can be summarised in a few words. The US 101st Division had to capture the four railway and road bridges over the river Aa and the Zuid Willemsvaart Canal at Veghel, the road bridge over the Dommet at St Oedenrode, the road bridge over the Wilhelmina Canal at Son, and the town of Eindhoven. The 82nd Division was to take the bridge over the Maas at Grave and the bridge over the Waal at Nijmegen. To enable them to carry out these orders it would be necessary—though the fact was not stated in their orders —to occupy also one of the four bridges over the Maas-Waal Canal.

The task of the British Airborne Division, assisted by the Polish Parachute Brigade, was the shortest of all to describe, namely to capture the road bridge over the Rhine at Arnhem. It was also the most audacious of the three airborne operations.

As there were insufficient aircraft available to transport these three and a half divisions (about 30,000 men and many hundreds of tons of equipment) in one lift, the job had to be spread over three successive days. This hard necessity naturally did nothing to decrease the risks. As might be expected, each of the divisional commanders who were responsible for the detailed preparation and the tactical execution of the orders they had been given, tried to get as many of the aircraft as possible for his own troops. Urquhart in particular, who had to carry out the trickiest part of the entire Operation MARKET GARDEN, three wide rivers and sixty miles away from the vanguard of the British Second Army, continued to press General Browning for more aircraft. He pointed out that the two American divisions at Eindhoven and Nijmegen were much better off in this respect. But Browning, probably putting Urquhart's remarks down to a rivalry between the British and American troops which undoubtedly also existed elsewhere, assured him that no other arrangement was possible. The line between XXX Corps and Arnhem had to be strongest near where it started, in order to give the advancing troops the greatest possible chance of success. If this priority were switched to Arnhem instead of Eindhoven and Nijmegen, it increased the danger of failure at one or both of the latter towns, bringing the advance of the ground army to a halt before the British division at Arnhem could be reached, in which case the fate of the division was sealed. Thus, although it was unavoidable, this circumstance necessarily meant a weakening of what was already the riskiest part of MARKET GARDEN.

But MARKET GARDEN was not the code name for a large-scale peacetime manoeuvre; MARKET GARDEN was war. And in war there is less time for long preparations which will limit risks to a minimum. In some cases a commander has to be ready to run the maximum risks. In practically all circumstances greater risk is the price that has to be paid for the advantage which the use of airborne troops gives in the form of surprise.

Military history shows that there has been no essential change for many decades in this respect, even if technical possibilities and terminology have changed. Once it was fast cavalry which protected the advance of the much slower infantry and paved the way for it by scouting on the flanks and occupying important points on the line of advance. The infantryman, marching at a maximum speed of two to three miles an hour, laden with a heavy rifle, a large quantity of ammunition, extra clothing and emergency rations, could, if necessary, operate independently for several days on end. But his speed excluded any possibility of surprise. This had to be provided by the cavalry. Their speed, however, was obtained at the cost of lighter arms, less ammunition and fewer supplies. With a fast unexpected attack they could capture a river-crossing or a village on a height and thus create positions to help the advance of the army behind them. But until the moment the army reached them they were extremely vulnerable to enemy counter-attacks.

Outwardly, much has changed since then. The infantryman no longer marches slowly; he drives. A time came when, motorised, he could move faster than the man on a horse. From then on it was all over for the cavalry. Reconnaissance was taken over by light, fast armoured cars and aircraft. And the rôle the cavalry had played in ensuring an unimpeded advance by the infantry—either by clearing obstacles on their way or by temporarily occupying their objectives—was on some occasions during the Second World War performed by a modern weapon, airborne troops. They, too, strike unexpectedly. And they have the further advantage that their approach cannot be reported until just before they land and that they can attack the enemy in the back, behind his lines, where troop concentrations are often thinner. Yet despite these advantages, despite the technical aids available to them, such as the great carrying capacity of modern transport aircraft and gliders, this modern cavalry—which also has inherited the romantic fame of its predecessor—remains a relatively lightly armed and vulnerable part of the whole. In other words, the valuable element of surprise has still to be bought by accepting greater risks. A price which can in turn be justified by the expected gain.

The Allied commanders who were responsible for MARKET GARDEN knew the risks involved in the operation; they knew the special risks of the airborne troops who would be used in the operation; and they had no delusions about the onerous task that the British division in particular had to carry out at Arnhem. But they accepted these risks in view of the profit they expected to reap: a speedy end to the war in the west.

During the first conference on 10 September at First Allied Airborne Army headquarters a large number of complicated problems was raised, all of which had to be solved within a few days. Among the most important was the question, already referred to, of the transport aircraft. The available aircraft consisted of some 1,250 Dakotas, which could be used either to carry paratroops or to tow gliders, and about 350 bombers which could only tow gliders. With this air fleet half of the airborne troops could be lifted to the landing and dropping zones on the first day of the operation. Another important question was the organisation of this lift. The airfields of departure in England had to be chosen so that the great streams of aircraft, which were to be protected by fighters, would not get in each other's way. The success of the operation depended to a large extent on a strict time-schedule which had not only to take the three separate air-landings into account but also to be co-ordinated with the start of the ground operations, ie xxx Corps' offensive. Over enemy territory the transport aircraft had to be routed round flak concentrations. The choice of landing and dropping zones was also dictated by the need to avoid flak, and this in turn once more raised the question whether there were strong enemy units stationed in the vicinity. Expectation of the various ways in which the enemy could offer resistance had, as far as possible, to be turned into certainty by aerial reconnaissance and information from other sources. And once the troops had landed, large numbers of aircraft and a clockwork organisation would be necessary to keep them supplied. One of the most uncertain factors in all this planning was the weather. Even an otherwise perfect plan could be wrecked by the whims of the weather, to which air transport is especially vulnerable. The weather gods were silent, unfathomable players in the game call MARKET GARDEN. In those September days of 1944 they were not always well disposed towards the Allies.

IV

When the commanders of the three Allied airborne divisions had received their orders, they set themselves and their staff officers to the task of working out the details. The objective of General Urquhart, the commander of the British Airborne Division, could be summed up simply: the road bridge at Arnhem. But the way to it was not so simple.

Urquhart, forty-two years of age, had assumed command of the Airborne Division in January 1944. Before that he had fought in Africa, Sicily and Italy. He had been slightly wounded in Italy. As he said, no one could have been more surprised than himself when he was given command of the First Airborne Division. He had never made a parachute jump or a glider landing, and he had an unfortunate and unpleasant propensity to air-sickness. When he suggested to General Browning that he should at least take some parachute training, Browning advised him against it saying: 'Your job is to prepare this division for the invasion of Europe. Not only are you too big for parachuting but you are also getting on.'

In the months which followed, Urquhart as a newcomer had to prove his worth to the naturally critical airborne troops, in addition to preparing the division for the invasion. On 6 June, however, another British airborne division (the 6th), landed in Normandy and Urquhart's division remained in England as a strategic reserve. An enervating period now began during which one plan after the other was conceived, worked out in a certain amount of detail and then abandoned: WILD OATS, RAISING BRITANNY, HANDS UP, TRANSFIGURE. They remained code names. In many cases the ground troops had advanced so swiftly as to render airborne operations unnecessary. Operation COMET was never carried out either, but planning for it had already made the division familiar with Arnhem at the beginning of September, although on a more modest scale than that now required.

In working out his plans for the capture of the road bridge at Arnhem Urquhart had first of all to bear in mind the limited number of aircraft which had been allocated to him. The capacity of approximately 150 Dakotas for transporting paratroops and the 350 gliders which could be towed by the remaining aeroplanes compelled him to spread the landing of his division over three successive days. The main force of the first lift (on 17 September) would consist of the 1st Parachute Brigade and the 1st Airlanding Brigade (glider-borne); each brigade consisted of three battalions. Also included in the first lift were the divisional staff and two detachments of the Light Regiment of Artillery. The three battalions of the Parachute Brigade were to secure the bridge; those of the Airlanding Brigade were to guard the dropping zones and thus cover the landing of the second lift (in the morning of 18 September). The second lift was to bring in the 4th Parachute Brigade, also consisting of three battalions. Finally, on 19 September, the Polish Parachute Brigade were to arrive; their equipment was to be landed in gliders on an area north of the Rhine, while the men were to jump south of the bridge which, it was hoped, would by then have been two days in British hands. The disadvantages of this arrangement are obvious. The very important element of surprise, which would be a considerable factor on the first day, would be completely lacking on the second and third. By that time the enemy would have had time for counter-measures and would certainly be expecting the arrival of reinforcements for the airborne troops. In addition, the need to guard the landing zones for the second and third lifts meant a reduction of the troops available for capturing the bridge. The weather risk, too, was considerably increased by spreading the operation over three days. If the weather on 17 September was exceptionally bad for flying, the entire operation could still be postponed, but once the first troops were landed, any postponement of the remaining lifts could have serious consequences.

The situation of the landing and dropping zones (for gliders and paratroops respectively) was also such as to contribute little to a speedy and efficient execution of the plans. The choice of these zones was based on the belief that the polder land to the south of the bridge and the immediate vicinity of the target at its northern end—the town of Arnhem and the woods around it—were unsuitable for mass landings by gliders. According to information received there were also many anti-aircraft guns in the immediate neighbourhood of the bridge. These various arguments led to the choice of several landing and dropping zones to the west of Arnhem, at distances of five to eight miles from the objective.

Few aspects of the airborne operation at Arnhem have been so thoroughly and critically examined in later studies as the choice of the landing and dropping zones. What has already been said about the loss of the surprise element on the second and third days was now also true to some extent of the first lift. This lift was to zones about six miles from the target. It would take at least several hours to assemble the troops and make them ready to move. The slightest setback might mean a delay of a few more hours, and this time, relatively short as it might be, could enable the enemy to take counter-measures.

Yet the distance between the landing zones and the objective and the fact that only a part of the division could be lifted on the first day could only have been considered unacceptable risks if there were reasons for expecting powerful enemy resistance. And there were none. On the contrary, the German armies in the west had suffered defeat after defeat. Some reserves had with difficulty been scraped together to man a weak defence line against the advancing Allied armies. It was known to the Allies that the German reserves even included 'ear and stomach battalions', units in which, for the sake of convenience (eg diet) men suffering from gastric disorders and others ailments were grouped together. What could an airborne landing far behind the thin crust of the enemy's forward defence line possibly encounter except a few scattered units of low fighting strength? Doubt had, of course, been expressed in several quarters. General Browning, for instance, on receiving his orders on the afternoon of 10 September, is reported by Urquhart to have said to Montgomery: 'I think we might be going a bridge too far.' General Gavin, the commander of the American division which was to drop at Nijmegen, recalls hearing experienced staff officers of another division discussing the British landing zones shortly before the operation; they called the plan one which they would be 'reluctant to attempt'. And one of the officers concerned in the preparations for MARKET GARDEN reacted to the statement that the ground army would advance like a bride to the altar on a carpet of airborne troops, with the grim question: 'Of living or dead airbornes?' A remark prompted not by cynicism but by genuine concern.

On the other hand in every undertaking the misgivings and the opposition to it are in direct proportion to its audacity. A war is no time for excessive caution. It is part of the job of great commanders to fight not only the enemy but also uncertainty and doubt in their own ranks. And if daring plans fail by a narrow safety margin, if a series of apparently petty setbacks and miscalculations finally accumulate enough weight to tip the wavering scales in the wrong direction, it is on those details that judgement is passed, after the event, by both parties to the struggle. After the event—when all the cards are on the table.

In *By Air to Battle*, a post-war publication of the Air Ministry in which the operations of the British 1st Airborne Division, *inter alia*, are discussed, we can read: 'Its [the plan's] success depended not only on the bravery and dash of the troops—these could be taken for granted—but on the inability of the Germans to react with sufficient vigour, weight and speed. That the enemy would be surprised seemed certain. How long he would take to recover from his surprise was a factor far less easy to calculate. Therein lay the risk which Montgomery and Browning did not hesitate to take, for the victor's palm falls to him who dares the most.'

In view of the expected inability of the Germans 'to react with sufficient vigour and speed', the disadvantages of the detailed plans for the Arnhem operation were felt to carry less weight. A six-mile march to the objective by only three battalions, and some sixty miles behind the enemy lines at that, might have seemed presumptuous but for a justified belief in the enemy's impotence.

Who was that enemy? And was the Allies' belief in his impotence in fact justified?

V

As we have seen, the area which the German Field-Marshal Model considered the probable battle-ground lay *south* of the line Brielle-Dordrecht-Nijmegen, and this area he, as commander of Army Group B, had divided into two halves by his order of 16 September. Von Zangen's Fifteenth Army occupied the western sector; in the eastern sector, where Model could expect the next

Allied offensive, there was Student's newly-formed First Parachute Army. To the *north* of the line Brielle-Dordrecht-Nijmegen, in the area where the British airborne division was to be dropped, the situation was somewhat different. It was there, behind the protection of three large rivers, that Model had set up his headquarters in the second week of September. Model, who was in command of all German troops in north-west Europe, had fallen back from Belgium to Holland with the retreating armies and finally moved into the Tafelberg Hotel at Oosterbeek, near Arnhem. If it had been possible at that moment to combine the German and British staff-maps of this area, there would barely have been room for a fingertip between the flag marking Model's headquarters and the edge of the landing zones of the British airborne division. A wonderful chance for the airbornes—if only they had known about it. And a precarious position for a field-marshal's headquarters, a fact which he not only failed to appreciate but which he regularly denied until the afternoon of 17 September, when the arrival of British paratroops forced him to abandon lunch hurriedly. He had denied it since 15 September, two days before the start of MARKET GARDEN, when the possibility of an Allied landing in the area had been the subject of a conversation between Model and Rauter.

Höherer SS-und Polizeiführer und General der Waffen-SS Hans Albin Rauter was, as his title indicates, the Commander-in-Chief of the SS and the German police in Holland during the occupation. On 15 September he received a Telex message from Germany. It was from his chief, *Reichsführer SS* Heinrich Himmler and instructed him to get in touch immediately with Field-Marshal Model. This was, as Rauter himself stated later, a normal and reasonable order. Model had entered Rauter's territory from the south and as Rauter was lower in rank, he was bound by military regulations to place himself at Model's orders. Rauter, who first expected to meet Model at Venlo, finally found him at Oosterbeek, where a talk took place between Model, Rauter and Model's chief-of-staff, Lieutenant-General Hans Krebs.

Rauter asked Model if there was any chance of Allied air-landings. (Rauter stated after the war that this question was prompted by the consideration that the Allies had previously made use of

49

airborne troops in Africa, Sicily, Italy and Normandy, and that they might do the same again in September 1944 in support of the new offensive that everyone was expecting.) But neither Model nor Krebs thought that there was any reason for Rauter's misgivings. They argued along the following lines: paratroops with their long specialised training were a precious commodity and the situation of the Allies was by no means such as to make the use of such troops necessary; secondly, Arnhem and Nijmegen were too far in advance of the spearhead of the British Second Army and the Germans would have wiped out the lightly-armed paratroops before they were relieved by the Second Army. Furthermore, Antwerp was within range of the V1, and the Scheldt estuary, which gave access to Antwerp, was still in German hands; the Second Army had therefore still to be supplied from Cherbourg and the Allies would be reluctant to lengthen their lines of communication still further and unnecessarily. Finally, Montgomery was a very prudent man and would not rush into such a reckless adventure. Model and Krebs assured Rauter that airborne troops might be used when and if the British Second Army reached the Rhine at Düsseldorf, but 'never over Dutch territory'. Model's remarks accorded closely with the forecast his chief Intelligence officer had compiled one day before (14 September) about the coming Allied offensive and the use of airborne troops; this officer was, in fact, so sure of himself that, as we saw, he couched his report in the form of an order by Eisenhower.

Rauter had no reasonable arguments with which to counter Model's. Nevertheless, he asked what troops Model had for his immediate defence. Krebs replied, '250 men of the Field Police'. That, too, illustrates the feeling of comparative security which prevailed at Model's headquarters. A troop of 250 Field Police would probably have sufficed temporarily in the event of an uprising by the civil population but was quite useless as a fighting unit.

The list of effective fighting units available to Model in the area north of the rivers was far from impressive. It was a mixture of small sections, often quite unsuitable for operations, of Army, Navy, Luftwaffe and Waffen-SS personnel. They were under the overall command of the Commander-in-Chief of the German Armed Forces in Holland, Luftwaffe General Christiansen. Christiansen's powers, however, were purely those of the commander of an occupied territory. His duties in this post, which he had held since 1940, were to ensure that the civil authorities met the wishes of the German Forces, to guard military installations and to co-ordinate the needs of the various German military units. He had little or nothing to do with civil administration in any shape or form or with German police services. He was under the direct orders of the *Oberkommando Wehrmacht* (OKW) in Berlin, except where tactical operations were concerned. For the latter purpose, his troops formed part of Army Group B and thus came under the command of Model.

When he took command of the German troops in Holland in 1940, Christiansen, a former tug-boat skipper, was not a newcomer to that country. He had paid a visit to Holland in the course of the much-publicised world tour of the Dornier Do-X flying-boat, of which he was captain. He was an uncomplicated, blinkered man. His devotion to Hitler was inspired less by Nazi convictions than by the firm belief that a ship could have only one captain, whether Hitler or another. This attitude ensured him the trust of the Nazi leaders. Although far from being a great soldier, he was regarded as a reliable and therefore useful officer, and those had been Goering's reasons for giving him the rank of *General der Flieger*.

Christiansen's chief-of-staff, General von Wühlisch, was a man of quite a different stamp. He was a typical Prussian general, whose father had served as a general in the Kaiser's army. The haughty von Wühlisch (who committed suicide after the war) had no high opinion of his chief. Within the small circle of trusted officers he had gathered round him he called Christiansen *bauernschlau*—as cunning as a peasant. A fairly accurate description, for Christiansen was in fact so cunning that he had arranged to be kept informed of what von Wühlisch said about him, but did not get rid of him. Von Wühlisch's advice on all kinds of strategic and tactical problems, of which he himself had not the slightest understanding, was indispensable.

In addition to these officers of the Wehrmacht there was the fierce Austrian SS general, Rauter. A fanatical supporter of Hitler, Rauter was head of the Security Police, the Security Service of the SS, the uniformed German police and the Waffen-SS in Holland. He was a harsh and feared man who held the lives of many thousands of Dutchmen in his hands, and, as a member of the SS, he was suspicious of everything in which the Wehrmacht was concerned. He could see some good in the simple Christiansen, but von Wühlisch he hated. In reports to his chief Himmler he repeatedly tried to undermine von Wühlisch's position. His feelings towards Christiansen's chief-of-staff were in fact reciprocated. (Rauter was condemned to death by the Special Court at the Hague in 1948 and shot some time later.)

There is no point in further unravelling the intricacies of German military command in those days. In some respects it was so complicated that the details could not have been quite clear to the Germans themselves. The problem of organisation was further complicated by the demarcation between the Wehrmacht and the SS. The SS (*Schutzstaffel*) was originally intended as a bodyguard for Hitler and was a picked body of trusted Nazis. At the start of the Second World War the SS units in Germany were incorporated in the Wehrmacht organisation by Hitler himself. The number of such Waffen-SS divisions was at first small, being not more than five in 1941. It was kept low for the first two or three years of the war by the principle of voluntary enlistment in the SS and by the regulation that SS divisions could not constitute more than ten per cent of the total strength of the Wehrmacht. When the pinch came, however, 'the principle of voluntary service had', in SS General Hausser's words, 'to be abandoned'. The number of SS divisions rose to about thirty-five, most of which were formed in the latter years of the war. This dilution obviously did not help to improve the quality. Despite Hitler's measure, a clear distinction continued to exist between the Wehrmacht and the SS. Not merely was there the external difference (in uniforms and equipment), but the SS also retained the aura they had originally acquired as élite troops. The result might be likened to a crack running through the entire German army from top to bottom. And the feelings exchanged across the rift certainly included animosity, resentment and contempt. Evidence of this dividedness and the suspicion it generated is found frequently in the history of the German Army during the Second World War, and the rift was further widened by the unsuccessful attempt by a number of Wehrmacht officers on Hitler's life in July 1944. More than ever before the SS badge was a guarantee of loyalty, and its absence was, at any rate in SS eyes, a reason for suspecting disloyalty to the German cause.

But it was not only these sentiments which had an inhibiting effect; the distinction was also extended to the organisational field. When the SS became part of the Army at the start of the war, *Reichsführer* SS Himmler lost his responsibility for training. Nor had Himmler, who was not a soldier, anything to do with the operational use of SS units. He did, however, continue to exercise an influence on the discipline and organisation of the SS and on appointments within it. It was only a matter of time before the lines separating one command from another were occasionally somewhat blurred.

Moreover, in the autumn of 1944 a number of German Army units were on the verge of disintegration as a result of heavy casualties. Men from coastal batteries were wandering round aimlessly, their guns having been abandoned on the French Channel coast. Ground personnel of the Luftwaffe had fled from their airfields in France and Belgium. The shortage of petrol kept many German aircrews grounded. Divisional and even corps commanders were in many cases left with troops who represented only a fraction of their original manpower and firing power. Some divisions now existed only on paper, and some commands and appointments only in name.

It is against this background that one should view the situation of the German troops north of the Dutch rivers in September 1944—forces which though under Christiansen's command were at Model's disposal for tactical operations.

V I

The decimated German divisions retreating in forced marches to the north towards the end of August 1944 included small groups of soldiers, and occasionally even individuals, who had lost almost all semblance of discipline. In many cases they were from the airfields in Belgium and France, and from positions along the coast — the Atlantic Wall. The Luftwaffe ground staff were grouped into *Fliegerhorst* battalions, a rather fancy name for troops whose only other training until then had consisted in rolling petrol drums.

The personnel from the Atlantic Wall consisted largely of older classes of the Navy and gunners from the garrison artillery. Many of them were old enough to remember the First World War, and they were witnessing the same fate befalling the Fatherland a second time. The Field Post had ceased to function, they were without news of their families and there was no question now of home leave. One thing they knew for certain, that Allied aerial bombing was leaving scarcely one stone upon another in their home towns and villages. So they wanted the war to end, whatever its end might bring. For them, all that now remained of Hitler's bragging slogans was a hollow echo. The idea of a 'hero's death' had lost all appeal. That was the frame of mind in which they trudged northwards, the road to the east having been cut off by Allied armies. They left their guns and transport behind. Without officers and NCOs they hovered on the verge of desertion.

When they reached Holland and crossed the bridges and ferries over the main Dutch rivers, the swelling numbers of these tattered, unarmed men began to form a danger to the already shaky morale of the troops still in Holland. General Christiansen found himself compelled to do something about it. Along the rivers, from Gorinchem to Arnhem, he posted small detachments with orders to intercept these fugitives and bring them under military discipline again. The gunners would be given new artillery, and horses requisitioned from the civilian population; re-formed into batteries these groups would be prepared to give battle again. The German Navy personnel were grouped into *Schiffstammabteilungen* (naval-manning divisions) and trained as infantry.

Christiansen placed this 'reception screen', consisting of very small detachments posted at bridges and ferries over the rivers, under the command of Lieutenant-General Hans von Tettau, who was attached to his staff as inspector of military training. Von

Tettau set up his headquarters in a villa on the Grebbeberg near Rhenen, approximately halfway along the reception screen. 'Headquarters' is rather an exaggeration, for there were hardly any officers to form a staff. Christiansen gave von Tettau for his chief-of-staff an officer called Ulrich, whom Rauter, with unconcealed contempt, was to refer to later as 'Actor Ulrich'. That von Tettau's staff did not exactly make an overwhelming impression is also clear from a remark made by the German officer Fullriede, who commanded several scattered battalions of the Hermann Goering Division. After a visit to von Tettau's headquarters Fullriede wrote in his diary, 'Tettau and his staff give one the impression of a club for old gentlemen'. In all fairness, however, it should be added that von Tettau's job was to operate a reception screen along the rivers, and not to form a first-class fighting unit. The fact that he suddenly found himself and his mixed bag facing the western flank of the British 1st Airborne Division on 17 September, was an unforeseen circumstance which was to cause him no end of headaches. It was probably the almost operetta-like operations which were carried out under his command, especially in the early stages of the air-landings, that later led some writers to speak, wrongly, of the 'Von Tettau Division'.

The reception screen along the rivers was divided into two halves. The western sector was held by an SS NCOs School from Arnhem under the command of Colonel Lippert, who had set up his headquarters in the deserted Luftwaffe huts at Schoonrewoerd near Leerdam. Lippert's men were young and well-trained. Some of them had already fought on the eastern front.

The eastern sector of von Tettau's screen was under the command of SS *Sturmbannführer* Sepp Krafft. Krafft and his SS training and depot battalion had originally been stationed at Arnhem, after which he was sent to the coast, leaving a company of convalescent troops behind. After von Tettau's screen was established, he was transferred with two companies to Oosterbeek, and he was still stationed there when the British paratroops and gliders landed near Heelsum and Wolfheze.

The adventures of Krafft's battalion are in fact only worth mentioning because of the effect they apparently had on the first phase of the battle of Arnhem. That effect was in fact very slight. The false impression was first of all created by the battalion's position. It was in Oosterbeek on the Wolfheze road, right between the British division's landing zones and the town of Arnhem. Later assumptions that this was due to deliberate forethought on the part of the German army leaders—whether prompted or not by information from a Dutch traitor—are amply disproved by the detailed *Gefechtsbericht* which Krafft himself composed after the battle of Arnhem and sent direct to his chief and personal acquaintance Himmler, thus by-passing his immediate army commander. This document, which provides further evidence of the cool relations that existed between the Wehrmacht and the SS, also contains several barely disguised hits at von Tettau. Himmler for his part did not bother to point out to Krafft that as a battalion commander he should have submitted this report via the official channels; instead, he thanked him in January 1945 for his 'excellent' report. It was perhaps partly on the basis of this vainglorious document, which was transparently designed to flatter Himmler, that Krafft had meanwhile been promoted. It is also, however, thanks to this report that we know exactly when Krafft and his two companies arrived at Oosterbeek. He writes: '3-4.9.44. Units of SS Pz Gren Training and Depot Bn 16 consisting of (inter alia) 2. Coy and 4. Coy with a total strength of twelve officers, fifteen NCOs and 229 men were detached from the 16th Battalion as "Battalion Krafft" and removed from positions on the coast. Battalion Krafft came under the orders of Lieutenant-General von Tettau in the vicinity of Oosterbeek.'

The date of transfer (ie 3–4 September, and not, as Chester Wilmot writes in *The Struggle for Europe*, 16 September) is repeated elsewhere in the report. At that moment neither a spy nor the German army leaders could have known about the plan that was only to be decided upon a week later in Brussels, for it was on 10 September that Eisenhower and Montgomery reached agreement on MARKET GARDEN. By his *Gefechtsbericht* Krafft himself disproves the rumour, which cropped up here and there after the war, that the battalion had been moved to Arnhem the evening before 17 September in connection with the impending air-landings. This rumour probably originated in some precautions which Krafft took against Allied airborne operations.

Some days before the British division landed, Krafft paid a visit to his chief, General von Tettau. After dinner, according to Krafft, von Tettau remarked that something was brewing. 'Today', he said, 'there has been magnificent weather all over Germany, and yet we haven't seen one enemy bomber. The British can't afford to let a single day go by unused' and if they do, it means they're preparing for a large-scale attack.' The remark sounds more penetrating than it was; the coming Allied offensive was the chief topic of conversation of all German officers, and not even a child would have supposed that the Second Army were planning to go into hibernation along the Maas-Scheldt Canal.

After his visit to von Tettau, Krafft returned to his headquarters in the villa Waldfriede near Oosterbeek. On 16 September he set up a look-out post in the turret of the villa. And when on the morning of 17 September Allied bombers attacked targets in the vicinity as a prelude to the air-landing, Krafft, again remembering von Tettau's words, put his two companies in a state of alert, a term which, in view of the liberality with which Krafft plied his troops with Dutch gin, soon proved to be a euphemism for 'state of intoxication'.

Even these measures were perfectly comprehensible from the German point of view—particularly when taken by a zealous and ambitious SS officer who still believed blindly in the military miracle with which Hitler would turn the tide of war.

Like other German commanders, Model, too, was reckoning with the new Allied offensive. Since he wanted to be prepared for any eventuality, he had, on hearing reports of concentrations of landing-craft in English ports, ordered Christiansen on 11 September to take steps to defend the Dutch coast. And as Model also suspected that the Allies would use airborne troops, eg to support an invasion of Holland from the sea, he had ordered the formation of mobile units which could be rushed to threatened areas. Von Tettau's pronouncements and Krafft's measures had thus been partly inspired by Model's own measures.

Time and again we see how the German leaders, for whom the

existence of an airborne army in England had not remained a secret, kept expecting air-landings. It is equally clear that they were completely in the dark about the time and place of the landings. Model's Intelligence officer, for instance, had on 14 September prophesied: east of the Rhine, near Münster. Von Rundstedt, C-in-C West, gave orders on 15 September to Air Defence Command in Germany to take precautionary measures against air-landings *east of the Rhine*. Yet on 16 September, one day before the start of MARKET GARDEN, Colonel General Alfred Jodl at Hitler's headquarters was expressing concern about the possibility of Allied air-landings in *Holland, Denmark or north Germany*.

The presence of Krafft's battalion at Oosterbeek on 17 September was an accident. An accident which hardly affected the course of the battle one way or the other, although Krafft, free from the restraint of excessive modesty, gives quite a different interpretation of events. It is grotesque to see him, in his report to Himmler, displaying a scorn for death and a heroic courage which in actual fact were never demanded of either him or his battalion. While he himself makes it appear—and perhaps even believed—that the entire British division swooped down on his two companies, consisting mainly of seventeen to nineteen-year-olds who were keen Nazis but only partially trained, it can be seen from the movements of the British units that they streamed all round his positions without sometimes even suspecting his existence.

VII

In addition to Krafft's battalion, there were also some units of von Tettau's stationed in the vicinity of Oosterbeek during the first fortnight of September. The gunners caught in von Tettau's net round the bridges and ferries across the Waal, Maas and Neder-Rijn were assembled at Wolfheze—about 600 men who had to be provided with guns and formed into batteries as quickly as possible. On Monday, 11 September, a train from Germany arrived at Wolfheze station with forty 105 mm howitzers straight from the factory and still in grease. For the next few days the gun-crews trained with these weapons under the command of Captain Breedemann, and that same week a number of them left with twelve guns for Doesburg, where they were to undergo further training. These howitzers crop up again later in a British Airborne Division report: 'A German gunpark of twenty-one 105 mm guns, new and still labelled . . ., was found. They were all spiked.'

And finally, quartered in two hotels at Heelsum, half a mile to the south of one of the landing zones, there were several dozen men belonging to administrative services, under the command of Major Krumpitz and Captain Seiler.

That was von Tettau's reception screen in the first weeks of September 1944: a mixture of small units spread out over an east-west line about thirty-seven miles long. There were some reasonably good battalions among them—Eberwein's, Lippert's and Krafft's—but also troops whose fighting value was next to nil, such as the *Schiffstammabteilungen*, the *Fliegerhorst* battalions and Captain Breedemann's collection of left-over gunners.

Among the enemy units whose acquaintance the British Airborne Division were also to make was a Dutch SS battalion which can scarcely have been Christiansen's pride and joy. The battalion had originally been formed to guard the concentration camp at Amersfoort. The *Sicherheitspolizei* (security police) had a free hand inside the camp but Rauter wanted to have a guard of SS troops outside the barbed wire. It was not so easy to satisfy his desire, for every usable soldier was needed at the front. Rauter nevertheless managed to have a German officer and German NCOs placed at his disposal for the purpose of rounding up Dutchmen for guard duties. The commander appointed to the battalion thus formed was the SS officer Paul Helle, a Tyrolean whose civilian occupation was described by the fairly elastic term 'engineer'. Helle soon found a devoted assistant in the Czech Franz Sokol, who for the purpose abandoned his Communist convictions in favour of National-Socialist principles. Sokol planned his propaganda work for the new battalion on an ambitious basis. He commandeered a fine house in Amsterdam and filled it with good-quality furniture. One of the upper floors was fitted out as a small cinema where propaganda films could be shown; Sokol's private black-market business was conducted in the basement.

Meanwhile, Helle himself was not standing still. He went to a criminal detention camp and told the inmates that the Germans had built new villages in the conquered areas of Russia and populated them with Jews from the west. Trustworthy officials, he said, were needed to run these villages, and volunteers for this task were promised extra rations for their families and, of course, safe careers for themselves. The prospective administrators would receive a short preliminary training at Amersfoort. Some fifty men fell into rat-catcher Helle's trap. He asked them to sign a German document, whose contents they scarcely understood. They signed and left for Amersfoort. For 'preliminary training'.

Sokol had tapped other sources. From the labour exchanges he obtained the names and addresses of young Dutchmen who had been called up for work in Germany. He visited these *Arbeitseinsatz* candidates and, speaking the truth for once, pointed out to them the unpleasant aspects of work in German factories, none of which was safe from Allied bombers. There was, however, a way out for them because he happened, he said, to need men to guard army stores in Holland. Once more a document was produced. Those who signed went to Amersfoort. For 'preliminary training'.

In addition, Sokol toured preventive detention centres where Dutchmen were awaiting trial (on black-marketing and similar charges) and boys' reformatories. Sokol guaranteed that all charges would be dropped and criminal records destroyed and that the prisoners would be released forthwith, if only they would sign a document. And go to Amersfoort for 'preliminary training'. And so Helle's surveillance battalion was formed. When they arrived in Amersfoort it was soon clear to most of the 'volunteers' that they had stuck their neck into a noose. But the German NCOs warned them that Helle was liable to fly into a rage. Nevertheless, there were a few who dared to ask Helle for their discharge. He then produced the signed forms in which they had undertaken, while remaining on Dutch territory, to fight shoulder to shoulder with their German brothers-at-arms against any possible invader. To break such a solemn promise was a grievous offence against SS discipline and would have a simple but drastic consequence, namely exchanging a position outside the barbed wire for one inside it. All those who were faced with this decision chose Helle's version of freedom. One of the few men in Helle's battalion who had had military training was his adjutant, Naumann. Helle's own training had been far from complete, but Rauter considered him good enough for this battalion and had chosen him because he had 'such a good military appearance'. Young Naumann, on the other hand, had originally studied law and entered the SS from the *Hitlerjugend*. He had fought and been wounded in Russia and was later declared unfit for active service because of permanent damage to his right arm—he could salute only with his left. He was a fanatical party-supporter who had no qualms about forcing political prisoners to dig their own graves and then shooting them down without any form of trial.

Helle's battalion also comprised a reconnaissance unit. Not that there was an urgent everyday need for such a unit, but it occasionally happened that an Allied aircraft was shot down near Amersfoort and the crew landed by parachute, or that a prisoner escaped from the concentration camp. In such cases it was the reconnaissance section's task to turn out in a few requisitioned lorries. As they were led by Drum-Major Sakkel and included most of the battalion band, this flying-squad was popularly known as the *Spielmannszug* (bandsmen's platoon). Drum-Major Sakkel, safe in Amersfoort, could never have dreamt that on that sunny, late-summer day of 17 September he would meet his death at the head of his bandsmen, struck by a bullet from the King's Own Scottish Borderers.

VIII

Apart from von Tettau's weak, scattered units and Helle's inferior surveillance battalion, there was not much that Christiansen could place on his list of troops on Dutch territory north of the rivers in the first fortnight of September: a few reasonable depot battalions of the SS, a few depot battalions of the Hermann Goering Division (very youthful soldiers, only partly trained but extremely fanatical), several police battalions, one or two anti-aircraft batteries, three battalions of Caucasians and Georgians produced by the Russian campaign, who were prepared at any time of the day to desert or even go over to the enemy, the modest coastal defence units, and finally some technical and other units which were completely devoid of fighting power. These were the troops with which Christiansen had to defend the whole of Holland north of the rivers, including a long coastline. And at the same time he had to be on his guard against a rising of the population.

Had these been Urquhart's only opponents on 17 September 1944, the battle of Arnhem would probably have followed an entirely different course; MARKET GARDEN would have succeeded; Holland would have been spared a disastrous six months of hunger and cold, and perhaps even western Europe a fifth winter of war. But on 7 September the remains of two fleeing German divisions arrived in the Dutch province of Gelderland.

IX

At the beginning of 1944 II SS Panzer Corps under the command of *General der Waffen-SS* Paul Hausser was among the crack corps of the German Army. The corps, consisting of the 9th and 10th Panzer Divisions, had fought *inter alia* at Tarnopol on the eastern front in 1944. At the time of the Allied invasion of Normandy, it was ordered to stand by to leave for the western front. The first units left Poland by train on 12 June; four days later they reached the Franco-German border. On 23 June Hausser reported his corps' arrival in France to Dollmann, the commander of the German Seventh Army, but he did not expect to be able to concentrate both divisions near Alencon before 25 June. The railway lines linking the east and west of France had been so badly damaged by aerial bombardment that the troops' journey had to be completed by road. The corps was intended to form the spearhead of an offensive which was being undertaken on Hitler's orders for the purpose of splitting the Allied invasion armies in Normandy in two.

But that offensive never came. One 28 June General Dollmann died of a heart attack; he had just heard that Hitler considered the loss of Cherbourg to be a matter for a court-martial. He was succeeded as commander of the Seventh Army by Hausser. The commander of the 9th SS Panzer Division, *SS Obergruppenführer und General der Waffen-SS* Wilhelm Bittrich replaced Hausser at the head of II SS Panzer Corps. Bittrich in turn was succeeded as commander of the 9th SS Panzer Division by *SS Brigadeführer und Generalmajor der Waffen-SS* Sylvester Stadler.

One day later II SS Panzer Corps went into action for the first time, near Caen. But Caen finally fell into Allied hands. A desperate new plan of Hitler's, an offensive aimed at Avranches in the hope of ripping the Allied front in two, almost resulted in the encirclement of the entire German Seventh Army. On 21 August II SS Panzer Corps gave battle for the last time in an attempt to relieve the German troops entrapped at Falaise. But by this time the entire German front south of Paris had collapsed. On 22 August the corps was ordered to withdraw northwards and seek safety across the Seine. They had fought almost uninterruptedly in Normandy from 29 June to 21 August without receiving any replacements during that time. A new threat to the two battered divisions developed, American troops having meanwhile reached the Seine near Paris and established a bridgehead on its north bank. II SS Panzer Corps was now in danger of being hemmed in between the Channel coast and the Americans advancing to the north, while in their rear they were being harried by the British Second Army. On 23 August Bittrich and his corps reached Elbeuf on the Seine, on 27 August they passed through Rouen, and on 28 August they appeared at Amiens.

An attempt to march eastwards from Amiens foundered against the flank of the American First Army. Cambrai was reached on 2 September. But the tanks of the advancing British Second Army had just arrived there. The corps now looked like being caught in the pincers formed by the British and the Americans, but by retreating rapidly via Valenciennes and Mons and brushing past the front of the American First Army, the German tank divisions succeeded in extricating themselves in the nick of time. At Mons the Americans took some men of the Frundsberg Division prisoner on 3 September. 'Frundsberg' was the historical, more romantic name of the 10th SS Panzer Division; the 9th was known as the 'Hohenstaufen' Division. (Although these names are never used in official German reports, they will, for the sake of convenience, be applied to the two divisions from now on in this book.)

After their lucky escape at Mons, the main danger for the Hohenstaufen and Frundsberg Divisions was over for the time being. Stadler, the commander of the Hohenstaufen Division, had been wounded and left behind in hospital, and his command was temporarily assumed by Lieutenant-Colonel Walter Harzer. The latter's reports show that the first units of the division arrived in Sittard on 4 September, having travelled via Hasselt and Maastricht. It was at Sittard, behind the shelter of the Maas, that the remnants of the division assembled. After shedding one detachment to reinforce the Maas defence line on orders from their corps commander, Bittrich, the Hohenstaufen Division marched on 7 September to their appointed encampment area, the Veluwe north of Arnhem (see map 2). The Frundsberg Division, under the command of Harmel, also moved northwards via Nijmegen and Arnhem. They were to be stationed in the Achterhoek, a district to the east of the Yssel.

The information given by Harzer accords precisely with orders which have survived in the *Kriegstagebuch* of Model (Commander of Army Group B). According to this diary Model issued an order at 10.15 pm on 3 September to the German Fifth Panzer Army (which was fleeing *eastwards* from France to Germany) instructing them to send the Hohenstaufen and Frundsberg Divisions *northwards* to Holland. This order, made out late in the evening, reached the corps commander, Bittrich, on 4 September. Bittrich reports that he arrived in the vicinity of Liége on that date and there received Model's order to send both divisions to the Arnhem-Apeldoorn area to refit and reorganise. This order was duly passed on to Harzer and Harmel.

The war diary of Army Group B records that at 12.30 pm on 5 September Model sent Bittrich another message ordering him and the headquarters staff of II SS Panzer Corps to follow the two divisions to Holland.

All post-war rumours that the presence of the Hohenstaufen Division on the Veluwe at the time of the air-landings was the result of espionage or betrayal are amply refuted by Harzer's report

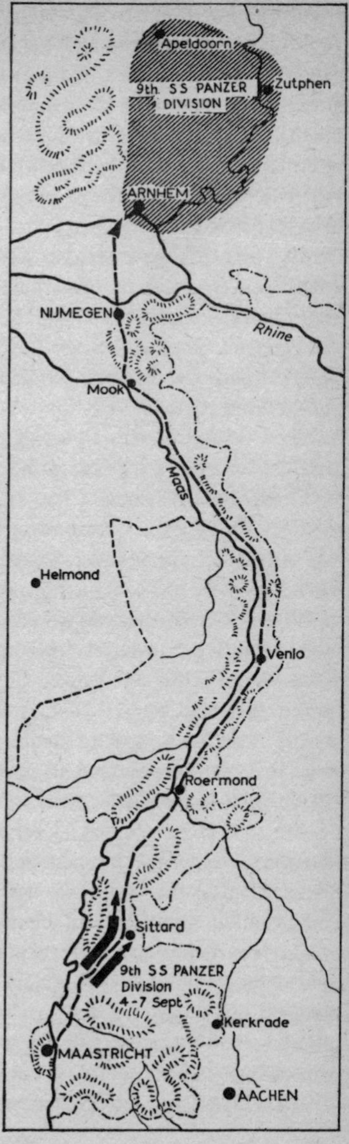

MAP 2   Route followed by the 9th SS Panzer Division from Maastricht to the Veluwe (4–7 September 1944).

and Bittrich's and also by the entries in Army Group B's war diary. The order for the Hohenstaufen and Frundsberg Divisions to march to Gelderland was issued on 3 September. It was not until 4 September that Montgomery suggested to Eisenhower that the Allies should push on to the north immediately after the fall of Antwerp. On 5 September Montgomery decided on a limited airborne operation in the Nijmegen area; this was COMET, fated to be cancelled several days later. It was not until 10 September that the first talk about MARKET GARDEN took place between Eisenhower and Montgomery—a whole week after Model's order. By then the Hohenstaufen Division had already been several days on the Veluwe.

As it proceeds, Harzer's report leaves not a single doubt about the German Army leaders' intentions with regard to the Hohenstaufen Division. Harzer writes: 'On reaching its appointed bivouac area, II SS Panzer Corps came under the command of Army Group B (Field-Marshal Model). The High Command at first intended to effect the necessary reinforcement [of both divisions] speedily but as unflurriedly as possible with men and equipment from the Reich. As early as 10 September the OKW decided that only one of the two Panzer divisions would refit in the forward area and the other would be transferred to German territory for the same purpose. As the 10th SS Panzer [Frundsberg] Division had been partly reinforced by . . . [names of two Panzer battalions] on its arrival in the area north of Arnhem, II SS Panzer Corps decided to let this division complete its refitting in the forward area. Army Group then ordered that before entraining for Germany the 9th SS Panzer [Hohenstaufen] Division should transfer all its effective units, weapons, equipment and vehicles to the 10th SS Panzer Division. After this order was carried out, all that was left of the Hohenstaufen Division were the nuclei of a number of units.'

The report continues: 'Transport of the remnants of the individual units by railway to Germany to the area of Siegen in Westphalia began on 13 September. Army Group B had nevertheless ordered stand-by units to be formed from the troops still awaiting transport, for use as combat groups in the event of any air-landing or other emergency. II SS Panzer Corps had issued instructions that troop commanders and smaller operational groups would be the last to be transported. The rest of the divisional staff and all officers who were not indispensable . . . were transported at the start of the movement.'

X

A number of legends grew up round the Hohenstaufen Division after the war. One alleges that it was sent to the Veluwe because the German High Command had somehow or other learned the plans of Operation MARKET GARDEN, another that it had sealed the fate of the lightly-armed airborne troops with its powerful Tiger tanks, a third that it happened by chance to be on its way from Germany to the front when the air-landings took place.

The reality was different, although the strange caprices of fortune make it no less fascinating than any legend.

The decimated Hohenstaufen and Frundsberg Divisions, fleeing from France, were, by an order of Model dated 3 September, sent to the Veluwe and the Achterhoek to recuperate. On the way the Hohenstaufen Division, badly mauled as it was, had nevertheless to provide one battalion for the defence of the line along the Maas. After the division arrived in Gelderland, the OKW in Berlin decided that only the Frundsberg Division would be refitted there (in his book *Arnhem* General Urquhart wrongly states that the Frundsberg Division was to be moved to Germany and the Hohenstaufen to remain in Holland). For the sake of convenience the Hohenstaufen Division had to transfer all the heavy equipment it still possessed (including two batteries of light field-howitzers) to the Frundsberg Division. All that then remained were small units, practically devoid of equipment, scattered in small groups over the Apeldoorn-Arnhem-Zutphen triangle. Harzer himself estimated his strength at about 2,500 men, consisting of signals' detachments, pioneers, military police, medical orderlies, headquarter personnel, *Panzergrenadiere* without heavy weapons, infantrymen and an anti-aircraft unit with four 20 mm AA guns (see map 3).

This unimposing skeleton of the former Hohenstaufen Division was to be moved as rapidly as possible to Germany where an entire new Hohenstaufen Division was already being formed by General

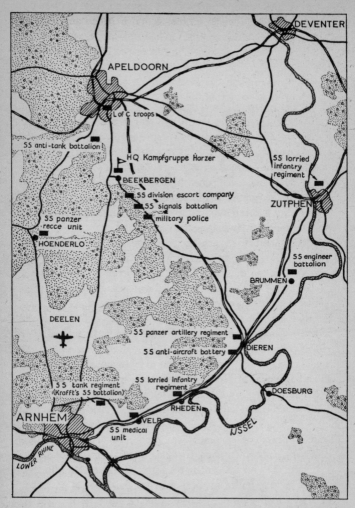

MAP 3 The positions of the various units of the 9th SS Panzer Division on the Veluwe and the Yssel (7–17 September 1944). Losses in France had reduced this division's strength far below establishment. The artillery completely lacked guns and the 19th and 20th *Panzergrenadier* (lorried infantry) Regiments (stationed at Zutphen and Rhenen, respectively) were without heavy weapons.

Elberfeld. While awaiting transport the remnants were to make up stand-by units which would go into action if Allied air-landings took place (which is also completely in line with Model's order of 11 September for constant readiness in this respect) or a rising of the Dutch people, which, in view of the weakness of the occupation force, the German High Command still considered possible. Entrainment of what was left of the division began on 13 September. In normal circumstances the movement would have been completed in several days, but railway traffic was rendered practically impossible in daytime by Allied fighters, while Resistance groups blew up the railway lines at night. Consequently, there was still a small number of units of the Hohenstaufen Division on the Veluwe the day the airborne operation started. The men and material that were ready to leave for Germany on that 13 September were, according to Harzer's report, quickly detrained on the order of Army Group B. Thus, despite what the legends say, *there was no German foreknowledge, and no well-equipped tank division happened to be passing through on its way from Germany to the front*. On the contrary, what we see is the chance encampment and departure to Germany of a defeated division. (Harzer estimates that the German fighting strength, including that of the Frundsberg Division, was at that moment no more than twenty per cent of the original.) In fact, there was not even a real division left. German reports on operations after 17 September no longer mention the Hohenstaufen Division but the *Kampfgruppe Harzer*.

And yet it was this *Kampfgruppe Harzer*, this shadow of a former tank division, which contributed decisively, particularly in the early stages, to the result of MARKET GARDEN. At a later stage in the battle the better-equipped Frundsberg Division was also to play an important part in the Betuwe, ie the area between the Rhine and the Waal, but it was Harzer who thwarted the British airborne troops at the most critical moment in the entire operation —the first few hours when the surprised enemy is still uncertain of the strength and objectives of the attackers and has still to organise his resistance.

If there is any question of a mystery, it is not the existence of Harzer's *Kampfgruppe* but the strength and speed with which it reacted in the afternoon of 17 September. This came as a surprise not only to the Allied commanders, from Montgomery to Urquhart. The German commanders, too, were astonished at the apparently unexplainable way in which Harzer produced armoured vehicles which at that moment should theoretically no longer have been in his possession. Even Field-Marshal von Rundstedt, the German Commander-in-Chief in the west, expressed his amazement. In the great game of MARKET GARDEN, these armoured vehicles were the trump card which Harzer had, not in his hand, but up his sleeve. Or rather, the card which, at the decisive moment, suddenly became a trump.

The explanation of this mystery was to be provided by events during the first few hours of MARKET GARDEN.

XI

After the war Montgomery wrote in his *Memoirs*: 'The 2nd SS Panzer Corps was refitting in the Arnhem area, having limped up there after its mauling in Normandy. We knew it was there. But we were wrong in supposing that it could not fight effectively: its battle state was far beyond our expectation.'

This miscalculation on the part of the Allies, as already said, considerably influenced the result of the battle of Arnhem and possibly also the duration of the war. The question, however, immediately arises whether Montgomery and other Allied commanders, or even staff Intelligence officers, could reasonably have been expected to see what the German High Command themselves had not seen: the card up Harzer's sleeve, a card whose full value even Harzer himself did not realise, not even when he saw with his own eyes the first British parachutes over Heelsum. And even if one assumes that in preparing for operations account must be taken not only of available information about the enemy but also of real possibilities about which no information has been obtained —if, in other words, every precaution is taken to guard against underestimating the enemy—the decision to go ahead with MARKET GARDEN cannot be viewed otherwise than against the background of the time and circumstances in which it was taken.

The Allied armies had reached a point which, according to the original time-table, they should not have reached until 180 days later; the German armies had suffered enormous losses and their reserves could not possibly be great; the Allied fleets and air forces controlled the sea and the air; the last enemy bulwark, Germany itself, was ripe for assault, and the fifth winter of war was approaching. The moment had now come to knock a hole in that bulwark with a lightning offensive and deliver the decisive attack through it. A combined ground-airborne attack in which a whole division was dropped more than sixty miles ahead of the ground troops from whom they would be separated by three large rivers and a number of canals, would have been an act of irresponsibility against a well-equipped enemy. But the state of the German troops in Holland about the middle of September 1944 made the risks undoubtedly attaching to MARKET GARDEN acceptable to Montgomery—and many with him.

What did the Allies know about the German troops north of the main Dutch rivers? A network existed for collecting and distributing information on this subject. That this entire system—from the man who gathered the information via the commander-in-chief who had to take it into account when making strategic decisions, to the field commander who was responsible for the tactical execution of these plans—could never be infallible, is obvious. The information had to be gathered in difficult conditions behind the lines by Resistance groups who had specialised in this type of work and by Allied agents dropped by parachute. Most of them had little if any military training. The German forces with their numerous kinds of uniforms and equipment, the cryptic designations of army units, the complicated organisation, the countless types and calibres of guns, the various makes of tanks and armoured cars—it was a subject practically impossible to master. Only a few experts were able to pick out the really important details from the mass. Then there is the fact that in September 1944 the confusion was further confounded by the disorganisation of some German army units. The term 'division' sometimes referred to a small group which in fighting strength did not much exceed a regiment.

If collecting and sifting information were difficult tasks, its transmission was no less difficult. Couriers, male and female, had to ride dozens of miles, sometimes even a hundred or more, on ramshackle bicycles (after four years of German occupation tyres were as scarce as most other commodities) in an occupied territory where they might be stopped and questioned at any moment by the Germans. It was sometimes possible to use the by now much-restricted telephone system, but only via secret lines. Journeys through the German lines to the Allies were dangerous. It was no less dangerous to operate transmitters; German radio direction-finder vans operated twenty-four hours a day. In any case, only a limited number of transmitters were available. Some of them were not even able to handle the large quantities of messages to be sent, and a backlog piled up or operators were obliged to make a selection. Under the circumstances it was a miracle that the Intelligence machinery was kept operating, a miracle made possible by the courage and perseverance of a small band of nameless men and women.

In addition to the information that reached the Allies in this way, information was also obtained by interrogating prisoners of war and by aerial reconnaissance. The interpretation of information often depended on the acuity, skill and interests of Intelligence officers on Allied staffs.

The overall picture thus finally formed of any particular situation was often very incomplete and had to be filled in with surmises which, in turn, naturally bore the personal imprint of the Intelligence officer concerned.

As to the enemy resistance that Operation MARKET GARDEN could be expected to encounter, the general opinion was that the ground troops (Horrocks' XXX Corps) would have to break through a hard but thin crust at the start of the offensive. Behind that crust the enemy—it was thought—had insufficient reserves to halt the corps' advance to the Zuider Zee. There were a few less optimistic voices but on the whole it was considered that the disorganised Germans could not have recovered sufficiently from their reverses and their flight to constitute a danger to the Allied troops.

Concerning the British 1st Airborne Division's knowledge of what awaited them north of the Rhine, Urquhart's information is very important. After all, as Commander of the division, he was responsible for the ground operations at Arnhem. In his book *Arnhem* he writes: 'I should have liked to put in troops on both sides of the river [the Rhine] and as close as possible to the main bridge. This was unacceptable to the RAF, however, because of the flak barrages which bomber crews on their nightly visits to the Ruhr reported as extremely heavy in the Arnhem area. It was also considered that the tug aircraft, in turning away after releasing their gliders in this area, would either have run straight into the flak over Deelen airfield some seven miles to the north or into a mix-up with the aircraft involved in the Nijmegen airlift [the American 82nd Airborne Division]. Furthermore, the intelligence experts regarded the low-lying polderland south of the bridge as unsuitable for both gliders and parachutists. These limitations were closely examined but the RAF had already conceded as much as they were ever likely to concede in agreeing to a daylight operation. An airborne operation remains the airmen's responsibility until such time as the troops are put on the ground. The airmen had the final say.'

Urquhart, who explains the choice of landing and dropping zones several miles from Arnhem as being due to the RAF's 'final say', nevertheless comes in his official report on the course of the battle to the conclusion that 'both the Army and the RAF were over-pessimistic about the flak. The forecast about the impossibility of landing gliders on the polder country [south of the bridge] was also wrong'.

Their estimate of the German flak was indeed too cautious. There were no longer any aircraft based on Deelen airfield and only a few Luftwaffe personnel were stationed there. Rauter declared after the war that the German flak at Deelen had been 'completely dismantled'. And Harzer states that on 18 September, the day before the first landings, his Hohenstaufen Division possessed only four 20 mm and two 88 mm guns. At the time of the first landings the 20 mms were at Dieren, where *SS Flakabteilung 9* was quartered as one of the stand-by units of the Hohenstaufen Division.

The plans for the actual *landing* operation were thus influenced by the available information about flak. At least equally important is what Urquhart knew about the resistance his troops would meet *on the ground*. On this subject he writes: 'The planning of the operation was not helped by the scanty intelligence that was coming our way. I knew extremely little of what was going on in and around Arnhem and my intelligence staff were scratching around for morsels of information. I knew that what information we had received from across the Channel was bound to be out of date: it had filtered through various offices in the Second Army and our own corps before it reached us. In the division there was a certain reserve about the optimistic reports coming through from 21st Army Group concerning the opposition we were likely to meet. Obviously we would have liked a more recent intelligence picture, but we were subordinate to corps in such matters. Browning himself told me that we were not likely to encounter anything more than a German brigade group supported by a few tanks. Already, however, Dutch resistance reports had been noted to the effect that "battered panzer remnants have been sent to Holland to refit", and Eindhoven and Nijmegen were mentioned as the reception areas. And during the week preceding the air-landing an intelligence officer at SHAEF, poring over reports and maps, came to the conclusion that these panzer formations were the 9th and possibly the 10th SS Panzer Divisions. It was likely that they were being re-equipped with new tanks from a depot in the area of Cleves, a few miles over the German border from Nijmegen and Arnhem. The SHAEF officer's opinions were not shared by others and, even as our preparations continued, 21st Army Group Intelligence were making it plain that they didn't see eye to eye with SHAEF over the panzer divisions. Nothing was being allowed to mar the optimism prevailing across the Channel. We all shared it to a certain degree, and this was particularly the case in our own Airborne Corps. On 13 September, four days before the attack, corps blithely passed on the information that the Germans in Holland had few infantry reserves and a total armoured strength of not more than fifty to a hundred tanks.'

That, then, was the British divisional commander's idea of what awaited him at Arnhem. A vague picture containing contradictory details, particularly as to the two German panzer divisions. Although, as already mentioned, it was not to be expected that the real mystery of the quick and drastic reaction of the Hohenstaufen Division would be revealed to the Allies in advance—it was not until 17 September that events gave an explanation which was almost disappointing in its simplicity—opinions in the Allied camp as to the two divisions in general, and whether they or any other forces were in the area or not, were somewhat divided. Had the certainty of the existence and quality of the two divisions been greater (although they were remnants, they consisted of crack troops with front-line experience), it might have been possible to avoid the under-estimation apparent in Montgomery's words: '... we were wrong in supposing that it [II SS Panzer Corps] could not fight effectively.' Both the activities of the Hohenstaufen Division in the very first stage of the fighting and those of the Hohenstaufen and Frundsberg Divisions in the later stages had a decisive effect on the result of the battle.

It is remarkable how contradictory the information and opinions about the two German divisions were at the various Allied headquarters.

The period which this information covers can be divided into the time before 4 September and the fortnight after it. The first of these constitutes no problem. During their forced march northwards from France the two SS divisions were then still in close contact with the American First Army, which was following on their heels. The reports of Intelligence officers agree in detail with the account of Harzer, the acting commander of the Hohenstaufen Division. These Allied reports contain the following entries:

30 August—9th SS moves from Amiens to St Quentin
1 September—10th SS battle units in Albert
2 September—9th and 10th SS battalions near Cambrai
3 September—men of 10th SS captured.

After that the two Panzer divisions slipped past the Allied advance posts and the Allies lost contact with them. For news of further movements of the divisions Intelligence now mainly depended on Resistance groups and agents in occupied territory. In *Top Secret* Ralph Ingersoll calls II SS Panzer Corps 'the one Panzer corps in the entire German Army of which British Intelligence had temporarily lost track'. That, as Urquhart's report shows, was not entirely true. The following was known about this corps at the various Allied levels of command:

SHAEF (Supreme Headquarters of the Allied Expeditionary Forces in Europe, under Eisenhower's command.) The Intelligence Summary for the week ending 16 September—one day before the air-landings—contained the statement that, according to information received, the 9th SS Panzer Division, and probably also the 10th, had been withdrawn to the Arnhem area where they would probably be issued with new tanks from a depot said to be in the vicinity of Cleves.

The *21st Army Group* (the most northerly of the Allied army groups, under Montgomery). According to Montgomery's *Memoirs*, this group was, as we have seen, aware of the divisions' existence but considered their fighting strength to be low. According to Urquhart, 21st Army Group 'did not see eye to eye with SHAEF over the Panzer Divisions'.

The *British Second Army* (one of the armies forming the 21st Army Group, under Dempsey's command). According to Chester Wilmot in *The Struggle for Europe*, General Dempsey had heard from his Intelligence officer before 10 September (!) that 'Dutch Resistance sources report that battered panzer formations have been sent to Holland to refit, and mention Eindhoven and Nijmegen as the reception areas'. This information, the origin of which is unknown, is dated 7 September in the report of the Second Army's Intelligence officer. (It was partly because of this message, writes Wilmot, that General Dempsey suggested to Montgomery on 10 September that the new offensive should be directed eastwards, to the Rhine near Wesel, instead of northwards. But that same day Montgomery decided on MARKET GARDEN.) On 12 September the Second Army reported that '9th SS and 10th SS (Panzer Divisions) were last identified in the great retreat on First US Army front . . . [what is left] may have made its way to Holland'. Finally, on 16 September, the Intelligence officer expresses the same opinion as SHAEF about the presence of the divisions in the Arnhem area. Concerning the importance which was attached to this information, Hilary St George Saunders (who was also commissioned by the British Air Ministry to write the official war history of the 1st and 6th Airborne Divisions) writes in *The Red Beret*: 'During the planning of operation "Market Garden" Dutch underground groups sent in information that there were SS troops with a not inconsiderable quantity of tanks just east of the Yssel and close to Arnhem. One of the Intelligence officers deduced from this that the 2nd SS Panzer Corps, which had been pulled out of the Normandy bridgehead in time to escape the final rout, was being reorganised in that area. This deduction was correct. His report, however, was received with incredulity at 2nd Army headquarters, which regarded the presence of tanks in or near Arnhem as highly improbable and asserted that no other source confirmed the information supplied by the Dutch resistance. Moreover, said the 2nd Army Intelligence, no tanks were to be seen on any of the reconnaissance photographs.'

XXX Corps (one of the army corps forming the Second Army, under the command of General Horrocks). Here, too, the Dutch Resistance group's report on the German Panzer formations was noted on 7 September, probably even before it was available to the Second Army. The normal procedure was for messages from occupied territory to be signalled first to London via secret transmitters and then passed on to the units concerned through the usual channels. The message dated 7 September about the Panzer troops, however, seems somehow or other to have reached xxx Corps direct from occupied territory and to have been passed on by them to the Second Army. Nevertheless, in his book, *A Full Life*, General Horrocks writes: 'Quite unknown to me, and, as far as I can make out, also to our own Intelligence service, a few days before, the 9th and 10th SS Panzer Divisions had arrived in the Zutphen area to refit.'

The *43rd Wessex Division* (one of the divisions in xxx Corps, commanded by General Thomas). On 16 September this division received orders for its part in the ground operations of MARKET GARDEN from the corps commander, General Horrocks: to advance via Eindhoven, Nijmegen and Arnhem to Apeldoorn, and to occupy the strip of territory between Arnhem and Apeldoorn. (A number of *Alarmeinheiten* of the Hohenstaufen Division were stationed along this strip.) Immediately after receipt of the order, General Thomas discussed its tactical execution with his staff officers. In *The 43rd Wessex Division at War, 1944–1945* Major-General Essame writes: 'He [General Thomas] opened up with the statement that the total German force ahead was quite inadequate to offer a prolonged resistance on any line and that armoured reserves of more than one squadron were most unlikely to be met.'

The *British I Airborne Corps* (forming part of the Allied First Airborne Army commanded by General Brereton which had been placed at Montgomery's disposal; the corps commander was General Browning). According to Urquhart, as already quoted, the mood here was 'optimistic'. Browning told Urquhart personally that he did not expect the opposition to be more than 'a few tanks'.

The *British 1st Airborne Division* (belonging to the British 1 Airborne Corps and commanded by General Urquhart). The information available to the division has already been summarised in the quotation from Urquhart.

The *2nd Battalion of the 1st Parachute Brigade* (part of the British 1st Airborne Division; the battalion, under the command of Lieutenant-Colonel J. D. Frost, fought at Arnhem bridge from 17 to 21 September). The *History of 2nd Battalion the Parachute Regiment* states: 'Information about the enemy was very favourable. It was thought that there were 2,000 SS recruits in Arnhem itself and that the only other opposition would come from Luftwaffe ground staff who manned an aerodrome some ten miles to the north (Deelen). There were, however, a large number of ack-ack guns defending the bridges.' The reaction when this information proved to be incorrect is described as follows in that same book: 'Another disturbing factor was that the prisoners taken during the evening were fully fledged SS Panzer Grenadiers, and it transpired that an SS Panzer Corps had been re-forming a very short way from Arnhem. Now, instead of dealing with raw recruits, the Battalion would have to beat off incessant attacks from well-seasoned and fanatical Hitlerite soldiers.'

XII

To what extent was information about the Hohenstaufen and Frundsberg Divisions (information which, as we have seen, did not get through to all Allied commanders and did not have the same impact at every level it in fact reached) based on messages from espionage groups in occupied Holland?

The source of *later* reports (eg SHAEF's of 16 September) is formed by a couple of messages which, according to copies which have survived, were dispatched from occupied territory on 14 September. The first message, from the 'Kees' espionage group, reads: *'SS divisie Hohenstrufl langs Ijssel, onderdelen hiervan waargenomen van Arnhem tot Zutphen, en langs de weg Zutphen-Apeldoorn. De staf wellicht in Eefde. Langs de Ijssel bouwt men thans veldversterkingen.'* The second message, from the 'Albrecht' espionage group stated that the Hohenstaufen SS Division was stationed along both sides of the Yssel between Zwolle and Arnhem and in the area to the east of this line, that Divisional HQ was probably at Doetinchem with other HQs at Beekbergen and Epse, and that 1,900 troops of the division were stationed north of a line Loenen–Zutphen. On 15 September the Military Intelligence Service of the British War Ministry recorded: 'SS Div. Hohenstrufl. along Yssel. Units from this division noticed from Arnhem to Zutphen-Apeldoorn. HQ perhaps at Eefde. Field fortifications are being built along Yssel.' In this English version of the 'Kees' group message the repetition of the spelling mistake ('Hohenstrufl' for Hohenstaufen) is a clear indication of the Dutch source.

It is possible after the event to see that these messages, too, contained inaccuracies, which is not at all surprising in view of the difficult circumstances in which the Dutch espionage groups had to operate. In fact, the headquarters of the Hohenstaufen Division were in Beekbergen, the Frundsberg Division's in Ruurlo and those of II SS Panzer Corps (to which both divisions belonged) at Doetinchem. The entire Hohenstaufen Division was stationed to the west of the Yssel. In the Albrecht message the Frundsberg Division (east of the Yssel) was mistaken for part of the Hohenstaufen Division. On 15 September the 'Kees' group sent another message which was recorded by the Intelligence Service in London as having been received on 16 September. It ran: 'At Arnhem MELDEKOPF HOHENSTAUFL. This is assembly place of members of the SS Division previously reported. Also at Arnhem MELDEKOPF HARZER presumably forming part of a unit situated south of Arnhem.' This incorrect message cannot have given the Allies anything to go on, although it at least confirmed the presence of the Hohenstaufen Division. Harzer, who commanded the division (the names 'Harzer' and 'Hohenstaufen' in the Dutch telegram were probably taken from signposts or boards in the town of Arnhem and both refer to the same unit) gave the following explanation of the word 'Meldekopf' after the war: 'My division had set up in Arnhem a "Meldekopf Hohenstaufen" where all men returning to their unit from ordinary or sick leave could find out where their unit was stationed. A "Meldekopf", then, was a purely administrative arrangement which could be found in any headquarters office.'

The scanty information circulating in Allied headquarters concerning the Hohenstaufen and Frundsberg Divisions shortly before the air-landings can thus be retracted to messages from Dutch espionage groups.

The origin of two other messages is shrouded in mystery. The first stated that the two German divisions were to be equipped with new tanks from a depot near Cleves; the second was the one which had been received a week earlier, on 7 September, by XXX Corps direct, the message from 'Dutch Resistance groups' about the battered Panzer formations which would probably be refitted in Eindhoven and Nijmegen.

There exists, however, a message dated 7 September sent from Roermond by the 'Albrecht' group: 'Large transports of SS Panzer troops have passed through here from the Maastricht direction and heading northwards to the Maas and Waal. Similar movements also went on throughout last night.' According to its commander, Harzer, however, the Hohenstaufen Division did not set out from Sittard in the direction of Roermond until 7 September. As the message talks of movements continuing throughout the night it could not have been passed on for transmission before the 8th. The leader of the 'Albrecht' group, who collected all incoming messages and passed them on to headquarters at Rotterdam, recorded that he received the message on 9 September and forwarded it to Rotterdam on the 11th. But it is not to be found among the copies of messages transmitted. Headquarters probably considered it out of date (there were days when the transmitter was on the air for six or seven hours, despite the unceasing activities of German radio direction-finding vans) and laid it aside.

These last few details are not of vital significance. It is certain that the presence of Panzer formations in Holland was known at the various Allied headquarters. The latter could probably only guess whether the Hohenstaufen Division reported from Holland was identical with the 9th SS Panzer Division which had last been identified on 3 September at Mons, retreating in a northward direction. Some commanders worried about the existence of those panzer formations, others considered their fighting power negligible. For a third group the reports were barely credible, and some commanders were simply not informed. But let us say it again: all these details must be seen against the background of the understandable optimism which had animated a number of Allied commanders after the resounding German defeats in France. It was probably this same confidence in the final results that pushed any thought of an alternative plan into the background during the tactical preparations for MARKET GARDEN. Even where the reports about the German Panzer divisions were known, they did not lead to any consideration of what was to be done if those divisions made it impossible to execute existing plans. As it turned out later, thought devoted to this possibility would not have been a waste of time.

XIII

Every great and audacious undertaking in which the margin between success and failure is so narrow that a freakish, practically unforeseeable, accident can decide the result, is a fruitful soil for the growth of legends. Small coincidences are seldom a satisfactory explanation of great consequences. Kings and generals do not trip over pebbles. But when they do, history is inclined to imagine a treacherous hand placing that pebble in their path. An insignificant stone is not acceptable as an actor in the drama; a human hand is called for. And from that need a legend is born.

MARKET GARDEN was no exception. Some persistent legends grew up round it. The presence of Harzer's armour in the path of the British airborne division was apparently inexplicable; it called for a deliberately malevolent brain. The facts provide another explanation—less romantic, but, on the other hand, historically correct. The only SS battalion in the immediate vicinity of the landing zones, Krafft's, had, according to Krafft's own report, been transferred there from the coastal area in the night of 3–4 September.

The battered Hohenstaufen and Frundsberg Divisions had, as an entry in Model's War diary shows, been ordered to Holland on 3 September. Their first units arrived in Arnhem on 7 September. On 10 September the German High Command decided that the Hohenstaufen Division (which was encamped on the Veluwe) would hand over its remaining equipment to the Frundsberg Division, to the east of the Yssel. The Frundsberg Division would be reorganised there; the last remnants of the Hohenstaufen Division would be gradually evacuated to Germany where an entirely new division would be formed. On Sunday, 17 September, after the first air-landings, a few railway coaches which were standing ready to leave for Germany were hastily unloaded again. Exactly when the first landing took place, Harzer, the commander of the Hohenstaufen Division was going to lunch with a number of other officers at Hoenderloo, a few miles north of the landing zones. They saw the paratroops coming down in the distance. And, according to Harzer's report, they went quietly in to lunch. 'I can', wrote Harzer, 'assure you that, so far as I know, no Dutchman betrayed anything that helped the German command. I should certainly have heard of it from Field-Marshal Model during the battle of Arnhem for he spent some time every day at my battle headquarters discussing the situation, and spoke very frankly to me.' The headquarters of Field-Marshal Model, the commander of Army Group B, were a mile or two to the east of the landing zones. Neither Model nor his chief-of-staff Krebs (to judge by the conversation they had with Rauter, the *Höherer SS-und Polizeiführer* in Holland, a few days before the landings) expected an Allied air-landing in this area: 'Montgomery will not rush into such a reckless adventure.' When the landings started, Model had just sat down at table. He had to depart hurriedly. Harzer, the commander of the Hohenstaufen Division, states: 'Field-Marshal Model had not received any information from agents about any impending air-landing in the Arnhem area, otherwise his advanced battle headquarters would not have remained in Oosterbeek until 13.00 hours on 17 September 1944 . . . The British did not know this, however, otherwise a capture would certainly have been possible.' And Krafft, the commander of the SS battalion stationed closest to the landing zones, wrote in the battle report which he later sent to Himmler: 'What is the enemy's aim in carrying out such a large-scale landing? Firstly, to neutralise or destroy the headquarters of Army Group B, of whose arrival in Oosterbeek he cannot have been ignorant . . .' Further on, Krafft comes to a different conclusion but he makes no mention of betrayal. Rauter, who as head of the Security Police in Holland must certainly have been well up to date with agents' reports, declared after the war: 'We were not informed, the air-landings came as a surprise to us all.'

At the time of the landing the Commander-in-Chief of occupied Holland, General Christiansen, and his chief-of-staff von Wühlisch were sitting lunching in an hotel outside Hilversum, far from their headquarters. After the war von Wühlisch told General van Hilten, head of the historical section of the Dutch General Staff, that for him, too, the air-landings had come as a complete surprise.

The American 101st Airborne Division were dropped north of Eindhoven, only a few miles from the headquarters of General Student, the commander of the German First Parachute Army. According to Student the air-landing operation was a 'total surprise'.

General Reinhard, the commander of the German LXXXVIII Corps, whose headquarters were at Moergestel near Tilburg, had gone to inspect his troops on the morning of 17 September. As he was returning, the Allied air armadas flew over him. For him, too— also according to a statement made to General van Hilten—the landings were a surprise. He quickly abandoned his car for the pillion-seat of a motor-cycle, and thus mounted returned to his headquarters.

Also on the morning of 17 September, the German supreme commander in the west, Field-Marshal von Rundstedt, ordered a thorough examination of the possibilities of Allied air and sea landings in the North of Holland. Von Rundstedt had decided on this order, which is recorded in the war diary of the *Oberbefehl-shaber West*, as a result of information about suspicious Allied reconnaissance activity in the area of the *West Frisian islands*. The result of the enquiry was to be reported to Hitler, but execution of this order was rendered superfluous a few hours later by the air-landings.

The details of German troop movements and the statements of the German commanders constitute incontrovertible proof that there was no betrayal.

The presence on the Veluwe of the Hohenstaufen Division—if this poor skeleton of its former self could still be called a division—is entirely explicable. The only remaining mystery is Harzer's armoured vehicles, which, according to orders could no longer have existed. This last mystery was to be cleared up in the afternoon of 17 September.

XIV

And thus Field-Marshal Montgomery and Field-Marshal Model faced each other on 17 September. The front followed a long stretch of the Maas-Scheldt canal through the north of Belgium, in a line from Antwerp to Maastricht. After a period of inactivity the Allied forces were about to open a new offensive. On the ground Horrocks' xxx Corps had to break out from the bridgehead at Neerpelt and advance to the Zuider Zee via Eindhoven, Nijmegen, Arnhem and Apeldoorn. All the German troops on the coast (including von Zangen's Fifteenth Army), the V1 launching bases and the ports of Antwerp, Rotterdam and Amsterdam would thus be cut off from their supplies from Germany. A bridgehead across the Yssel north of Arnhem would be the point of departure for an offensive round the northern end of the Siegfried Line to the open North German plain and the Ruhr, which was so important for German war efforts. The offensive of xxx Corps (part of Dempsey's Second British Army) was to be supported by three airborne divisions who were to capture the bridges at Eindhoven, Nijmegen and Arnhem. It was expected that xxx Corps would take about four and not more than five days to reach the Zuider Zee.

Operation MARKET GARDEN was audacious and in many respects unique. Expectations about German opposition were, with a few exceptions, generally optimistic. The ground forces would have to break through the hard but thin crust, with behind it no German troops of any significance. The presence of two battered Panzer divisions in the Arnhem area was known or suspected in some headquarters, and opinions as to their fighting power ranged from slight concern to carefree optimism. The weather was an uncertain factor; since a shortage of aircraft meant that the divisions could not be flown over in a single lift but only in several lifts spread over successive days, bad flying weather could delay the arrival of reinforcements and also of supplies for the tens of thousands of men involved. The Germans were expecting a new Allied offensive. They thought it would be directed over the Maas-Scheldt Canal towards Roermond and thence through the Siegfried Line to the Rhine. It was on the far side of the Rhine, to the North of the Ruhr, that Allied airborne landings were expected 'at an as yet indefinite date' (see map 1). Model, commanding Army Group B, had established his headquarters securely behind the Dutch rivers, at Oosterbeek. The battle area south of the rivers was divided into two. In the western sector (Zeeland and West Brabant) was von Zangen's Fifteenth Army. The eastern sector, opposite the British Second Army, was held by Student's new First Parachute Army. North of the rivers command was theoretically exercised by the *Wehrmachtsbefehlshaber Niederlande*, General Christiansen, who was considered unsuitable for battle command. The forces in his area included some reasonably good SS battalions (such as Eberwein's, Lippert's and Krafft's) and a number of units of low fighting value made up of Luftwaffe ground staff and gunners from the French Channel coast: the harvest of General von Tettau's reception centre, later sometimes loosely called von Tettau's division. They also comprised several depot battalions of the Hermann Goering Division—very youthful and untrained but fanatical recruits—a surveillance battalion of Dutch SS from Amersfoort concentration camp under the command of Helle, and Bittrich's II SS Panzer Corps, consisting of the 9th SS Panzer Division (Hohenstaufen) and the 10th SS Panzer Division (Frundsberg). All that was left of the Hohenstaufen Division under Harzer was a number of *Alarmeinheiten* (about 2,500 men in all), scattered over the Veluwe. The Frundsberg Division under Harmel, which was stationed to the east of the Yssel, was somewhat better equipped because it was being refitted there.

X V

The last few hours before the start of MARKET GARDEN passed. At Hitler's headquarters, the Wolfschanze, an important conference was held on Saturday, 16 September. It was here that Hitler first revealed his plan for the Ardennes offensive.

In the night from Saturday to Sunday the Allied air forces bombed the German airbase of Rheine, where the Luftwaffe's latest acquisition was stationed: the Me 262, a fighter with a turbo-jet engine.

The Sunday brought good weather. On a number of airfields in England the engines of the hundreds of aircraft which were to take part in MARKET GARDEN started up. The officers and men of the British 1st Airborne Division slowly realised that the moment for which they had so often prepared had now finally arrived. Time after time they had had to study aerial photographs, always of a different area. And every time a plan had been cancelled, something of the tension had remained, a dissatisfied feeling. For some it was a relief on that 17 September to know that within a few hours they would be in action on Dutch soil.

About noon on the same Sunday General Christiansen and his chief-of-staff von Wühlisch were sitting down to table in the Crailoo Hotel near Hilversum.

At Oosterbeek Field-Marshal Model was preparing to have lunch with his officers in the Tafelberg Hotel.

At Amersfoort 2nd Lieutenant and Adjutant Naumann was on duty in the office of the SS surveillance battalion. He was reading a novel. His commanding officer Helle was away on a visit. And Naumann knew better than to bother Helle when he was away on special visits such as this one was. In any case, there was not the slightest reason for doing so on that sunny Sunday. All was quiet.

The commander of the Hohenstaufen Division was driving with Captain Scheffler and 2nd Lieutenant Engel from Beekbergen, where his headquarters were, to the village of Hoenderloo on the Veluwe. Harzer was going there to decorate Gräbner, the commander of his reconnaissance battalion, with the Iron Cross. Gräbner had won this distinction in Normandy.

'It was a sunny day,' Harzer recalls, 'a typically quiet and peaceful Sunday.'

Major General R. E. Urquhart, C.B., D.S.O., commander of the 1st British Airborne Division.

British parachutists jumping over one of the dropping zones near Arnhem on 17 September 1944. Bottom left, parachutes with containers in which supplies were dropped.

CHAPTER THREE

MODEL MISSES HIS LUNCH

(*17 September 1944*)

I

The Gelderland countryside on a sunlit Sunday in September. The late summer lies silent and unsuspecting over the high, sloping sandy ground on the north bank of the Rhine. Villages and pieces of flat farmland dot the expanse of forest. Roads and paths wind through woods and housing estates. Behind thick bushes and tall trees the distant white of a stretch of wall: a country house, a hotel, a convalescent home, a conference centre. Tall gates and thick hedges shield them from the world outside. Behind them, in the distance, the green edge of the pinewood reappears. An occasional wide view to the south: the wilfully rippling silver strip of the Rhine. On the far side, beyond the dyke, the low polders of the Betuwe with their orchards. On this side, straight through a region of woods, moorland, villages and country estates, Arnhem's connections with the west of Holland extend like the outspread fingers of a hand: a few wide main roads, a railway line, a narrower path —the little finger of the hand—along the Rhine. They join in Arnhem. Even the Rhine there makes a wide bend to converge with the built-up areas of Gelderland's capital.

A sunny Sunday in September 1944.

In wartime.

From the early morning hours until noon Allied bombers have attacked German anti-aircraft positions at various places in Holland. Along the Rhine, for instance, at Rhenen and Arnhem. Now all is quiet again. In Oosterbeek Field-Marshal Model is sitting down to lunch. Rauter has left his headquarters at Apeldoorn for the weekend and gone to the Hague. Christiansen and von Wühlisch are lunching in an hotel outside Hilversum. At Amersfoort, in Helle's battalion orderly-room, Naumann is on duty —reading.

And Harzer, the commander of the Hohenstaufen Division, is delivering a speech at Hoenderloo. That, in the middle of the Veluwe, ten miles north of Arnhem, is where the reconnaissance unit of this division is stationed. The entire unit, 500 strong, is formed up in a square. On either side stand a few troop-carrying armoured vehicles, with wheels in front and crawler tracks in the rear, ie half-tracks, not tanks. Gräbner, the commander of the reconnaissance unit of the Hohenstaufen Division, had been detached to the 277th Infantry Division for a time during the fighting in Normandy. He fought to such good purpose that he won the Knight's Cross of the Iron Cross. That distinction was now, on 17 September, being presented to him by Harzer. Harzer says there was no music. 'I made a speech in which I referred again to the bravery of the troops and their commander, Gräbner, in Normandy. Then I pinned the Knight's Cross on his breast.'

At that moment some British aircraft were approaching from the west. They were flying low and slowly. They were the advanced elements of a long stream of Dakotas, bombers and gliders.

A few hours earlier the largest air fleet ever used for an air-landing operation had taken off from twenty-four airfields in England; it consisted of 1,545 powered aircraft and 478 gliders. Off the English coast they had formed into two elongated groups. One flew via Belgium to Brabant: the American 101st Division which was to drop north of Eindhoven. The second group followed a more northerly course over the islands of Zeeland: the American 82nd Division and General Browning's headquarters staff, who were to land near Nijmegen, and the British 1st Airborne Division, whose landing and dropping zones were near Arnhem. Both routes across the North Sea had been carefully marked with radio beacons. A chain of aircraft and launches of the air-sea rescue service stood by along the routes to give immediate assistance in case of ditchings. This precaution was instrumental in saving over 200 men from the sea.

When the two air fleets arrived over occupied territory about

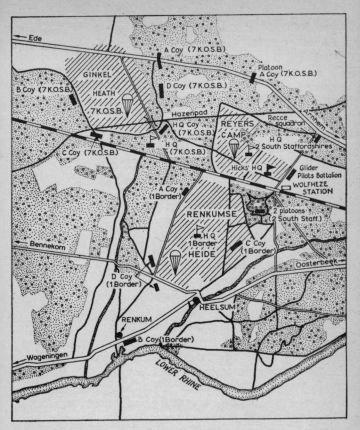

MAP 4 Sketch map of the area west of Arnhem, showing the three landing and dropping zones and the dispositions of the British battalions which were detailed to protect them (situation in the afternoon of 17 September 1944). The 'European' highway E 12 now follows the line of the 'Hazenpad'.

1 pm several dozen aircraft were lost by flak. In relation to the total number of aircraft involved, however, losses were remarkably low. There was practically no opposition from German fighters. The air transports were protected by some 900 American and British fighters.

General Horrocks watched the more southerly of the two streams cross into enemy airspace. The commander of xxx Corps was sitting on the flat roof of a factory on the bank of the Maas-Scheldt Canal. Now and then there was the thud of an exploding shell or the staccato rattle of a machine-gun. But apart from that, this Sunday here, too, was—in Horrocks' own words—'peaceful and sunny'. This state of affairs was not to continue long.

Horrocks knew that on the ground below him 350 camouflaged guns stood ready to fire. The Allies were counting on the Germans having sent all their reserves to this threatened part of the front (the bridgehead at Neerpelt). The British artillery had to batter this enemy resistance flat to enable xxx Corps to advance. When Horrocks saw the air armada approach, he gave the final orders for the ground operations of MARKET GARDEN. And as the British artillery burst into action, the tanks of the Irish Guards trundled to the point from which they would start attacking half an hour later. Thirty thousand men and many tons of equipment were about to be delivered to the dropping and landing zones at Eindhoven, Nijmegen and Arnhem. The northern stream had meanwhile divided into two, one half flying to Nijmegen, the other to the Heelsum area. Ahead of each division flew a marker force of pathfinders, who arrived first at the landing and dropping zones and marked the way for the main force with smoke signals.

'As the troops were moving off to their quarters and the officers and myself were making for the officers' mess for lunch, we saw the first British parachutes in the sky over Arnhem,' says Harzer, the commander of the Hohenstaufen Division. 'It could not be deduced at this stage that a large-scale operation was under way and we sat down quietly to lunch.'

But while here and at other places in Holland German commanders at various levels were sitting at their midday meal, American and British paratroops were dropping like confetti from a clear sky over Brabant and Gelderland, and gliders were tracing out strange patterns on the dry sandy soil with their undercarriages.

It was about 13.30 hours.

At practically the same time the tanks of the Irish Guards started moving off at Neerpelt. Less than a hundred yards ahead of them the curtain of exploding shells from their own guns moved forward at the same speed. Now the German anti-tank guns went into action. One British tank after the other was hit and disabled. Two hundred Typhoons of the RAF intervened in the fight and sent their rockets screaming into the German defence lines. Slowly the British advance gathered speed.

Sixty miles further north, near Heelsum, the reception was quieter. On two sites, one on either side of the Arnhem-Ede railway, the Renkum Heath and Reyerscamp Farm, Major Wilson's 'marker force' had marked the destination of some 350 gliders and over 150 transport aircraft with smoke signals and coloured nylon sheets. On the arable land of Reyerscamp Farm, north of the railway line, only gliders landed. On Renkum Heath, in addition to gliders, hundreds of paratroops came down.

Before the eyes of the people living round about, as they watched liberation descend upon them from the skies, there unrolled a picture of seemingly infinite chaos on the landing and dropping zones. Jeeps and light guns were wheeled from the landed gliders. Some gliders had been damaged on landing and had to be hacked open before they could be unloaded. Jeeps were driving straight through hedges and barbed-wire fences. Terrified horses and cows were caught by farmers with the assistance of British paratroops and led to their stables and byres. Renkum Heath was strewn with parachutes. Here and there green, yellow or purple smoke rose to mark the assembly points of various units. Wireless operators hunted about for their transmitters, doctors for their ambulance jeeps, pioneers for their implements. One officer asked for a farm-cart and horse to take the scattered ammunition containers to a central depot. Dutch civilians were asked questions such as: 'Does anyone here speak English?', 'Are there Germans round about here?', 'Can you show me where I am on the map?' or 'What's the way to Arnhem?' Ankle injuries sustained in the landing were being treated in a barn. A room in a large farm was evacuated and fitted up as a temporary headquarters. Trenches were dug in the rose-beds round the farmhouse. Machine-guns were set up at the open upstair windows.

An apparently inextricable confusion, the vulnerable opening phase in an airborne operation, when units have not yet formed up and individuals have not grouped themselves into disciplined units under familiar NCOs and officers. But there were also gaps. Some aircraft had been lost during the lift; officers and men were missing from some units; other units were without transport and heavy weapons. An enemy attack during this stage would have placed the airborne troops in a difficult, well-nigh impossible predicament. On the other hand, the enemy, too, needed time to recover from his surprise and take counter-measures.

I I

Within an hour and a half the British airborne troops under General Urquhart's command were ready to march off. Apart from unavoidable small incidents the airborne landing was a success. The only real drawback was the extreme difficulty, if not impossibility, of establishing radio contact between the various units. The radio sets were not designed for this wooded and steeply sloping terrain. This was a handicap which would be felt more and more sorely in the days that followed.

Viewed as a whole, the first task of the landed units consisted of two main parts (see maps 4 and 5).

The 1st Parachute Brigade under the command of Brigadier G. W. Lathbury was to move off as quickly as possible to Arnhem. It was planned that the Reconnaissance Squadron of this brigade, which was scheduled to land first with its vehicles, should set off immediately, capture the bridge in a surprise attack and hold it until the arrival of the main force of the brigade.

The three battalions of the brigade were to march by three gradually converging routes from Heelsum to Arnhem. The 2nd Battalion, under the command of Lieutenant-Colonel J. D. Frost, was to follow the narrow road along the Neder Rijn through Oosterbeek-Laag, reinforce Major C. F. H. Gough's Reconnaissance Squadron at the bridge, occupy the northern and southern approaches and guard it against attacks from the west and northwest.

Simultaneously the 3rd Battalion, commanded by Lieutenant-Colonel J. A. C. Fitch, was to follow the Utrecht road from Heel-

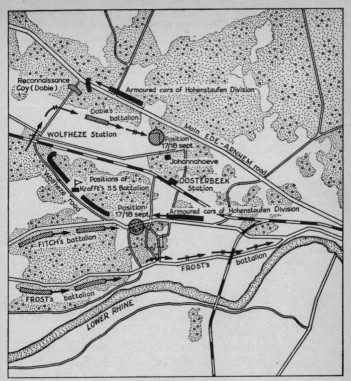

MAP 5 The advance of the three parachute battalions. The 1st Battalion under the command of Lt-Col Dobie reached the wood NW of Johannahoeve Farm in the evening; the 2nd Battalion led by Lt-Col Frost succeeded in occupying the road bridge at Arnhem; the 3rd Battalion under Lt-Col Fitch ran into enemy units and dug in round the Koude Herberg café.

sum to Arnhem, and upon arrival at the northern end of the bridge, guard it against attack from the north-east and east.

The 1st Battalion, under Lieutenant-Colonel D. Dobie, was to wait until it was definitely known that the other two battalions were making satisfactory progress. It was then to take the most northerly route, the main Ede-Arnhem road. Its instructions were not to go to the bridge but to occupy the high ground immediately to the north of the town.

If everything went according to plan, Dobie's 1st Battalion would by the evening of 17 September be guarding the Ede and Apeldoorn approaches to Arnhem and forming a cordon round the 2nd and 3rd Battalions occupying the bridge.

The first setback, however, was received immediately after the landing. Major Gough's Reconnaissance Squadron, which was supposed to drive to the bridge as quickly as possible without waiting for the parachute battalions to assemble, could not carry out its assignment because most of its vehicles were missing. They were in some of the gliders which had failed to reach their destination. Urquhart accordingly ordered Brigadier Lathbury to speed up the departure of Frost's 2nd Battalion—which was to take the most southerly route along the bank of the Rhine. The road bridge at Arnhem was the goal of the entire operation; it had to be captured before the Germans had a chance to demolish it.

That, then, was the job of the 1st Parachute Brigade.

The 1st Airlanding Brigade (which had landed not by parachute but in gliders) had a different job. The three battalions of this brigade, which was under the command of Brigadier P. H. W. Hicks, were to remain behind at the landing and dropping zones and occupy them in preparation for the second lift which was due to arrive next morning (18 September).

The 1st Battalion of the Border Regiment, under the command of Lieutenant-Colonel T. Hadden, occupied Renkum Heath; Reyerscamp was occupied by the 2nd Battalion of the South Staffordshire Regt, under Lieutenant-Colonel W. D. H. McCardie. These zones had already been used on 17 September. The 7th Battalion of the King's Own Scottish Borderers, commanded by Lieutenant-Colonel R. Payton-Reid, moved off to Ginkel Heath, a mile or two to the west of Reyerscamp, between the Utrecht-Arnhem railway line and the Ede-Arnhem road. This landing zone was to be used for the first time on 18 September.

The three battalions (1st, 2nd and 3rd) of the Parachute Brigade thus marched towards Arnhem; the three battalions (1st Border, 2nd South Staffs and 7th KOSB) of the 1st Airlanding Brigade stayed behind to guard the landing zones for the second lift on the morning of Monday, 18 September (see map 4).

At 3 pm Frost's and Fitch's battalions were ready to go. Frost's 2nd Battalion had in fact already taken twelve German prisoners of war at the collecting point: an administrative unit under the command of the German Colonel Krumpitz. As the 2nd Battalion was about to march off, the commander of the Parachute Brigade, Lathbury, received a message stating that Gough's Reconnaissance Squadron had lost practically all their transport and could not carry out their orders to occupy the bridge. Lathbury therefore ordered the 2nd and 3rd Battalions to march to the bridge as quickly as possible. After all, not much opposition was expected. Between 3 and 3.30 pm the two battalions set off in the direction of the bridge, following different routes. Brigade Commander Lathbury and his headquarters staff joined Frost's 2nd Battalion which was taking the southern route along the Rhine. About half an hour later Dobie's 1st Battalion also set off, making for Wolfheze station. This battalion was taking the northern route.

III

Meanwhile various things had been happening on the German side. The air-landing had descended like a bolt from the blue upon the unsuspecting Germans on this peaceful September Sunday. Field-Marshal Model, the commander of Army Group B, received the message just as he was about to sit down to eat with his officers in the Tafelberg Hotel at Oosterbeek: Allied airborne landings only two or three miles to the west. Model himself rushed to his room and crammed a few personal belongings into a suitcase. His officers rapidly and nervously gave orders for the headquarters to be evacuated. Outside the hotel, an uneasy driver was sitting in his car, sounding the hooter to urge his superior officers to still greater haste. Model, lugging his suitcase along, ran down the steps. It would be an inglorious end to a brilliant career if he were captured now, sixty miles behind the lines. Outside the hotel the lid of his suitcase burst open, spilling the contents all over the road. But seconds later, he was speeding on his way to Arnhem. There he quickly visited the *Feldkommandantur* (Area Command HQ) where he ordered General Kussin to radio the latest developments direct to Hitler. He could not refrain from mentioning that he had escaped through the eye of a needle—a detail which Kussin considered so important that he also telegraphed it to the Führer. Neither of them suspected that the British were at that moment busy forming up on the landing and dropping zones, quite unaware of the fact that Model had almost been theirs for the taking.

In Hitler's East Prussian headquarters at the Wolfschanze the news of the Allied air-landings caused great consternation. Just the day before, 16 September, Hitler had revealed his plans for the coming Ardennes offensive. Discussion of it was to be resumed on 17 September, but the report of the new Allied offensive caused a rapid change of topic. Model's close escape in particular made a deep impression on Hitler. The shorthand records of his conferences which have survived report him as having said: '. . . At any rate the business is so dangerous that you must understand clearly: if such a mess happens here—here I sit with my whole supreme command; here sit the *Reichsmarschal* [Goering], the OKH, the *Reichsführer*—SS [Himmler], the Reich Foreign Minister [Ribbentrop]!—Well, then, this is the most worthwhile catch, that's obvious. I would not hesitate to risk two parachute divisions here if with one blow I could get my hands on the whole German command.'

Model meanwhile continued his journey to Doetinchem, to the headquarters of General Bittrich, the commander of II SS Panzer Corps.

General Kussin decided to drive westwards with a few staff officers to assess the situation personally and see what measures had been taken by Major Krafft, whose battalion was stationed in the area. Several hours later Kussin was killed by a bullet from a British bren-gun.

IV

Höherer SS-und Polizeiführer Rauter was in the Hague when he received a message via the Luftwaffe signals network to the effect that large groups of aircraft, including a number of gliders, had crossed the coast. Everything pointed to air-landings. The strength of the Allied troops was estimated at one and a half divisions at least. Rauter immediately passed this message on to his superior officer Himmler in Germany and added that he was going to his headquarters at Apeldoorn to place himself at Model's orders.

Before leaving for Apeldoorn he first made two telephone calls. The first was to Amersfoort, to Helle's surveillance battalion. Helle himself was not there. He was paying a Sunday visit to a female acquaintance. This affair of Helle's was a constant source of quiet amusement to the strange collection of press-ganged young men who formed his SS battalion. From time to time Helle used to make impassioned speeches to his soldiers on the superiority of the fair-haired blue-eyed Nordic race, while everyone knew that his female acquaintance possessed none of the characteristics of that race.

So Helle was away. Second-Lieutenant and Adjutant Naumann was on duty in the battalion office. He was interrupted in his novel-reading by the telephone. It was Brinkmann, the town major of Amersfoort, telling him that large numbers of parachute troops had been dropped in the Betuwe area, between the Neder Rijn and the Waal, and asking whether it would not be a good idea for Naumann to despatch his *Jagdkommando*. Naumann put Brinkmann off with a few vague remarks and returned to his book. He had no intention of following Brinkmann's advice. How could he possibly get his *Jagdkommando* together? It was Sunday and his men had gone out walking with their girl-friends. And to disturb Helle at this time of day with Brinkmann's somewhat hysterical suggestion seemed about as sensible to Naumann as pulling a sleeping tiger's tail.

The telephone rang again. This time it was the hard, clipped tones of Rauter, telling him to get the battalion ready to move off and then await orders, and that the commander and staff officers were to report to General von Tettau at Grebbeberg, near Rhenen. This time Naumann was more inclined to act. He began by calling the company commanders together. Then he sent for a car and discreetly alerted Helle. He left the necessary orders for the officers and, when Helle arrived, was able to accompany him straight to Grebbeberg. He thus forestalled Helle's angry blustering. By presenting him with the fact that he, Helle, the military nonentity, had to go to war at the head of a battalion of loafers, Naumann rendered his dreaded commander as meek as a lamb.

Rauter's second telephone call before leaving the Hague for Apeldoorn was to General Christiansen's headquarters. The call was taken by von Wühlisch and the conversation between the two arch-enemies did not have the result that the energetic SS general was expecting. Rauter explained the situation to von Wühlisch, and advised that all available Wehrmacht units should be directed to the threatened areas. Nothing was further from the matter-of-fact Wehrmacht general's intention. So far as he was concerned, the end of Germany's senseless resistance could not come quickly enough. The war was lost—why go on fighting? And anyway, why should he accept orders from this SS general who had spared no effort to get him out of the way?

Von Wühlisch told Rauter he could not spare a man: he wanted to keep his last remaining reserves in case the civil population rose. Rauter replied that any such rising would have to be put down by batmen and telephone operators, and that every fighting man was needed at the front. He, Rauter, had at any rate sent his SS units there. Von Wühlisch coldly and ironically wished him luck in this undertaking and hung up.

Christiansen was not so happy about the way his chief-of-staff had dealt with this call. He himself was still under an obligation to use the troops in his command area in case of emergency, and this was unmistakably such a case. Though they did not constitute much of a deterrent, his troops came under the command of Army Group B for tactical operations. Christiansen therefore tried to get in touch by telephone with Model's headquarters at Oosterbeek. Perhaps Model could make do with the remnants of the Hohenstaufen Division, who were stationed not far away, on the Veluwe. Christiansen was not a minute too early. The only response from Oosterbeek was the excited voice of a staff officer shouting: 'We're getting out of here!' Then there was silence. A second attempt to establish telephone contact with Oosterbeek failed completely.

While he was not entirely unresponsive to his much more competent chief-of-staff's argument that it would be military madness to go on fighting, Christiansen was also apprehensive of his Führer Hitler, to whom he did not wish to be unloyal and who, he knew, would refuse to capitulate. He therefore made a final attempt to shed his personal responsibility, at least in part. He tried to make direct contact with the remnants of the Hohenstaufen Division on the Veluwe. But when he was told that this division was already carrying out orders from another source, he had no choice but to take action himself. He ordered Colonel Lippert, who commanded the western wing of General von Tettau's 'reception screen' to report to von Tettau with every man he could get hold of from his SS school for NCOs. Not until the next day did he dispatch any more units; there were two companies of the Field Security Regiment which was actually his personal bodyguard, and he sent them straight to the Veluwe.

V

In the 'Old Gentlemen's Club' at Grebbeberg—General von Tettau's headquarters—the days of peace and quiet came to an end on 17 September. Early in the morning Allied aircraft had destroyed the quiet of the Sabbath with their attacks on the German anti-aircraft guns mounted on boats on the Rhine. Von Tettau and his officers could not know that these attacks were part of the preparations for an airborne operation. Peace returned temporarily. But about half-past one von Tettau and his chief-of-staff Uhlrich received their second shock. And this time it looked more serious. A huge air fleet roared low over their heads in an easterly direction: transport aircraft and bombers with gliders in tow. It was obvious that the landing zones could not be far away. Von Tettau stood staring impotently; the flak on the river had already been silenced that morning. He tried to find out what was going on but the incoming reports were contradictory and confused. And what could he do with his 'division'—that strange conglomeration which included only a few battalions that were of any use?

At 16.20 hours von Tettau sent a wireless message to SS Major Krafft, who commanded the eastern wing of the screen and was stationed at Oosterbeek with two companies of his training battalion. The message ran: 'Enemy air-landings at Driel, Culemborg,

Zaltbommel and Nijmegen. Attack independently.' But there was no question of air-landings at Driel, or Culemborg, or Zaltbommel. There was at Nijmegen—by the American 82nd Airborne Division. Von Tettau appeared to know nothing about Arnhem. That was nearly three hours after the start of the air-landings, which had taken place less than ten miles from his headquarters.

VI

Although Krafft, knowing the fighting strength of his troops (some being practically untrained recruits, some older men declared medically unfit for active service), was not immediately capable of developing a large-scale attack, he had nevertheless displayed some initiative in the meantime. When he saw the British troops dropping to the west near Heelsum and Reyerscamp Farm, he decided to evacuate his position at Oosterbeek and occupy a more westerly one along the Wolfhezerweg, the road which runs from Wolfheze station in a south-easterly direction to the main Utrecht-Arnhem road. For the subsequent course of the battle it is important to know that Krafft's line did not quite extend to the station but curved to the north-east a short distance from it, joining the railway line at a point about 500 yards to the east of the station. The station and the railway-crossing were therefore outside his position (see map 6). One of his two companies (the 4th) was already along the Wolfhezerweg. The other (the 2nd) was now sent to join it there; Krafft himself chose the Wolfheze Hotel in the middle of the line as his command post.

The logic on which Krafft's measures were based reveals a certain degree of intelligence. When he observed the British air-landings about 1.30, he must quickly have concluded—at least to judge by his battle report—that Model's headquarters could not have been the target of the British, otherwise they would have organised their landings so that Model was surrounded right from the start. The Deelen airfield to the north was not their objective either—it had been bombed earlier that same morning by Allied aircraft. Moreover, it was too far from the landing and dropping zones. The bridge at Arnhem was the likeliest objective of the British operation. Krafft quickly calculated that his was the only

German unit between the British and the bridge. He had to delay the advance of the airborne troops as long as possible, at least until Harzer with the remains of his Hohenstaufen and Harmel with the battered Frundsberg Division could get through to him. The British would naturally try to get from their landing zones near Heelsum to Arnhem as quickly as possible. The main road from Ede to Arnhem in the north and the narrow road along the Rhine could therefore be ignored. The shortest way was the main Utrecht road, which was also suitable for their heavy equipment, while the British infantry could move unseen through the woods to the north of that road. A second possibility was that the British would follow the Utrecht–Arnhem railway line, which was a still shorter way. Krafft therefore took up a position between these two approaches, concluding that whether the enemy attacked his position or executed an outflanking movement, it would cost them precious time. Time which the Germans could put to good use by bringing up reinforcements.

For the civilian residents at Wolfheze Hotel, Krafft's choice of headquarters was not a very happy one. Two sisters, who had previously kept a rest home for the aged at the Hague and been compulsorily evacuated from that city, had decided after long deliberation to transfer their institution to this country hotel at Wolfheze with its magnificent surroundings. Now suddenly, on 17 September, the aged ladies and gentlemen found themselves occupying the middle of Krafft's position.

Krafft ordered all his heavy weapons to be transferred to a new position; these comprised anti-tank guns, anti-aircraft guns, a mortar section, a flamethrower and a *Werferrahm*.[1]

As the presence of Krafft's battalion has, as already mentioned, had the effect in some quarters of strengthening the betrayal myth, it is important to examine the subsequent adventures of this battalion on 17 September. From Krafft's own battle report we have already seen that some companies had arrived in the area before the plans for Operation MARKET GARDEN came into existence. The rest of the report reveals—at any rate to those who know the plans and

[1] A German projector frame from which several heavy shells could be fired simultaneously.

movements of the British paratroop battalions—how little effect Krafft's operations had on the advance of the British to the bridge at Arnhem.

At 13.45 hours Krafft ordered his 2nd and 4th Companies to take up their positions along the Wolfhezerweg. At the same time he sent an order to Arnhem to his 9th Company, which consisted mainly of diet cases, instructing them to march to his previous headquarters and await fresh orders there. He also sent out two scouting parties. One in fact stumbled upon the British and was captured; the other returned to report that they had not contacted the enemy. Krafft then sent General von Tettau a wireless message stating that in his estimation the enemy strength was two battalions and that he was going in to attack.

At 14.00 hours his 2nd Company opened fire with machine-guns on the British, but it quickly withdrew to its own position for fear of being encircled.

Krafft, who had still no clear idea of what exactly was happening, decided to do some personal reconnaissance. After passing over the railway-crossing at Wolfheze station, he came within several hundred yards of running into the enemy on his motor-cycle. At least, according to his own account, he barely managed to escape capture.

It is probably owing to the confused and uncertain picture created by any airborne operation that Krafft, like several other commanding officers on 17 September, did the thing that General Gavin—the commander of the 82nd American Airborne Division which landed at Nijmegen—so expressly warned against after the war in his book *Airborne Warfare*. Gavin writes that in the event of an air-landing the commander of the opposing forces can probably do his job best by remaining at his headquarters instead of going personally into battle.

Krafft was not the only one who failed to observe this wise rule. A few hours later the German Area Commander of Arnhem, General Kussin, made the same mistake. He was less fortunate than Krafft. Even General Urquhart, the commander of the British Airborne Division, was to learn on that same day, and in a not particularly pleasant manner, the lesson that Gavin teaches in his book. At 15.30 hours Krafft's 9th Company arrived from Arnhem. It was held in reserve for the time being. It brought the total strength of the battalion up to: 13 officers, 73 NCOs and 349 men (see map 6).

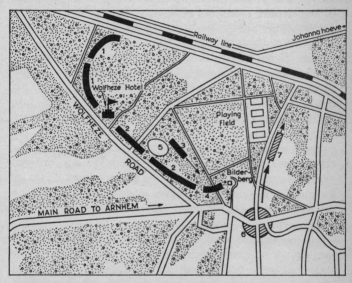

MAP 6 Disposition of Krafft's SS Battalion on the Wolfheze road (headquarters in Wolfheze Hotel). 1, 2 and 3: positions of 4th, 2nd and 9th Companies respectively. The 9th Company, originally in the second line, moved in between the 2nd Company and the Bilderberg Hotel (4); 5. mortar position; 6. position of Fitch's parachute battalion in the night of 17–18 September; 7. C Company was ordered to advance to the bridge at Arnhem via the railway line.

At 15.35 Krafft informed General von Tettau by radio of the measures he had taken.

At 16.20 he received from von Tettau the message, already referred to, about 'enemy air-landings at Driel, Culemborg, Zaltbommel and Nijmegen'. And the order to attack. This message revealed how much von Tettau, four hours after the air-landings had started only some ten miles from his headquarters, was still in the dark about the facts.

At 17.00 Krafft's 2nd Company, which was holding the southern part of the position round the Bilderberg Hotel, reported enemy opposition at a strength of about two companies. (This was Fitch's 3rd Parachute Battalion which was following the middle route to Arnhem.) About the same time Krafft received a visit at his headquarters from General Kussin, who had been alerted in Arnhem by Field-Marshal Model during the latter's precipitate flight, and who had now come to find out personally what was happening. He did not stay long. Krafft, however, had meanwhile heard that the 2nd Company at the southern end of his line had made contact with the enemy. He therefore advised Kussin not to take the road by which he had come. To judge by the 2nd Company's message it was not impossible that the advancing enemy had cut this road; it would be safer, said Krafft, to follow the northern wing of his position and return to Arnhem along the railway line. But Kussin was anxious not to lose any time and wanted to return to Arnhem by a proper road, so he took the risk. A few minutes later his car was riddled by dozens of bullets from a British bren-gun. The occupants, General Kussin and some of his officers, must have died instantly.

The incident also shows that the situation on Krafft's southern wing was not improving. Fitch's 3rd Parachute Battalion advancing along the Utrecht-Arnhem road captured the junction of that road with the Wolfhezerweg and then passed by the southern wing of Krafft's line. At 17.30 Krafft sent his 9th Company, which had been held in reserve, to the threatened point, together with reinforcements for the mortar section, but the German mortar fire on the left flank was unable to halt the British paratroopers. Fitch's battalion, however, was brought to a standstill shortly afterwards by other German units. Fitch therefore decided, probably about 18.00 hours, to divert his C Company under Major Lewis to the north and the railway line in an attempt to outflank the opposition and arrive in Arnhem by that route. Krafft consequently concluded that the entire enemy forces had concentrated on his position and were trying to surround him.

At 18.25 he decided to evacuate his position as darkness fell and to break through to the north-east. At 20.05 he gave orders for this break-out because the entire battalion was 'surrounded by the enemy'. At 20.20 he informed von Tettau that he was abandoning his position. Just over an hour later he was ready to move off. He was no doubt astonished to find he could withdraw without any enemy opposition. And at 22.30 he ran into another German unit. This encounter promptly put an end to Krafft's independent operations—actions which he sprinkled liberally with the salt of heroism in his later report to Himmler but which in reality contained more than an element of the ridiculous. He had fought against an enemy who was barely aware of his existence and who had certainly never planned to surround him. But despite all the boasting with which Krafft larded his battle report—a report which brought him a letter of thanks from Himmler, plus promotion—we can scarcely blame him for describing the situation as it seemed from where he stood. He saw only his cards and could only reconstruct his opponent's hand by guesswork. Which, in fact, is true of both sides. We, however, can see the cards of both parties.

After landing, the British troops had divided into two parts, according to plan: three battalions remained behind to guard the landing zones for the following day's lift; three parachute battalions marched to Arnhem by three different routes which met in a central point like the spokes of a wheel. Between the northern and middle routes—and very roughly at right angles to them both—Krafft had occupied a line along the Wolfhezerweg. He would thus, he thought, be able to delay the enemy's advance on both flanks. The most northerly parachute battalion, however, Dobie's 1st, slipped unseen past Krafft's northern wing because, as we saw, his line curved away somewhat at that point. The two opposing forces saw nothing or hardly anything of each other.

When Dobie was brought to a halt later, it was by different German units. Those units belonged to the Hohenstaufen Division—the mysterious German trump card.

On his southern flank Krafft in fact made contact with the British parachutists. There Fitch's 3rd Battalion streamed along the Utrecht-Arnhem road, past Krafft's line. The German mortar fire on his left flank, however, could not stop Fitch's advance. He therefore passed the end of Krafft's line—without suspecting its existence—but ran later into units of the same mysterious Hohen-staufen Division. To get round this opposition Fitch sent his C Company to the north-east with orders to try to reach Arnhem by that route. C Company of the 3rd Parachute Battalion thus unwittingly and unintentionally passed along the rear of Krafft's position. The two parties would probably not have noticed each other (for C Company was marching towards Arnhem and therefore away from Krafft) if the parachutists had not made contact with an ammunition lorry on its way to Krafft's position on the Wolfhezer-weg. When Krafft had occupied this new position on 17 September, he had left his ammunition dump behind at the site, further to the east, where he had originally had his headquarters. He later ordered the ammunition to be transferred to his new headquarters. The fact that Krafft's line of communication with former head-quarters crossed the route of march of Fitch's C Company brought the British and the Germans into contact with each other.

Sergeant-Major Mason of the British C Company, in reporting this incident, states that B Company of Fitch's 3rd Battalion had been brought to a standstill and that C Company was therefore ordered to carry out a flanking movement to the left as far as the railway line and then to follow that line to the bridge. 'We . . . ran into a German DR whom we captured,' says Mason. 'We . . . sent the prisoner back to Bn HQ with Private Davis, who had a gammy leg. About ten minutes later we came to a fork road and met a German MC with two men up. We killed them. We then found that we had lost the other two platoons. We did not want to go along the railway, as this was in a cutting. So we went along the road which ran parallel with the railway. After about twenty yards, we saw one of our own jeeps coming towards us, filled with Germans. We got down but they opened up on us and wounded Private Tindle in both legs. We left Private Madigan, RAMC, with him. The jeep turned round and made off, leaving one man behind to snipe us. We took him prisoner immediately . . . We proceeded down the road and on hearing a truck coming up from behind us, laid an ambush. Private Gooseman wounded the driver and set the truck alight . . . The driver got out and Lance-Corporal Newbury killed him. Sergeant Graham stood up to shoot another

German, riding in the back of the lorry, but the German shot him first. Sergeant Graham was very seriously wounded in the stomach. That German was shot by Corporal Burton. By this time the other two platoons had linked up with us. They said that they had attacked an ammunition lorry which they had set on fire and killed the four German passengers. It was now dusk, so we proceeded down the railway cutting until we reached Arnhem Station.'

If we consider the situation from Krafft's point of view, it is not very surprising that he thought he was surrounded. To his front he was making occasional contact with patrols of the 1st Battalion of the Border Regiment (one of the battalions left behind to guard the landing zones). On his right wing Dobie's 1st Battalion was advancing towards Arnhem. On the left his 2nd Company was having brushes with Fitch's 3rd Battalion, also moving towards Arnhem. And at his rear C Company of Fitch's battalion had attacked his ammunition transport. So Krafft withdrew, his shadow-boxing completed.

What Krafft did not know was that further south, via the narrow road along the Rhine, Frost's 2nd Battalion had succeeded in marching to Arnhem, and the bridge, practically unopposed. And what Frost in his turn did not know was that in his rear a German line was being formed which would separate him from the rest of the British division for the duration of the battle. The German wall against which Dobie's 1st and Fitch's 3rd Battalion had come to a halt that same day; the mysterious Hohenstaufen Division, which did more to nurture the betrayal myth than Krafft's accidental presence in the area.

VII

While the three battalions of the British 1st Parachute Brigade were trying to reach Arnhem by three different roads, the three battalions of the British 1st Airlanding Brigade, as we saw, remained behind at the landing and dropping zones. The 1st Battalion of the Border Regiment was to guard Renkum Heath, the 2nd Battalion of the South Staffordshire the Reyerscamp zone, and the 7th Battalion of the King's Own Scottish Borderers the still more westerly Ginkel Heath. Unlike the other two zones, Ginkel Heath had not been used on 17 September.

This division of duties by the British resulted in the division of German counter-measures into two groups. Thus an eastern group was formed which tried to prevent the parachute battalions from reaching the bridge. This group included the Hohenstaufen and Frundsberg Divisions and, towards the end of the day, Krafft's battalion which had fled in an easterly direction. The western group's task was to deal with the three airlanding battalions left behind at the dropping zones, whose task was primarily not offensive but defensive.

For General von Tettau the situation was extremely obscure. He did not know the position or intentions of the enemy, and he had hardly any troops at his disposal. Krafft's battalion, to which after some delay, he had given a vague order to attack, withdrew in the evening and was absorbed in the German east group. In the course of the afternoon Helle and his adjutant Naumann reported at von Tettau's headquarters. After Rauter's telephoned order they had rushed at full speed by car from Amersfoort, where Naumann had left the necessary instructions for the company commanders. Von Tettau now ordered Helle to proceed with his battalion to Ede and attack the enemy. Helle, the military nonentity, accepted this order without question, but his more experienced adjutant Naumann was not to be sent off with such vague instructions. He asked for details of the enemy's position, plans and probable strength. Von Tettau shrugged his shoulders. He said Helle would have to find out for himself – that was what he had a *Jagdkommando* (raiding detachment) for. That this *Jagdkommando* was only intended for tracking down escapees from Amersfoort concentration camp and crews from shot-down British aircraft seemed a matter of minor importance to von Tettau. Naumann telephoned Amersfoort and ordered the battalion to march to Ede. In circumstances such as these Helle, who was not completely unaware of the narrow range of his own military experience, was amiability personified to Naumann, and addressed him paternally as 'Bubi', the Tyrolean word for 'boy'.

After Naumann had ordered the SS surveillance battalion at

Amersfoort to march to Ede, Helle and 'Bubi' drove to the Langenberg Hotel on the Ede-Arnhem road and set up their headquarters there. Opposite the hotel was a low barracks building, surrounded by trees. Beyond this lay Ginkel Heath which was being guarded by the 7th Battalion of the KOSB in preparation for the landings on the following day—a fact of which Helle and Naumann were naturally unaware. In the barracks Helle found the German commander, *Obersturmführer* Laban, with 183 men who had been turned down for active service and were now being used to guard military stores. Helle found Laban in a fairly nervous state. The day before, two young members of the Dutch Resistance had been brought to him for handing over to the Security Service. To simplify matters Laban had had them shot in a wood opposite the barracks. He had then informed the Ede police that two bodies had been found there and he gave the police permission to collect them. But now that the English had landed in the immediate vicinity of the barracks and the liberation of Holland seemed to be at hand, Laban feared the vengeance of the 'terrorists'. He was in fact so worried that he had taken no action when he saw a British patrol peering through the bars of the high railing that surrounded the barrack grounds. The patrol had moved on, however, and Naumann concluded that there were enemy units on the far (eastern) side of Ginkel Heath but that they were small and awaiting reinforcements before they could advance over the heath in a westerly direction. Westerly, because Naumann thought that the aim of the British air-landings must be to support an invasion of the Dutch coast, and that the airborne forces would consequently try to break through in that direction. 'We must attack them', said Naumann, 'but we must not wait till their reinforcements have arrived. We must have reached the woods on the far side of the heath before first light.' Helle nodded approvingly—'Bubi' was right.

Only Sakkel and his *Jagdkommando* turned up in the course of the evening; the Amersfoort battalion possessed only a few vehicles. As senior company commander, Bartsch had claimed the remaining transport, and he was now on his way to Ede with his company. The other companies were left to fend for themselves.

When Drum-Major Sakkel and his 'Spielmannszug'—his Jagdkommando's nickname—arrived at Helle's headquarters, he was ordered to follow the road which skirts the Ginkel Heath, infiltrate into the woods at the far side of the heath, and reconnoitre the enemy positions. The British—a platoon of the 7th KOSB—allowed them to come quite close and then opened fire. Sakkel was badly wounded. The rest of the men fled. They were so terror-stricken that most of them took the chance to desert. Only four men turned up at Helle's headquarters to report what had happened. Helle, who had to wait till his companies arrived from Amersfoort, could for the moment do nothing but send a sergeant and some medical orderlies out to bring in the wounded Sakkel. This the British made no attempt to prevent. Drum-Major Sakkel was taken to a hospital in Apeldoorn, where he died.

At about 21.00 hours Bartsch reported from Amersfoort with his company. He was given the same orders as the ill-starred Sak-

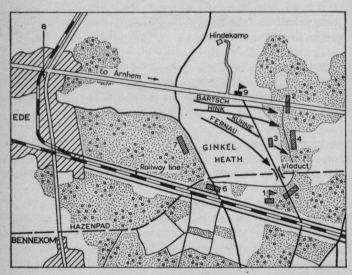

MAP 7 Fighting between the 7th Battalion of the KOSB and the SS Battalion under Helle: 1. Headquarters of Lt-Col Payton-Reid; 2. A Coy; 3. platoon of D Coy; 4. D Coy; 5. HQ Coy; 7. B Coy; 8. Helle's first command post (Langenberg Hotel); 9. Helle's second command post (Zuid-Ginkel Restaurant).

kel; to move along the Ede-Arnhem road and through the woods to the far side of Ginkel Heath.

Bartsch marched off. Once more the British allowed the Germans to come close before opening fire. Bartsch failed to reach the wood. About midnight another company from Amersfoort reported at Helle's headquarters. Helle ordered its commander to take up position on Bartsch's right flank. It was a dark night and many of Hink's men took advantage of it to desert. After all they had been enlisted to do guard duties at Amersfoort concentration camp, not to fight against trained British airborne troops. Thus weakened, Hink's company met the same fate as Bartsch's. The British allowed them to come within a certain range and then brought them to a standstill in the light of their flares (see map 7).

At his headquarters, the distracted Helle turned to his adjutant and asked for the hundredth time, 'Bubi, what now?'

VIII

It was about 5 pm on 17 September when Colonel Lippert—who, as already mentioned, was in command of the right wing of von Tettau's reception screen—received a telephone call at his headquarters in Schoonrewoerd from the headquarters of the *Wehrmachtbefehlshaber in den Niederlanden,* General Christiansen. The latter's chief-of-staff, General von Wühlisch, ordered Lippert to report with his men from the *Unteroffizierschule*—young, well-trained soldiers—at General von Tettau's headquarters near Rhenen. This order was thus not issued until several hours after the Allied air-landings. The delay was due to the difference of views between General von Wühlisch and General Christiansen.

But it was already dark when Lippert reported to von Tettau. His unit consisted of men who were following a course and it was not an organic whole. Transport had still to be requisitioned and considerable talent was required in various other directions. Lippert himself had gone on ahead in a car, but his journey to Rhenen had been slowed down by the frequent necessity to take cover from strafing by British fighter aircraft. When he finally arrived at von Tettau's headquarters, he was ordered to march his troops to Renkum via Wageningen and attack the enemy. But as it would still be hours before his men arrived, Lippert went and had a chat with von Tettau's chief-of-staff, Uhlrich. Not that it made him much wiser. Uhlrich knew as little about the situation as von Tettau himself, and Lippert confessed after the war that the impression he formed of both men at that moment was not very favourable (see map 8).

The evening hours of that September Sunday passed. A German naval lieutenant reported to von Tettau with a manning division—a *Schiffstammabteilung*. This unit was placed under the command of Lippert, who did not greatly benefit by this addition, for, as the lieutenant told him, he had practically no NCOs and neither he nor his men had the faintest idea of infantry fighting. Lippert's own men arrived towards midnight. Lippert picked out several NCOs and assigned them to the sailors. He had hardly started out when a *Fliegerhorst* battalion was sent by von Tettau to join him. These men, supernumerary ground personnel from German air-fields, were, if possible, even less useful than the sailors. Lippert had no illusions about the fighting power of this battalion. He placed it on his left wing—the *Schiffstammabteilung* was on his right, along the Rhine—with only one order, to advance to the east. He left it to these superfluous airmen to decide their own speed of advance. And he did not expect them to walk fast.

Von Tettau and Uhlrich had scarcely retired for the night when yet another battalion arrived, an SS depot battalion under Major Eberwein. This battalion was ordered to go to Bennekom, contact Helle, march eastwards and engage the enemy.

And so, by the end of the first day of the air-landings, a German west group had been formed which was very slowly following the movements of the airborne forces in an easterly direction; their speed was about two miles a day. This group had been scraped together with difficulty and in West Holland there was now scarcely a German soldier left who could be used for combat. Not that the west group had much effect on the course of the battle of Arnhem. According to General Bittrich, the Commander of II SS Panzer Corps which formed the nucleus of the east group, the west group's only real task was to cordon off the airborne troops' terrain on the

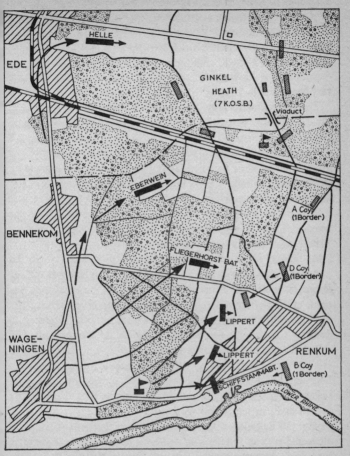

MAP 8 The German western group advances. In the north Helle moves towards Ginkel Heath (see Map 7); the SS depot battalion under Eberwein
operates south of the railway line; the *Fliegerhorst* battalion and the men of
Lippert's NCO school, together with a naval manning division, advance eastwards on the Bennekom–Renkum and Wageningen–Renkum roads or within
the triangle formed by these three towns. All of these units except Helle's
were faced by companies of the 1st Battalion of the Border Regiment.

west. This cordon, this German line, was thus formed on the night from Sunday 17 to Monday 18 September by the following units, from the north to south: Helle's battalion near Ede (facing the 7th Battalion of the KOSB), Eberwein's battalion near Bennekom, the *Fliegerhorst* battalion, Lippert's NCO cadets north of Renkum, and finally the *Schiffstammabteilung* along the Rhine to the south of Renkum. All units other than Helle's faced various companies of the 1st Battalion of the Border Regiment, which occupied Renkum Heath.

To speak of this German western group as the '*Kampfgruppe* von Tettau' or even the 'Von Tettau Division', as was done later, is, of course, nonsensical. It is nevertheless remarkable that this group, which was in fact under von Tettau's command (but received little or no guidance from him) operated independently from the beginning until 21 September, when all the troops encircling the British came under a single command.

As already observed, the operations of the western group did not greatly affect the battle. The real battle of Arnhem was the one fought without quarter between the airborne forces and the remnants of the Hohenstaufen Division: the *Kampfgruppe* Harzer.

Meanwhile, 17 September had not gone entirely according to plan for the airborne forces. After landing, the various units had assembled and prepared to march off.

The three battalions of the 1st Airlanding Brigade—under Brigadier Hicks—were, as we saw, now occupying the three landing and dropping zones where the 4th Parachute Brigade, and other units, were to arrive the following day.

The 7th Battalion of the KOSB had their positions in the wood along the edge of Ginkel Heath. There, in the course of the day, they had skirmishes with units of Helle's battalion: Sakkel's *Jagdkommando* and the four companies of the battalion proper. The 2nd Battalion of the South Staffordshire Regiment occupied the Reyerscamp landing zone, where they themselves had landed in gliders. In a South Staffordshires report on the 1939–45 period we read: 'It was a strange sensation to be deep in enemy territory and miles from one's own troops. However, the Huns either did not know where the battalion was, or were being kept too busy to come and cause any trouble. There was spasmodic fighting from the direction of Arnhem during the night, but as it did not come any nearer most of the men were able to get what was to be their only real night's sleep during the operation.'

The third airlanding zone, Renkum Heath, was guarded by the 1st Battalion of the Border Regiment. Immediately to the south of this zone lie the villages of Renkum and Heelsum. Immediately after the airborne forces had landed, the leader of the Dutch Resistance group in Renkum tried to contact them. He was instructed to get as many vehicles as he could, collect the scattered ammunition containers and take them to a central point. While returning to Renkum to execute this order, he met up with B Company of the 1st Border Regiment who were marching in the same direction. The British commander told him he had been instructed to occupy the brick-factory at Renkum in order to seal off the western end of the road along the Rhine. The leader of the Renkum Resistance acted as guide and then chose as his own headquarters a café opposite the British position. From there he telephoned to Wageningen, further to the west, to obtain information about the German troop movements. The people of Renkum thought that their moment of liberation had arrived. They flew Dutch flags from their houses and decked themselves out in the royal orange, while members of the Resistance movement wore their official armbands in public. The officer in charge of the British company was not very enthusiastic about these manifestations of joy. Especially when he sent a patrol out on reconnaissance; half the population of the village marched after them as if it were a procession. Since the British knew they would not be staying on in the village, they advised the people to take in their flags and allow the patrols to carry out their duties undisturbed. As long as it was still daylight, the Resistance also sent out patrols, but after nightfall they were forbidden to do so by the British company commander. During the night the British patrols appeared from time to time in the café where the Resistance group had its headquarters; they would drink a glass of beer, get the latest telephoned news about German troop movements to the west and then proceed on their rounds. The headquarters of the British airlanding brigade was established slightly to the east of the Reyerscamp landing zone. A little further to the east was a battalion consisting of the pilots of the gliders which had landed; it was commanded by Colonel J. Place. Their job at this stage of the operation was to occupy Wolfheze.

Finally, in addition to the units already mentioned, the troops who landed on 17 September included the 1st Airlanding Light Regiment of Artillery, (under Lieutenant-Colonel K. Thompson). The 1st Battery was intended to support the Airlanding Brigade in guarding the landing zones, and the 3rd to support the three parachute battalions as they advanced towards Arnhem. The 2nd Battery was to arrive next day. During the night of 17–18 September the guns of both batteries (in all, fifteen 75 mm howitzers) were sited to the south of Wolfheze.

While the situation in the west was at first not unfavourable, the eastward advance of the three parachute battalions did not go so well.

As we saw, the 1st Parachute Brigade—under Brigadier Lathbury—had landed on Renkum Heath at 1.30 pm. By three o'clock the brigade's three battalions were ready to move off, each following a different route into Arnhem.

While still at the assembly point on Renkum Heath Frost's 2nd Battalion heard from Dutch civilians that there were few Germans in Arnhem. By 3 pm the battalion had assembled its anti-tank guns and the bulk of its transport. In addition, they had already captured six vehicles from a German supply post; the stores staff, twelve men in all, were taken prisoner. Lathbury, whose jeep had meanwhile turned up, joined the battalion. Just as they were about to leave the landing zone, Lathbury was told that Major Gough's Reconnaissance Squadron was without most of its transport. This made it impossible for the squadron to make a quick attack and surprise the German force occupying the road bridge at Arnhem. Lathbury therefore ordered the 2nd Battalion (Frost) and the 3rd (Fitch) to advance as rapidly as possible and not to hesitate to send a company on ahead in jeeps since there would not be much enemy opposition.

It was about 3.30 when the 2nd Battalion left. Half an hour later Lathbury joined Frost's battalion which was following the most southerly of the three routes, the narrow road along the Neder Rijn. A mile or two further on, the battalion was fired on from the woods on their left flank. As there were no large German units in that area, the shots were presumably fired by a patrol from Krafft's battalion—which was occupying positions further north—or from a sentry-post guarding Field-Marshal Model's headquarters which had been overlooked at the time of his hasty departure.

The presence of Germans in the woods between the southern and middle route caused Lathbury to return to the point of departure and take the middle route to find out how Fitch's 3rd Battalion was faring. Meanwhile, Frost's battalion continued on its way. Beyond the small church in Oosterbeek the main road is joined by a narrow one which leads across the low-lying polder land to the railway bridge over the Rijn. While the rest of the battalion advanced along the main road to Arnhem, Major V. Dover's C Company turned down the narrow polder road with the intention of occupying the railway bridge. The battalion's objective, the road bridge several miles further to the east, was naturally much more important for the further course of MARKET GARDEN than the railway bridge, for the latter did not connect with any road network on which highly motorised troops could move at speed. It was nevertheless very desirable to gain possession of this crossing of the broad Neder Rijn intact. In any case, C Company's job was not only to occupy the bridge but to send a part of its strength along the south bank of the river to the road bridge and capture its southern end (while the rest of the 2nd Battalion was marching along the north bank of the Neder Rijn to capture the northern end of the road bridge).

Wehrmachtbefehlshaber Niederlande Christiansen had insisted several times (but *after* the air-landing, when the railway bridge was already blown up) that the road bridge should be demolished but Field-Marshal Model was apparently so certain he could beat off the British attack that he refused to let this drastic operation be carried out.

The embankment on the north side of the railway bridge had already been damaged by British bombers at eleven o'clock that morning, causing suspension of the train service between Arnhem and Nijmegen. A small gang of Dutch workmen appeared between 1 and 1.30 pm to repair the damage, but they were chased away by fire from British fighter aircraft. The same aircraft also attacked a small German detachment which was guarding the northern end of the bridge with three anti-aircraft guns. This detachment consisted of *Reichsdeutsche*. These were Germans who had been resident in Holland before the outbreak of war but had never acquired Dutch nationality; when Holland came under German occupation, they were conscripted into the German Army. The men, who, of course, could also speak Dutch, had been billeted on civilians in the area since the spring of 1944. When Dover's C Company approached the bridge about 5 pm, the leading platoon was fired on by the German detachment. The British quickly silenced this fire. The *Reichsdeutsche*, thinking, no doubt, that they had expended sufficient effort in serving Hitler's interests, fled to their civilian billets, asked for civilian clothes and deserted to their families elsewhere in Holland.

So the north side of the bridge did not give much trouble. Since the invasion of Normandy, however, a German demolition party consisting of an NCO and some ten men had been stationed at the southern end. They had placed a demolition charge at that time and were quartered in the immediate vicinity.

A Dutch farmer living on the south bank of the Neder Rijn near the bridge was an eye-witness of what now happened. He had watched the British approaching the bridge along the north bank and he saw the commander of the demolition party and his assistant on the bridge. As he was curious about what was going to happen he went to the café where the other men of the demolition party were billeted. An excited German corporal advised him to get back home as quickly as possible, for something might happen at any moment. The farmer went back to his house at the foot of the Neder Rijn embankment. But the dyke there is so high that it projects above the roof of the house. The farmer nevertheless intended to witness what happened, so he climbed up and along the embankment until he had a good view of the bridge. He saw a group of British troops approaching the bridge but at the same instant there was a blinding flash of fire. He heard the loud explosion of the charge and saw a section of the bridge collapse first slowly, then increasingly quickly, until some of the buckled girders disappeared below the water of the Neder Rijn. The demolition party disappeared; they had done their work.

Dover, with his C Company on the other side of the Rhine, had now no choice but to return to the main road and follow the rest of the 2nd Battalion to Arnhem. He wanted, however, to wait until nightfall before doing so. Before then he had a brief exchange of fire with a small German column on the south bank. But the fight stopped when darkness fell. C Company returned via the polder road and resumed its march in the direction of Arnhem, following the route which the rest of the 2nd Battalion had taken several hours earlier. A part of that battalion had meanwhile reached the road bridge—or at least its northern approach.

Shortly after C Company had turned off into the polder road, the rest of the battalion had had some trouble with a German armoured car. The vehicle turned up several times, but on each occasion disappeared before the battalion could use its anti-tank guns. Frost, who had already been expecting enemy opposition near the high ground called Den Brink, sent his B company up there to push the Germans back and occupy the position. Den Brink dominates the western approaches to the town. B Company had another job to do, namely to capture the pontoon bridge over the Neder Rijn between the railway bridge and the road bridge. This bridge was still undamaged but the Germans had removed some sections from it and towed them to a dock east of Arnhem.

While Frost was continuing his march to the road bridge with A Company, wireless contact with both C and B Company failed. A Company nevertheless pushed on into the town, keeping close to the river. In the failing light there was an occasional short exchange of fire with small German patrols. In the course of this advance A Company took several dozen prisoners of war. It must have been about 8 pm when A Company reached the northern approach to the bridge. German military vehicles were observed crossing the bridge from south to north. The company took up positions near the northern approach in order to block this traffic. At about 20.45

hours a platoon of A Company tried to cross the bridge to the southern end, but the attack was soon repulsed by fire from a light anti-aircraft gun sited in a bunker at that end. The commander of this platoon, Lieutenant Grayburn, was wounded during this operation but remained at his post. A day or two later he was wounded again. He fought on. On 23 September, when he had been wounded three times, he was killed in action by a German flame-thrower. He was posthumously awarded the Victoria Cross.

The enemy now opened fire on A Company with mortars, followed shortly afterwards by an attack which was beaten off. Then the British got a flame-thrower into a position from which they were able to aim it at a bunker on the other side of the bridge. The flame-thrower failed at the critical moment but with the aid of a Piat (an anti-tank gun for infantry use) the desired result was obtained; the fire from the bunker was silenced and a German tank on the bridge withdrew to the southern end. Before the British could mount a fresh attack, three German lorries carrying soldiers appeared from the south. The lorries were set on fire and the occupants taken prisoner.

In the meantime, battalion commander Frost had arrived at the bridge with his headquarters staff. He reckoned that B Company must have overcome enemy opposition at Den Brink and be by now at the pontoon bridge. He gave orders for B Company to cross the Rhine in boats which he had seen in a small dock near the pontoon bridge. B Company could then attack the southern end of the bridge along the other bank of the Rhine. Radio contact with B and C Company was still interrupted, so Frost sent some men to convey his instructions to B Company. But the company was not to be found at the pontoon bridge and it was not until five o'clock the next morning that they managed to force their way through to the rest of the 2nd Battalion at the road bridge.

Meanwhile, Dover's C Company had still not reappeared either. In addition to being ordered to capture the pontoon bridge in which they had not succeeded, this company had also been instructed to take the *Ortskommandantur* (town major's office). Frost sent a patrol to these headquarters, but the patrol returned with the news that the company was completely surrounded by the enemy and could not be reached.

Nevertheless, C Company of Fitch's 3rd Battalion arrived in the course of the night, together with brigade headquarters, though minus Brigadier Lathbury.

And so the first day of Operation MARKET GARDEN ended for Frost's 2nd Battalion. In all, six or seven hundred men of various units had succeeded in pushing through to the coveted objective of the entire operation, the road bridge at Arnhem. But they were not in control of the bridge—only the northern approach. And six or seven hundred lightly-armed men are not much with which to occupy and defend a position over sixty miles behind the enemy lines. But wasn't Horrocks' XXX Corps approaching from the south? And closer by, somewhere in the dark, weren't there the other battalions of the division? And reinforcements were to arrive the next day and the day after: Hackett's 4th Parachute Brigade and Sosabowski's Poles. In any case, there were no German troops worth talking about left here.

But in the hours of darkness of that same night the German wall which had already brought Fitch's battalion and Dobie's to a premature halt was extended further and further south and increasingly strengthened, dividing the small group at the bridge more effectively from the rest of the division.

IX

The advance of Fitch's battalion and Dobie's—the 3rd and 1st Battalions of the 1st Parachute Brigade—had been brought to a standstill within a few hours of their leaving the landing zones.

Dobie's battalion, which was to follow the most northerly of the three routes, had left the assembly point about 4 pm and marched in the direction of Wolfheze station. There Dobie met the commander of the Reconnaissance Squadron who reported enemy activity along both the railway line to the east—in the direction of Arnhem—and the road to the north—which Dobie had to follow in order to reach the Ede-Arnhem road. The opposition on the railway line was offered by infantry; that on the way to the Ede-Arnhem road consisted of armoured vehicles.

The presence of German infantry is easily explained. It was the northern end of Krafft's position. As we have already seen, Krafft's northern wing curved round slightly to a point several hundred yards to the east of Wolfheze station (see map 6). But Krafft— whose movements we know almost from hour to hour—had scarcely any influence on the course of the battle. The armoured vehicles along the line of advance were a more serious matter. Lightly-armed parachutists, however great and undoubted their courage, are no match for armour. And particularly in the first few hours of the attack, when surprise is still the main trump in the hand of paratroops, an enemy who happens to be on the spot and heavily armed can affect the chance of success drastically if not decisively. These armoured vehicles of the Hohenstaufen Division appeared suddenly and they took the airborne forces by surprise. Like phantoms they rose between Dobie and his objective. But they were not phantoms—as Dobie was soon to discover.

'As we could not get transport along railway any further', he records, 'moved north up road. Tanks withdrew. 17.00 R Coy attacked infantry positions. Enemy withdrew . . . R Coy reached road junction (Ede-Arnhem) after more fighting. Were heavily engaged at that point by tanks and infantry. R Coy . . . attacked again.'

But the enemy was too strong and Dobie, wishing to reach his allotted objective as quickly as possible, decided to try and by-pass the enemy positions with the rest of the battalion. Perhaps he could reach the Ede-Arnhem road at another point.

At 19.00 hours some fifteen armoured vehicles approached. They took up positions in a wood. Radio contact with R Company had meanwhile been lost. Dobie sent out one of his officers and decided once more to by-pass the enemy opposition on the southern side. It was now 19.30 hours. Half an hour later an enemy attack supported by an armoured vehicle was beaten off. Then the enemy's main force which had taken up positions in the wood opened fire. Dobie was forced to dig in for the rest of the night in the wood near Johannahoeve. At 22.00 the officer who had been sent to R Company returned; that company had already suffered casualties amounting to fifty per cent of its strength. Dobie sent orders to R Company to turn about and join the rest of the battalion.

X

The 3rd Battalion under Fitch also came to a standstill on the same evening. The battalion was following the middle route—the route which ran past the end of Krafft's southern wing (Dobie was moving round the northern end). Although Krafft's mortar fire on Fitch's left flank naturally caused the battalion some trouble, it was not Krafft who brought Fitch's paratroopers to a halt, any more than it was he who halted Dobie's. At 16.30 hours the brigade commander, Lathbury, joined the battalion. He was, as already mentioned, somewhat alarmed by the strong fire that Frost's battalion had met from the north, and he had left the latter to go and see how Fitch was progressing. He had scarcely joined the battalion, he himself relates, when two enemy tanks arrived to impede the advance. The well-wooded terrain with its many solidly-built houses lent itself admirably to defence. Lathbury decided to wait.

Very soon afterwards a message arrived from the divisional commander, Urquhart, saying that progress was not satisfactory. Lathbury decided they must not allow themselves to be held up by slight enemy opposition on their proposed route of advance. As in Dobie's case, the opposition consisted of infantry with automatic weapons on their flank and of armoured vehicles ahead of them. The only difference was that the fire on their flank now came from the southern end of Krafft's position. The armour, however, belonged to Harzer's *Kampfgruppe*, the remnants of the 9th SS Panzer, or Hohenstaufen, Division.

Fitch finally moved past the extremity of Krafft's southern wing, at a position due south of the Bilderberg Hotel. He did not get much further. The battalion was forced by the head-on opposition of the German armour to dig in for the night near a restaurant called De Koude Herberg on the Heelsum-Oosterbeek road. The divisional commander, General Urquhart, had also joined Fitch's battalion about 18.00 hours. Both he and Lathbury decided to stay the night with the battalion.

It is readily understandable that these two officers, with the over-optimistic reports of their Intelligence services about the probable enemy opposition still fresh in their memories, were eager to reach the objective of the operation—the road bridge at Arnhem—as quickly as possible. They had both left their respective headquarters and joined one of the three battalions marching towards the bridge. But by the end of the day, the conclusion that remained to be drawn was different. Two of the three battalions (Dobie's and Fitch's) had been brought to a standstill by the enemy—and by armoured troops at that. Only Frost's 2nd Battalion had reached the bridge. As soon as Lathbury had received news of Frost's good progress—it was then about 17.30 hours—he had ordered his headquarters staff to follow the same route as Frost. They in fact reached the bridge and came temporarily under Frost's command.

The result of all this, however, was that two commanding officers, both without their headquarters staffs, found themselves in the front line at a critical moment, for it must certainly have become clear to them in the course of the night that the enemy opposition would have to be taken more seriously than they originally thought. It remains, of course, very doubtful whether any carefully-planned measures could have been taken which would have sufficiently counteracted the sudden appearance of the armour, but it is less open to doubt that the divisional commander and his deputy (for Lathbury had been appointed to that post) should not have been together in the front line at a critical moment. And the situation was to become much worse, for when Fitch's spearhead moved forward again in the early hours of 18 September, Urquhart and Lathbury went with them. Shortly afterwards they became involved with German patrols in the outskirts of Arnhem, with the result that Urquhart and Lathbury had to hide in the attic of one of the houses.

Lathbury's report contains a laconic sentence which partly explains the lack of a centralised command which could have directed the British units. 'From now on [the evening of 17th September]', he writes, 'the wireless link was useless for the rest of the night.' Similar observations keep recurring in battle reports on the fighting at Arnhem. But the Oosterbeek-Arnhem area is a well-to-do area. Very many houses there have telephones. Why did the airborne forces not use them? There were odd occasions when they did, and successfully. For example, on the night of 17–18 September when Fitch's battalion wanted to evacuate their wounded (thirty-five in all, including some badly wounded), patrols reported enemy activity both in the west and in the east. It was thus impossible to get the wounded either back to the 1st Airlanding Brigade Headquarters at Wolfheze or forward to St Elisabeth's Hospital in Arnhem. 'This latter', Lathbury's report states, 'was incidentally confirmed by the Bn MO, Captain Rutherford, who telephoned the hospital on the civil line.' In other words this doctor had talked from the British position to a point in German-occupied territory. But that was only one case. This unique opportunity was not exploited on any scale, at least not at Arnhem. When a member of the Dutch Resistance pointed out to a British officer the great advantage the airborne forces could derive from the private telephone system of the Gelderland Provincial Electricity Board, he was informed that the paratroopers' own field transmitters would do.

The failure to take this chance of a reliable means of communication is all the more regrettable since the network was controlled at a number of junctions by the Resistance. The Arnhem exchange was naturally occupied by the Germans, who had disconnected practically all private telephones. Realising the great importance of a telephone link, eg for the purpose of espionage, the local Resistance leaders had made sure that the operators at the German-occupied exchange included a number of reliable Dutch girls. In this way the Arnhem headquarters of the Resistance movement had three telephone lines at their disposal.

In addition to this public telephone system, there was an entirely separate network belonging to the Gelderland Provincial Electricity Board (Dutch initials PGEM). Every transformer sub-station in the province of Gelderland was connected to this network, which in turn was linked to similar networks in the other provinces of Holland. Moreover, it was possible to obtain access to the public telephone system from the PGEM network by dialling a secret number.

When the airborne forces landed on 17 September, the German

supervisors at the telephone exchange disabled the trunk circuits and fled. This was not an insuperable loss for the Resistance in Arnhem because they could use the network of the PGEM, whose management co-operated fully with them. The reliable Dutch operators who had stayed on at the public exchange meanwhile restored circuits connecting them with equally reliable friends in the surrounding area. And so it happened that civilians who had for some time been unable to make use of their telephones suddenly heard their sets ringing again. This made it possible for the headquarters of the Arnhem Resistance groups to collect numerous details of German activities by telephone—details which were placed at the disposal of the British troops.

Another point about the telephone networks was that they provided a link with Nijmegen. The assistant manager of the PGEM had left on 16 September to spend the weekend at Nijmegen. By the time he set out on the return journey, the air-landings had taken place and he found his path blocked by German lines. On the morning of Monday, 18 September, he tried to ring his superior from Nijmegen via the PGEM network. He succeeded. It was almost two whole months before the Germans discovered this telephone link between occupied Arnhem and liberated Nijmegen. The line was cut on 16 November, having meanwhile been used to convey many espionage reports.

These few examples illustrate the effectiveness of a communication system which could have been of great benefit to the British airborne troops during the battle of Arnhem. That the Germans realised its importance is obvious from a report by the commander of the Hohenstaufen Division, in which he says: 'It was an advantage for our command that an excellent telephone system existed in Holland and particularly in Arnhem. This made it possible to dispense almost entirely with radio communication during the battle, especially as our signals section possessed very few transmitters that were of any use.'

XI

Early in the evening something had happened in Fitch's battalion which, though not very important in itself, perfectly explains

128

Krafft's impression that the airborne forces were trying to surround him. As we saw, Fitch and his battalion moved past the southern extremity of Krafft's position but was brought to a standstill slightly further to the east by the tanks of Hohenstaufen Division. About 17.30 hours, therefore, C Company under Major Lewis was ordered to make for the railway in a north-easterly direction. Lewis' company thus moved to the left to avoid a head-on collision with the Hohenstaufen Division and consequently arrived in the rear of Krafft's position. Neither party would probably have noticed the other's existence (C Company, by moving towards Arnhem, was receding from Krafft), if the airborne forces had not run into some Germans who were guarding Krafft's lines of communication. These meetings have already been described; they gave Krafft the impression that he was surrounded and that the British were about to attack him. The contrary was the case, and so Krafft's efforts to 'break out' did not meet with the slightest opposition. The main body of Fitch's battalion also did not know what had happened to C Company. A scout was sent out to try and contact them but he returned to say that the only trace he could find of C Company were a few dead Germans and burning ammunition lorries.

The report by Sergeant-Major Mason of C Company, to which reference has already been made, states: 'It was now dusk, so we proceeded down the railway cutting until we reached Arnhem Station. A recce was made by 8 Platoon and when they returned, we moved off towards the bridge . . . The town was deserted except for two Dutch policemen who gave us a great welcome. We walked down a main street of the town towards the bridge. Just before reaching it, a German car was blown up by . . . the leading platoon . . . On the way to the bridge Private McKinnon in the hope of finding food entered a butcher's shop, of which the owner, having no meat, gave him bread, wine and cheese. He asked, said McKinnon, if he could bring his daughter down to see me. She was twelve years old and she had one line of English to say: "Many happy returns after your long stay away." '

XII

We have seen how in the course of 17 September a German western group, opposing the battalions of the 1st Airlanding Brigade who had been left behind on the landing zones, was gradually and hesitantly formed. Similarly and simultaneously a German eastern group was built up facing the three battalions of the 1st Parachute Brigade who were marching on Arnhem. And it soon became clear to the parachute battalions that this eastern group were much tougher opponents than they had originally assumed. While the western group the 'Von Tettau Division'—formed an incohesive whole and included only a few good battalions, the eastern group had armoured cars and tanks at its disposal and reacted quickly and effectively. As the battalions of Fitch and Dobie discovered.

What had happened on the German side immediately after the air-landings?

At half-past two on the Sunday afternoon General Bittrich, the commander of II SS Panzer Corps, was sitting in his headquarters at Doetinchem, like a spider in its web. The threads linked him with his superior, Field-Marshal Model, at Oosterbeek, with Harzer, the commander of the 9th SS Panzer (Hohenstaufen) Division at Beekbergen, with Harmel, the commander of the 10th SS Panzer (Frundsberg) Division, in Ruurlo; with the Luftwaffe Communications Network, and the Luftwaffe Station, Doetinchem. Bittrich had an excellent line to Harzer, whose division had been badly battered in France and—as we have already seen—consisted of little more than a number of *Alarmeinheiten*, now that the transport of the remaining troops to Germany, where a new Hohenstaufen Division was to be formed, was in full swing. Harzer still had with him at Beekbergen a signals unit comprising eighty men and amply equipped. Harmel (whose Frundsberg Division was to be re-fitted east of the Yssel) had lost many of his signals personnel and much of his signals equipment in Normandy, but he was quartered in an area where an extensive public telephone system was at his service. Both Harzer and Harmel, therefore, were in touch with all their units by telephone, although these were scattered over the Veluwe, north of Arnhem, and the Achterhoek, east of the Yssel.

Within five minutes of the start of the air-landing Bittrich received the first report about them via the Luftwaffe Communications Network. The message was too vague to enable definite orders to be given but important enough to alert the Hohenstaufen and Frundsberg Divisions. When this alert reached Harzer's headquarters at Beekbergen (about 1.40 pm, according to Harzer), Harzer himself, of course, was not there, having gone to Deelen airfield, where he was to decorate the commander of his reconnaissance squadron, Gräbner, with the Knight's Cross of the Iron Cross. During lunch news came from Beekbergen that Bittrich had put the division in a state of alert. Harzer was able to take measures immediately. He ordered the 'tanks' of Gräbner's reconnaissance squadron to be got ready for action.

The 'tanks' which, contrary to all expectations, were to thwart Dobie's and Fitch's battalions. The 'tanks' whose existence came as a surprise even to Rundstedt, the German supreme commander in the west. The 'tanks' which, according to one of the most persistent of the betrayal legends, rumbled quietly into position in the Arnhem area after dark on the night of 16–17 September. The 'tanks' whose presence was later to be cleared up by Harzer himself.

Shortly after the message from the Luftwaffe Communications Network, Bittrich at Doetinchem received another report on the air-landings, this time from the Luftwaffe Station at Doetinchem. 'This second message', Bittrich writes, 'indicated that the main centres of the air-landings were in the Arnhem-Nijmegen area. In view of this information I issued the following orders by telephone:

'To the 9th Panzer Division:

1. Division to reconnoitre in the direction of Arnhem and Nijmegen.
2. The Division to go immediately into action, occupying the Arnhem area and destroying the enemy forces which have landed to the west of Arnhem at Oosterbeek. Immediate attack is essential. The aim is to occupy and firmly hold the bridge at Arnhem.

To the 10th SS Panzer Division:

1. Division to proceed immediately to Nijmegen, occupying the main bridges in strength, and defending the bridgeheads [south of the Waal].
Traffic over the Rhine bridge at Arnhem to be controlled by the Field Security Police of II SS Panzer Corps.'

Although Bittrich was, of course, ignorant of the plan for MARKET GARDEN the experienced SS general grasped the situation quickly. This is even less surprising if we consider the theoretical training he had had in dealing with air-landings. In 1943, when the 9th and 10th Panzer Divisions were stationed in Belgium and northern France (Bittrich was then in command of the 9th SS or Hohenstaufen Division), the then commander of *Panzergruppe West,* Geyr von Schweppenburg, had both divisions thoroughly trained for operations against the air-landings he was expecting. September 1944 thus gave Bittrich an opportunity to put his specialised training into practice. He knew that troops who have landed so far behind the lines can never hold out very long without support. The first essential in this case, therefore, was to prevent access to these troops of any assistance from the south, which meant securing the bridges at Nijmegen and Arnhem. Once these were firmly in German hands, the annihilation of the Allied airborne forces was just a matter of time.

After Bittrich had issued his orders, he received a visit (at 3 pm, if he recalls correctly) from Field-Marshal Model and his chief-of-staff, Krebs. Model was still so deeply affected by his narrow escape from Oosterbeek that he first gave his personal impression of the air-landings which had caused him to abandon lunch abruptly, before allowing Bittrich to speak and tell him what measures he had taken. Model agreed with them in their entirety and placed Bittrich in charge of the whole operation in the Arnhem and the Nijmegen area. In addition, II SS Panzer Corps was now reincorporated as a combat unit in Army Group B, and thus came under the direct command of Model. The period of rest and reorganisation was over for the Hohenstaufen and Frundsberg Divisions. Model decided to remain in Doetinchem and set up his headquarters there provisionally, so that contact with the corps and its two divisions was strengthened.

Harzer had meanwhile carried out Bittrich's orders. He had sent a part of his reconnaissance squadron via the Rhine bridge at Arnhem to reconnoitre the situation at Nijmegen. Another part of the squadron, accompanied by several groups of *Panzergrenadiere* (infantry attached to panzer divisions), was operating in the direction of Oosterbeek. Bittrich instructed Harzer to move his headquarters to Velp, and the units forming the division were also directed there. Late in the evening of 17 September Harzer moved to the Area Command Headquarters at Arnhem.

On the same evening Bittrich tried to find out the situation for himself by paying a visit to Arnhem. If his orders had been carried out, Arnhem should now be clear of British troops. But Frost's battalion had meanwhile reached the northern approach to the bridge and other British units were trying to join them. 'In the evening of 17 September the situation in the Arnhem area was completely obscure', writes Bittrich, who, as he drove through Arnhem, became involved in the turmoil resulting from a confused day's fighting. He went back to his headquarters at Doetinchem and kept in contact with Arnhem from there by telephone. Two women operators from the Luftwaffe who had remained on duty at Arnhem told him late that evening that the Rhine bridge was in British hands. The mere presence of experienced commanders such as Model and Bittrich partly explains the quick reaction of the German troops. Then there is the additional fact that in 1943 the Hohenstaufen and Frundsberg Divisions (Bittrich was still in command of the former) had been trained to oppose enemy air-landings. The speed of the German reaction cannot be used to support betrayal legends; many high German commanders, as we have already seen, flatly deny that there was any such betrayal. Nevertheless, there still remains the mystery of the Hohenstaufen Division which suddenly proved to possess a number of 'tanks'. The veil of legend which has shrouded this division since 1944 can probably best be sundered by quoting the statement of its commander, Colonel Walter Harzer. In his report on *Die Mitwirkung der 9. SS-Pz. Div. (Kampfgruppe) an der Schlacht von Arnheim vom 17.9–26.9.44* he writes: 'The German High Command, it is true, considered enemy air-landings behind the front to be possible but were definitely not informed of intended large-scale landings involving several divisions, otherwise the repatriation of the 9th SS Panzer Division would not have begun and the headquarters of Army Group B . . . would not have been set up at Oosterbeek near Arnhem.'

Harzer repeats this declaration in a personal letter: 'Field-Marshal Model had not received any report from an agent about imminent air-landings near Arnhem, otherwise his advanced head-quarters would not have remained at Oosterbeek until 1 pm on 17 September. As we know, the field-marshal was himself at Oosterbeek when the air-landing took place. The English did not know that, otherwise it would certainly have been possible for them to make a capture.' A little further on in the same letter, he writes: 'We [he and Harmel] were definitely not aware of any reports by agents about forthcoming parachute landings in the Arnhem-Nijmegen area, for the evacuation [of the Hohenstaufen Division to Germany] continued and was not halted until the afternoon of 17 September.' And again in the same letter: 'I can assure you that to my knowledge no Dutchman betrayed any information [about the airborne operation at Arnhem] which helped the Germany army command; I should have heard of it from Field-Marshal Model during the fighting near Arnhem, for he visited my headquarters every day to discuss the situation and spoke very frankly to me.'

Those, then, are the words of the commander of the German division which looms so large in the betrayal legends. In this report, he also clears up the mystery of his 'tanks' or armoured cars.

Let us quote from that report: 'The 17 September was a bright, sunny Sunday. While visiting the SS–Pz AA 9 [the reconnaissance unit of the 9th SS Panzer Division] to award the Knight's Cross [to its commander], the divisional commander personally wit-nessed the first parachute and glider landings. The aircraft were first thought to be a large daylight bomber force on its way to Germany, a fairly common sight for the troops even then . . . It was 1.30 pm when the first parachutists jumped. By 1.40 II SS

Panzer Corps had alerted the 9th SS Panzer Division. I received this message at the battle headquarters of the Reconnaissance Unit of the 9th SS Panzer Division.'

He continues: 'By the time I returned to my headquarters at Beekbergen my staff officers had alerted all stand-by units and these reported within an hour that they were ready to move, except the Reconnaissance Unit of the 9th SS Panzer Division, which *had to fit tracks on their* Schützenpanzerwagen (*armoured troop-carrying vehicles*) *and mount part of the armament, since these vehicles had been reported unserviceable to Corps in order to avoid handing them over to the 10th SS Panzer Division.*'

In other words, Harzer had concealed the existence of his reconnaissance unit's *Schützenpanzerwagen* (SPW).[1] The Hohenstaufen Division had been ordered to hand all its heavy equipment to the Frundsberg Division, which was to be brought up to strength in the area east of the Yssel. Anything left after this transfer was to be gradually moved to Germany, where a completely new Hohenstaufen Division was being formed. Pending that removal the remnants of the division had to be formed into stand-by units which could go into action in an emergency such as a rising of the Dutch population. In order not to be weakened completely, however, Harzer had evaded these orders in one respect: he had partly dismantled his reconnaissance unit's armoured cars and then reported them unserviceable. He thus avoided having to hand them over to the Frundsberg Division.

Harzer continues his report: 'Within two hours the Reconnaissance Unit also reported it was ready to move . . . About 16.00 hours II SS Panzer Corps issued the following order: "Harzer's Division to collect in Velp area and there prepare to attack enemy forces which have landed near Oosterbeek, west of Arnhem . . . Advance headquarters to be set up in Velp."

'About 16.30 hours the division was ordered by General Bittrich to reconnoitre via Arnhem in the direction of Nijmegen, using the larger part of the Reconnaissance Unit, and in the direction of

[1] The SPW (of which various types existed) was distinguished by the fact that it was a semi-tracked vehicle, ie an armoured vehicle with wheels in front and tracks behind. Some had guns mounted in them.

Oosterbeek using smaller units . . . In addition, it was ordered to occupy the bridge over the Waal at Nijmegen and prevent the enemy forces which have landed near Arnhem and Nijmegen from making contact with each other . . .

'At 17.30 hours II SS Panzer Corps headquarters issued the following instructions: "Strong enemy parachute forces landed in and to west of Arnhem and also in Nijmegen area. II SS Panzer Corps will immediately attack and destroy the enemy.

"Troops to be used:

"*In Arnhem area*: *Kampfgruppe* 9th SS Panzer Division towards Oosterbeek and northern approach to bridge over Neder Rijn.

"*In Nijmegen direction*: 10th SS Panzer Division

"*Orders*:

"*Kampfgruppe* 9th SS Panzer Division to throw back enemy who has entered Arnhem, first westwards, then to Neder Rijn. 10th SS Panzer Division to attack enemy who has landed near Nijmegen, occupy and hold bridges over Waal, and push on to southern outskirts of Nijmegen. It is particularly important to prevent the enemy who has landed at Nijmegen from advancing northwards." '

These orders from Bittrich and particularly the last sentence, show that this experienced SS general had quickly grasped the situation. It was not the British air-landings near Arnhem which gave him most concern but the situation at Nijmegen. Nijmegen was the gateway through which the Allies in the south could come to the assistance of the British north of the Rhine. Once the Germans had blocked that gateway, they could more or less concentrate on the task of liquidating the British division at Arnhem. That was why Bittrich instructed the Reconnaissance Unit of the Hohenstaufen Division to direct its main force towards Nijmegen and ordered the Frundsberg Division to occupy the bridge over the Waal there and establish a bridgehead to the south. To enable these operations to be carried out quickly, however, the bridge over the Rhine at Arnhem had necessarily to remain in German hands, because it was on the route that the main forces and reserves were to follow to reach the critical point, Nijmegen.

This was also the reason for Harzer's secondary instructions, to drive the enemy westwards from Arnhem: Arnhem had to be kept clear to guarantee the German armoured troops uninterrupted access to the south and Nijmegen.

Things turned out differently.

In carrying out Bittrich's order to reconnoitre in limited strength against the enemy who had landed west of Arnhem, Harzer dispatched his *Panzergrenadiers* with some SPWs along the two main roads leading westwards from Arnhem: the road to Ede and the road to Utrecht via Bennekom. That accords completely with the reports from Dobie and Fitch, whose battalions were halted on those roads about 5 pm by German armoured units; Harzer had received his orders about 4.30. But Harzer apparently overlooked the southern road, the narrow road along the Neder Rijn. This enabled Frost and his battalion to slip past the panzer units and to reach the northern approach to the bridge about eight. German transport had started streaming over the bridge in a southerly direction at six o'clock; it was Harzer's reconnaissance unit heading for Nijmegen. When it returned late that evening, it found the bridge over the Rhine cut off by the British. On his own initiative the commander of the German detachment occupied the southern approach to the bridge to prevent the British from breaking through to the south, into the Betuwe.

Harmel, the commander of the Frundsberg Division, had apparently taken longer to get started than his opposite number, Harzer. On that Sunday evening only the reconnaissance unit of the Frundsberg Division was ready for battle. As most of the Hohenstaufen Division's reconnaissance unit was cut off in the Betuwe—its return route across the Rhine bridge at Arnhem was, as we saw, blocked by Frost's battalion—the entire unit was transferred to Harmel's command. In exchange Harzer was given the reconnaissance unit of the Frundsberg Division. Its commander, Major Brinkmann, was entrusted with the task of encircling Frost's battalion at the bridge. In addition, the Hohenstaufen Division was reinforced with a mortar battery from the Frundsberg Division. Every hour gained was to the advantage of the Germans; although their reserves were not great, they could set considerable machinery in motion to obtain reinforcements from a large number of sources and direct them to the threatened points.

Kampfgruppe Harzer (for simplicity's sake, we will continue to call it the Hohenstaufen Division) was now divided into two parts. The first was Brinkmann's group, whose task was to clear Arnhem of the British in order to keep the road to the south across the Rhine bridge open. The second was the *Sperrgruppe* (blocking-group) Spindler. Major Spindler (who died several months later during the Ardennes offensive) had previously commanded the artillery of the Hohenstaufen Division. As he had no guns left, however, his remaining men were employed as infantry. Spindler's task for the time being was to form a defence line to prevent the British troops at Oosterbeek from linking up with Frost's battalion at the bridge. All reinforcements as they became available were to be sent into this defence line which even in the course of the night from 17 to 18 September stretched from Arnhem Station via the Nieuwe Plein and Roermondse Plein to the old pontoon bridge.

Thus a wall, still weak, it is true, of German units had been constructed straight through Arnhem. And as soon as this *Sperrlinie* (blocking-line) had been made sufficiently strong, Harzer would go over to the offensive and drive westwards. On the way next day, Monday 18 September, the *Sperrlinie* was shifted to the west. It ran along the Dreyenseweg to Oosterbeek Station, then followed the railway to the high ground known as *Den Brink* and then went southwards along the Arnhem-Nijmegen railway line to the Rhine (see map 9).

XIII

That was how the cards lay at the end of the first day. Even at this early moment time and chance were trumps in the German hand—not in the British. Without any doubt the Germans had also had their setbacks; the chief one at this decisive stage was certainly that one British battalion had succeeded in reaching the Arnhem bridge, so that the quickest way to Nijmegen was blocked against the Frundsberg Division. Later on, even the German General Bittrich was to admit the great effect that this fact had on the battle for the bridge over the Waal and on the formation of an

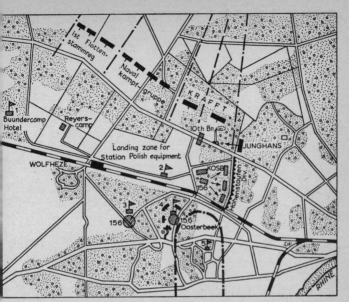

MAP 9 The advance, fighting and withdrawal of the 4th Parachute Brigade under Brigadier Hackett (18–20 September). After the brigade landed on Ginkel Heath on 18 September, the 7th KOSB and the 10th and 156th Parachute Battalions moved via Wolfheze to woods east of the Polish landing zone, where they were halted by the German line along the Dreyenseweg. After the landing of the Polish brigade's equipment, the British battalions withdrew, finally reaching Urquhart's divisional area in the night of 19–20 September. 1. Hackett's HQ (18–20 September); 2. Hackett's command post; 3. Wolfheze Hotel; 4. Units of the German west group; 5. Hartenstein Hotel (Urquhart's HQ).

Allied bridgehead in the Betuwe (the area between the Neder Rijn and the Waal) which enabled some 3,000 British airborne troops to escape to Nijmegen and freedom in the night of 25–26 September.

But despite that fact, the Allied objectives had not been attained by the evening of 17 September. While the American divisions dropped at Eindhoven and Nijmegen had had encouraging results —after, in many cases, hard fighting—and the advance of the ground forces (xxx Corps under Horrocks) was not so slow as to generate alarm, signs could already be seen of the approaching crisis at Arnhem.

The three battalions which had been left behind on the landing zones to guard them for the lifts on the next few days were still having no difficulty in coping with the 'division' which von Tettau had hastily scraped together, but the three parachute battalions that had marched off by three different routes in order to occupy the road bridge at Arnhem had unexpectedly encountered tough opposition—two armoured divisions which, though possessing only a fraction of their original fighting strength, nevertheless consisted of trained and hardened soldiers under competent commanders. One of the parachute battalions had succeeded in reaching the northern approach to the bridge; the southern end remained in German hands. A wall of enemy units, equipped with armoured vehicles, was erected between two of the battalions and Frost's isolated battalion at the bridge. That wall was growing stronger by the hour. A quick decision was necessary. Whether to force a breakthrough to the bridge with the reinforcements which were to land on the Monday—they included the 4th Parachute Brigade—and to concentrate the entire division there, or to start now and look for a point on the Neder Rijn downstream from Arnhem where it would be possible to defend a bridgehead with some hope of success? At Driel ferry, for example, which gives access to Westerbouwing, a hill on the north bank of the Neder Rijn which is ideally suited for defence. No operation of this sort had been prepared, although it is not wise to assume that a plan can never go agley.

So a quick decision was called for. But the man who had to make the decision, the divisional commander General Urquhart, had gone with the advanced guard of Fitch's battalion when they set off again in the Arnhem direction at first light on Monday, 18 September. A few hours later Urquhart was in the garret of a house on the edge of Arnhem; in the street below, German soldiers were on patrol. Urquhart's deputy, Brigadier Lathbury, was with him.

Just when decisive action was necessary, the commander of the division had lost contact with his headquarters and could no longer see the battle as a whole.

CHAPTER FOUR

THE GERMAN RING CLOSES

(18–21 September 1944)

I

Helle, the commander of the SS surveillance battalion from Arnhem, had meanwhile not been having an easy time near Ede, for although von Tettau had sent him with vague orders to attack the enemy, he had still not succeeded in crossing Ginkel Heath in an easterly direction. In his attempts to do so he had lost Drum-Major Sakkel; and the companies of Bartsch and Hink, which had arrived later in the evening, had also been brought to a halt by the fire of the 7th Battalion of the KOSB.

'*Bubi, was nun?*' Helle kept asking his more experienced adjutant Naumann, '*Bubi, was nun?*' Naumann concluded that it was not possible to attack the enemy head-on but that they must now try to execute an outflanking movement to the south.

At that moment yet another company of Helle's battalion arrived: Fernau's. Fernau was ordered to occupy the sector to the south of Bartsch and Hink and to reconnoitre the enemy's southern wing. Fernau marched off, but however far he moved to the south, he kept running into opposition. Finally he discovered a concrete tunnel standing ghostly, weird and useless amidst the heath. It was a tunnel under the Utrecht-Arnhem motorway[1] which was then under construction. When Fernau and his men tried to pass through this tunnel, they were driven off by fire from the 7th KOSB. Fernau took up a position and informed his commander, Helle, that no further progress was possible. Helle was at a loss what to do. He still appeared not to realise that the British battalion facing him, the 7th KOSB, was not interested in attacking to-

[1] The present highway No 12 from Utrecht to Arnhem (see map 7).

wards the west but had merely to guard Ginkel Heath for the coming landing of the 4th Parachute Brigade. That was why Lieutenant-Colonel Payton-Reid had stationed his companies round the edges of the wood surrounding the heath. Wherever Helle's companies went, they were bound to run into opposition. '*Bubi, was nun?*' Helle asked his adjutant for the hundredth time. Naumann, who, like Helle, still believed that the airborne forces would attack at dawn, had meanwhile discovered that a gap had been created between Hink's company and Fernau's company, which had swung to the south, and he reasoned that, if the English attacked the next day, they would concentrate on that weak spot.

Just then Kühne's company arrived and Kühne was ordered to march to and occupy the sector between Fernau and Hink. On his way there, he discovered a wooden hut on the heath and surrounded it. By doing so he was responsible for the only success of Helle's battalion that night; the hut was occupied by a platoon from D Company of the 7th KOSB, who were taken prisoner. The commander of D Company counter-attacked in an attempt to recover his men but in vain.

Helle's only success in the night of 17–18 September—yet practically the whole of Ginkel Heath, where the British 4th Parachute Brigade was to land in the morning of 18 September, was in his hands. The companies of the 7th KOSB, spread out thinly round the edge of the wood enclosing the heath, were too weak to sweep the plain clear by a counter-attack.

Helle moved his headquarters from the Langenberg restaurant opposite the barracks to the Zuid-Ginkel hotel-café on the main road a mile or so to the east, where he knew he would be protected by Bronkhorst's company (which was being held in reserve) and by the heavy weapons of Einenkel. The latter, a German Army veteran, was one of the few competent soldiers in the entire battalion.

The transfer of Helle's headquarters was followed by a lull which was only interrupted once when both sides opened up briefly with heavy arms. Then all was quiet again. Both sides were just waiting. Helle had come to the conclusion that it would not be possible for his battalion to advance unless von Tettau sent reinforcements;

Helle's opponent, Payton-Reid, and his battalion were waiting on the edge of the wood for the arrival of the 4th Parachute Brigade. According to the time-table the brigade were to jump at ten o'clock on Monday morning. In view of the advanced positions of the Germans on the eastern edge of the heath, the British parachutists would land in the rear of Helle's companies.

In the meantime the German company commander Fernau went to Helle's headquarters to ask for reinforcements. His company, furthest to the south, was also the one most exposed to attack. In addition, the only machine-guns he had were of Czech manufacture and they kept jamming. So he wanted not only more men but also some mortars. When Fernau arrived at headquarters, however, he was amazed to find Bartsch, one of the company's commanders, acting as battalion commander. Helle had gone. He had just left, Helle's adjutant Naumann explained, but he might be back any minute. Fernau informed Bartsch of his requirements, and Bartsch promised to send him the reinforcements he wanted. Bartsch kept his promise but the reinforcements did not reach Fernau. The snipers of the 7th KOSB at the edge of the wood made it impossible for a platoon of Bronkhorst's reserve company to join Fernau, and all that arrived of the mortars were the base-plates—the men despatched with the other parts had taken cover on the way.

Fernau's persistent suspicion about the reason for Helle's absence has never been completely confirmed. Even after the war Fernau was still convinced that Helle had left his command post to pay a short visit to Amersfoort—to the woman whom the British air-landings had forced him to leave at a moment's notice the day before. The woman herself no longer remembers the exact details. Which is remarkable, for a woman who loves a man—and she loved Helle—has a memory like an elephant's for things like that.

11

Hour after hour passed by. The men of the 7th Battalion of the KOSB listened hopefully, trying to detect the sound of aircraft engines in the distance. Ten o'clock came, eleven o'clock, twelve. Ground fog on the English aerodromes had delayed the 4th Parachute Brigade's departure. Meanwhile, German patrol activity was increasing. There was occasional skirmishing between individual soldiers on the edge of the woods.

Noon came. Then one o'clock, two, half-past two. Helle had returned to his headquarters. He was now sleeping on the café table. The battalion paymaster and his clerk were bringing their accounts up to date. Only Naumann was on the alert; in the dull silence of the tap-room he was the only one who heard the sound of aircraft engines at three o'clock. 'On their way to Berlin to kill innocent women and children', thought Naumann, forgetting Coventry and Hitler's order to wipe it out. He got up and walked to the window.

He saw the aircraft coming. They were flying low. They came from the south-west in wave after wave across the heath. And then he also saw hundreds of parachutes burst into bloom. For an instant Naumann stood stock-still. But there was no time to lose. He shook Helle roughly to wake him up and Helle gazed up astonished. The sight of a British parachutist looking in at the window quickly brought him to his senses. He leapt from the table and rushed to the back door, followed by Naumann and the two accountants. The commander of the more heavily-armed troops, Einenkel, who saw a number of British running to the café, was the only one who kept his head. He opened fire on his own headquarters. This not only had the effect of hastening Helle's flight, but also caused Bronkhorst's reserve company to panic and take to their heels.

Helle's other companies fared no better. This was the moment for which the men of the 7th KOSB had waited. When the headquarters staff and three battalions (the 10th, 11th and 156th) of Brigadier Hackett's 4th Parachute Brigade landed in the rear of the enemy, a part of the 7th KOSB went over to the offensive. Of Helle's company commanders, Fernau was captured almost immediately and Kühne fled to the north where he found Bartsch and Hink still trying to hold on. When their positions were overrun, however, they too were taken prisoner. Kühne continued his flight. He remained in hiding for several days, then he reported to Helle. He was immediately relieved of his command and sent back to Amersfoort.

During his precipitate flight from his headquarters Helle had run into another of his company commanders, Bronkhorst, with a part of his company. Bronkhorst was ordered to prepare a neighbouring farm for defence. Helle continued his flight behind the protection of this position. At Ede he met the commander of *Sicherheitsregiment* No 42, which had been sent to the front—a day late—by General Christiansen. The excited Helle asked him why he had not come to his assistance. The commander of the *Sicherheitsregiment* looked at Helle in silence for a moment and then answered drily: 'Be glad you're still alive. A report I received said you and your whole battalion were killed or captured.'

The only man who refused to be disconcerted by the British landing was again the veteran Einenkel, who made another attempt to save the situation with his heavy weapons. A vain attempt. Hackett's men came down in hundreds on the heath, which was burning fiercely as a result of the fighting between Helle's battalion and Payton-Reid's. As they floated down on their parachutes, they could see the dirty white smoke of the burning moorland below them and hear rifle fire, the staccato rattle of machine-guns and the explosions of mortar bombs.

But the landing was successful. Even before the commander of the 4th Parachute Brigade, Brigadier Hackett, had extricated himself from his parachute, he had taken two prisoners. And this pair had grown into a small group by the time he started to set up his headquarters. SS men made for the Britons from all directions, not to attack but to surrender.

The 7th Battalion of the KOSB had carried out their first assignment. At 19.00 hours they marched off to the positions they were to occupy for their second assignment: to guard the landing zone at Johannahoeve Farm, a mile or two to the east, where the equipment of the Polish Airlanding Brigade was to be put down on Tuesday, 19 September.

What Payton-Reid did not know was that this landing zone lay immediately in front of the 'blocking-line' which the German east group had originally formed straight across Arnhem, but which by Monday had already shifted westwards, to prevent contact between Frost at the bridge and the other troops who had landed.

By marching eastwards the 7th KOSB were making straight for this *Sperrlinie* of Major Spindler, the commander of Harzer's artillery regiment. In their rear they were followed by the reluctant 'Von Tettau Division'; to the south ran the wide, swirling waters of the Neder Rijn. And in the north German units which included Krafft's SS battalion were getting into position.

When the 3rd Battalion (under Fitch) of the 1st Parachute Brigade was brought to a standstill on its way to the bridge early in the evening of Sunday, 17 September, by units of the Hohen-staufen Division, the divisional commander, General Urquhart, set up his headquarters in the Hartenstein Hotel at Oosterbeek because it happened to be nearby. Both Urquhart and the commander of the 1st Parachute Brigade, Brigadier Lathbury, had—as we saw—gone along with Fitch's battalion. At 9.30 that same evening they heard over their field wireless sets—it was the last such message, for radio communication failed for good shortly afterwards—that Frost's 2nd Battalion had reached the bridge and that the bridge was intact. Urquhart and Lathbury decided to spend the night with Fitch's battalion, which was to resume its advance towards the bridge before dawn on the following morning. As Lathbury says in his report: 'The CO and I agreed during the night, and as a result of patrolling, to disengage the Battalion before first light and to move south through Oosterbeek and thence via Lion [Frost's route] to the bridge.'

This decision by the divisional commander and his deputy had, like all decisions, its pros and cons. If the operation had been successful, if the other battalions had managed to reach the bridge, if they had captured it and held it until the arrival of the British Second Army—everyone afterwards would have had nothing but admiration for Urquhart and Lathbury. Everyone would have deeply respected the general who at danger to his own life had fought his way through to the bridge in order to conduct the rest of the battle from there. But all those 'ifs' could only have become reality had the enemy opposition been weak. In making their decision both Urquhart and Lathbury must have under-estimated that resistance. And now their courageous initiative was to do more harm than good.

Right from the early hours of Monday morning Urquhart and Lathbury became involved in the hurly-burly of battle in the maze of streets to the west of St Elisabeth's Hospital in Arnhem. The situation there was not quite clear. The enemy was busy building up and strengthening a barrier to prevent the British battalions from joining Frost's 2nd Battalion at the bridge. On their march eastwards Fitch's battalion ran into this blockade, and during the fighting which ensued the advanced guard of the battalion was in fact cut off from the rest. Urquhart and Lathbury, who were moving about in the midst of this fighting, were forced to take cover in one of the houses. 'There was a good deal of small-arms fire across this area', writes Urquhart in his book, 'and I was told that there were Germans in the upper rooms of the houses across the gardens. My prospects of returning to Divisional HQ appeared for the present more remote than I would have liked . . . Our situation quickly took on the appearance of a siege.'

That situation did not improve as Monday morning wore on. During an attempt to break out, Urquhart and Lathbury had to stride over a fence and Lathbury's sten-gun accidentally went off. The shot narrowly missed Urquhart's foot and the general—rightly—comments: 'It was bad enough for a divisional commander to be jinking about in what was now hardly more than a company action, and it would have been too ironic for words to be laid low by a bullet fired by one of my brigadiers.'

A little later Lathbury was hit by a bullet from a German machine-gun; the wound was not serious but it meant that the commander of the 1st Parachute Brigade had to be left behind in the care of a Dutch couple. Urquhart continued on his way with two other British Officers. They finally got into a house, occupied by a Dutch family, just as the Germans were entering the street. They ran up some stairs that were pointed out to them, and looked cautiously out of a bedroom window. The neighbourhood was crawling with Germans. Urquhart and his two companions sought cover in an attic which was only about half the height of the bedroom. Then they pulled the detachable steps up after them. In that position, armed with pistols and hand-grenades, they awaited the arrival of the Germans. They heard a German gun approaching; it drew up practically below the bedroom window. As the commander of the British division sat cooped up in an attic somewhere in Arnhem, the rest of that Monday passed. 'I was frustrated,' writes Urquhart, 'at my inability to influence the battle, and the minutes dragged through the evening and night. If I had known just how badly the battle was going elsewhere, I would certainly have attempted to reach my HQ. It is doubtful, however, if I could have succeeded.'

I V

Back at headquarters, Brigadier Hicks had already taken charge in the early hours of Monday. Since the time Urquhart had joined Fitch's battalion towards evening on Sunday, little more had been heard of him. The officers still at divisional headquarters had taken several independent decisions on matters of minor importance during the night from Sunday to Monday, but by Monday morning the situation clearly called for drastic measures. It was of urgent importance that Frost's battalion, the only one which had reached the bridge, should be reinforced. A search was made for the sole remaining brigadier, Hicks, the commander of the 1st Airborne Brigade. Hicks handed the brigade over to his second-in-command and went to divisional headquarters, where he did his best to familiarise himself with the situation in which the division found itself. In his diary he noted: '07.30 hours. Brigade Commander to Div the GOC being reported missing.'

Rarely can an officer have been obliged to assume command in such difficult circumstances. The entire, rather complicated operation had been carefully planned in England on the basis of maps and aerial photographs. Every officer had learnt his own precisely-defined task by heart. But fairly soon after the landing, when the various units were dispersed far from each other deep behind the enemy lines; when the failure of wireless links rendered intercommunication practically impossible; when the German opposition proved fiercer and more effective than had been expected—then the danger of confusion arose. A danger that could only be exorcised by a vigorous central command. But within twenty-four hours of the start of the air-landings the commander-in-chief had to be presumed missing at divisional headquarters. That can happen in any battle; and there is always a deputy ready to step in. But now the deputy, too, was missing. Brigadier Hicks can never have thought that the probability of his assuming command was very great. And yet now, when the operation was not developing according to plan, he was called upon to make vital decisions.

Had Urquhart been there, he might well, in view of the enemy's strength, have abandoned the advance to the bridge, recalled Frost's battalion (if that was still possible), concentrated his six original battalions and the three battalions of the 4th Parachute Brigade which landed at Oosterbeek on the Monday, and tried to establish a firm bridgehead somewhere else on the north side of the Neder Rijn, for example between Heveadorp and Oosterbeek with the high ground at Westerbouwing, which dominated the Driel ferry across the Neder Rijn, as the centre of the bridgehead. There they could have awaited the arrival of the British Second Army.

But such a drastic alteration of the original plan could not be expected of Hicks, for it was still not certain that Urquhart could be presumed missing for the rest of the action; contact with him had only been lost temporarily. He might return to his headquarters at any moment. And when he did, would he necessarily concur with the measures Hicks had taken? There was still a second possibility. Even if neither Urquhart nor Lathbury returned, the 4th Parachute Brigade would be dropping within a few hours. Its commander, Brigadier Hackett, was senior to Hicks. Hackett would never be prepared to place himself at Hicks' orders. And yet something had to be done, measures had to be taken which departed as little as possible from the original plans.

It was clear that Frost had to be reinforced at the bridge. But where could Hicks get the troops he needed to do so? Every man already had his hands full and there were no reserves. But Frost's situation was so precarious that it took priority over the rules of tactical warfare. Hicks came to the conclusion that the 2nd Battalion of the South Staffordshires was practically inactive at that moment. The battalion had landed on the Sunday and was now occupying the Reyerscamp landing zone in preparation for the arrival of the rest of the battalion. That landing was timed to take place simultaneously with the dropping of the 4th Parachute Brigade over Ginkel Heath and the landing of the brigade's transport on Renkum Heath. Hicks decided to send the 2nd South Staffordshires to the bridge; the inevitable disadvantage of this was that the landing of the rest of the battalion would be unprotected and the second lift would be immediately given the unexpected task of following the first lift of the battalion to the bridge.

But one battalion was not enough. Hicks therefore decided that as soon as the 4th Parachute Brigade landed, it would have to part with the 11th Battalion. That battalion, too, would be ordered to get to the bridge as quickly as possible. Like the first decision this one, too, had its drawbacks. The 11th Battalion, as part of the 4th Parachute Brigade, was to land by parachute on Ginkel Heath. But the battalion's transport was scheduled to come down in gliders on the Reyerscamp landing zone, several kilometres to the west. The battalion would therefore not be ready to advance until it had collected its vehicles at Reyerscamp.

There was yet another cause for anxiety. The task originally planned for the 4th Parachute Brigade was to occupy the high ground to the north of Arnhem and to form a bridgehead round the town. The loss of the 11th Battalion, however, entailed a considerable weakening of the brigade. Hicks was consequently forced to take a third decision, that, after completing the task on which it had been engaged until now—guarding Ginkel Heath for the landing of the 4th Parachute Brigade—the 7th Battalion of the KOSB should join the Parachute Brigade in order to make good the loss of the 11th Battalion. It was not a fair exchange. The 11th Battalion was fresh; the 7th KOSB, on the other hand, had already been fighting for a day against Helle's battalion. Moreover, the KOSB had to be at the Johannahoeve landing zone on Tuesday, 19 September to protect the landing of the Polish Parachute Brigade's transport, while the *men* of this brigade were landing on the *south* bank near the Rhine bridge. That, at any rate, had been the original plan . . .

V

In that one day, however, events had led to a situation which differed radically from the plans. Of the six British battalions that had landed on Sunday, only the 2nd Battalion under Frost had managed to push through to the bridge over the Neder Rijn: the goal of the entire operation. By energetic and effective counter-measures the Germans had succeeded in cutting off this battalion from the rest of the division—a separation which might not only mean destruction for the isolated battalion but also deny the other battalions access to their coveted objective. And every hour that passed saw fresh reinforcements reach the German lines.

The measures that Hicks was obliged to take in Urquhart's absence were designed to force, as quickly as possible, a decision in keeping with the original plan: the capture of the Rhine bridge and the formation of a firm bridgehead north of the Rhine in order to ensure the British Second Army, now advancing via Eindhoven and Nijmegen, a rapid break-through to the Zuider Zee.

The battle of Arnhem was now divided into several parts. At the bridge Frost's isolated battalion was fighting stubbornly against forces which were becoming stronger all the time.

Four battalions were on their way to relieve Frost: the battalions of Fitch and Dobie, the 2nd Battalion of the South Staffordshires, and the 11th Battalion which had been taken from the 4th Parachute Brigade after the latter landed on the Monday. This attempt to break through took place on a narrow front, several hundreds of yards across, among the houses of Arnhem, approximately level with St Elisabeth's Hospital.

And some kilometres to the west the three battalions of the 4th Parachute Brigade (the 10th and 156th Parachute Battalions and the 7th KOSB) were marching eastwards to carry out their task: to occupy the high ground to the north of Arnhem.

Both the attempt by the four battalions to break through to the bridge and the advance of the 4th Parachute Brigade (see map 9) must obviously and necessarily run into Major Spindler's *Sperr-front*, whose formation had been ordered as early as Sunday afternoon by Harzer, the commander of the Hohenstaufen Division.

From the reactions of the Germans it must quickly have become clear to the British that the enemy opposition was much stronger than had been expected; Harzer's and Bittrich's reports show how the counter-measures were taken and constantly strengthened. And this was happening about the same time that Hicks, uncertain of Urquhart's fate, was taking far-reaching decisions at British headquarters to make a success of the plan and capture the Rhine bridge.

'About 23.59 hours [Sunday]', writes Harzer, 'Spindler reported that despite strong enemy opposition the western edge of the centre of Arnhem had been reached and that the *Sperrfront* was being built up ... About midnight Captain Knaust, commanding the "Bocholt" training and depot battalion of *Panzergrenadiers* reported at ... [Harzer's] headquarters ... They had with them ten obsolete tanks which at home were used only for ... training. The first units of this battalion reached Arnhem about 4 am [on Monday] ... the 9th SS Panzer Division attached this battalion to Brinkmann's *Kampfgruppe* at the bridge to enable the enemy who had dug in there to be destroyed, because the 10th SS Panzer Division needed the bridge urgently for the movement of reinforcements, heavy arms and supplies.'

As already said, Major Brinkmann's task was to destroy Frost's battalion; the bridge had to be cleared to allow the Frundsberg Division through to Nijmegen.

Harzer continues: 'In the course of the night [from Sunday to Monday] Krafft's battalion retreated to the north ... It collected to regroup on the southern edge of Deelen airfield.'

This observation accords with the previously described movements of Krafft's SS Battalion, which originally formed part of von Tettau's western group but fled eastwards on Sunday evening because its commander mistakenly thought the British were trying to encircle him. Krafft ran into the arms of Spindler who incorporated him in the eastern group.

On Monday, 18 September, General Bittrich, the commander of II SS Panzer Corps issued the following orders: 'II SS Panzer Corps will resolutely direct its main effort against the enemy who has landed at Nijmegen (the American 82nd Airborne Division).

For this purpose further forces will be ferried across the Neder Rijn (at Pannerden) and a firm bridgehead will be maintained south of the Waal at Nijmegen. The 9th SS Panzer Division will also destroy as speedily as possible the enemy parachutists who have established themselves at the bridge, continue to attack, and reduce the area held by the 1st Airborne Division and, after the arrival of fresh reinforcements, destroy it.' Harzer comments: 'So the bridge at Arnhem has first to be recaptured, since the destruction of the enemy troops who had landed at Nijmegen depended on the supply of reinforcements with heavy arms and tanks (for the Frundsberg Division). The task of destroying the enemy at Arnhem rested mainly on the *Kampfgruppe* Harzer (9th SS). Von Tettau's group to the west of the landing area had at first only a containing function. The 9th SS Panzer Division therefore gave orders for Krafft's battalion, after reforming on the southern edge of Deelen airfield, to move towards Oosterbeek and push the enemy parachutists back to the northern edge of the town and at the same time establish contact with von Tettau's group.'

In other words, Krafft's battalion was the lid being placed on the box. The sides of the box were formed by von Tettau's west group and Spindler's east group and the bottom was the Neder Rijn. And Krafft's battalion was now to act as a lid which was hinged at the east and would come down and close on the west (von Tettau's group). The British parachute battalion commanded by Frost was the only battalion outside the box; the rest of the division was inside it.

Harzer also ordered the Spindler group to continue its attack against Oosterbeek on a wide front. He goes on: 'Brinkmann's group encountered very stubborn resistance to its renewed attacks . . . In the forenoon Field-Marshal Model (commander-in-chief of Army Group B) appeared for the first time at the battle head-quarters of the 9th SS Division in Arnhem . . . The field-marshal announced the arrival of another *Panzergrenadier* battalion . . . [from Germany] under the command of Captain Bruhns. The newly formed 506th Heavy Tank Battalion from Ohrdruf was also promised and could be expected to arrive about 22 September. In the course of the day (18 September) other stand-by units sent by the *Wehrmachtbefehlshaber Niederlande* arrived in Arnhem, most of them by way of Apeldoorn. These units used improvised transport or rode bicycles. They included the 1st Labour Service Battalion, completely unarmed (aged sixteen to seventeen). These forces were added to the *Kampfgruppe* Spindler. As there was a shortage of officers with actual fighting experience in the stand-by units which were now being added to his own *Kampfgruppe*, Spindler formed two more such groups under the command of ... Captain von Allwörden and ... Lieutenant Harzer. On 18 September *Kampfgruppe* Spindler succeeded in consolidating the front to such effect that the British battalion fighting at the bridge could not receive reinforcements or supplies. It was thus possible to calculate roughly when that battalion would run short of ammunition.'

The threat inherent in this situation was, of course, obvious and it did not escape Hicks. That was why on Monday he sent two more battalions (the 2nd Staffordshires and the 11th Parachute Battalion) after Fitch's and Dobie's battalions, which had been halted on their advance to the bridge even before Sunday was over. These four battalions had therefore to break through the east side of the 'box' in which they were enclosed. The attempts to break through are also mentioned in Harzer's account. But before that, Harzer states: 'In the afternoon the attack against the bridge was renewed by Brinkmann's group assisted by the *Panzergrenadier* battalion under Knaust. On 18 September the sky was overcast and cloudy and not favourable for the British Air Force. Nevertheless, new landings by British parachutists and gliders took place ... Our air defence was still weak on 18 September ... and could not prevent the landings or inflict heavy losses on the enemy. At that moment the 9th SS Panzer Division had still only four 2 cm and two 8.8 cm anti-aircraft guns, the bulk of the original units ... having already been transported to Germany.'

This last observation also proves once again that the disbandment of the Hohenstaufen Division was in full swing before and at the time of the air-landings.

Harzer continues: 'In the confused street and house-to-house fighting at Oosterbeek contact between individual assault groups frequently failed in the night of 18–19 September. The German front line was completely irregular. This often made it difficult for the heavier arms to support the attacks of the assault groups. The British and Germans were extremely close to one another there . . . Immediately north of the Neder Rijn the British repeatedly mounted heavy attacks in the hope of forcing their way through to the encircled battalion at the bridge. It could be deduced from this that the British were anxious to hold on to the bridge . . . All fighting units were also ordered to attack unceasingly in the night of 18–19 September in order to give the British no chance to reform or to launch an attack . . . Even with the thinned-out ranks of the 9th SS Panzer Division and the stand-by units formed from them, the experience acquired from TEWTs on maps and in the anti-parachutist training which had previously been received under General Geyr von Schweppenburg, now proved very valuable in fighting the British airborne forces.

'By the second day of the battle [at Arnhem] a considerable amount of improvisation was already necessary. None of the units involved in the fighting had sufficient transport. At the same time it was becoming more and more difficult to provide essentials for the stand-by units that arrived daily without supply vehicles. These troops were completely without field kitchens. Their only arms were weapons captured from many different European armies, with little ammunition that was suitable for them . . . On 19 September the headquarters personnel of an anti-aircraft brigade under the command of Lieutenant Swoboda arrived. In addition, several AA units with guns of various calibres were brought in from the Ruhr. The 9th SS Division headquarters decided that all AA units deployed in the Arnhem area would come under the unified command of the AA brigade HQ staff. By the afternoon of the 19th, this brigade was able to announce its preparedness to fight . . . The position with regard to AA ammunition was very satisfying.'

The German reserves were very far from inexhaustible; in many cases they had to be taken from units defending German soil. In some cases their fighting value was small; in others, the Germans had to adopt primitive means to be at all effective. Harzer says, for instance, that the AA units from the Ruhr were not designed for operating in the field. They had no transport of their own and on this particular occasion they were moved from the Ruhr to Arnhem in trailers drawn by tractors and wood-burning lorries. But despite all that, reinforcements continued to pour in, and it was particularly the heavier units that caused the balance to swing against the lightly-armed airborne troops.

Harzer, still speaking of Tuesday, 19 September, says: 'A liaison officer from the 1st *Jagddivision* also reported. This *Jagddivision* had been placed at our disposal for the battle of Arnhem . . . At that time it still had about 300 operational aircraft consisting of Messerschmitt 109 Fs and Focke-Wulf 190s. The flying time from the Ruhr to the Arnhem airspace was about ten to twenty minutes after the alert . . . Field-Marshal Model was now appearing daily at the 9th SS Division's battle headquarters in Arnhem and was having a noticeable effect on the fighting spirit of all the troops with his enthusiasm and dynamic personality. The AA brigade reported that the disposition of its batteries was now such as to enable the more than 100 guns of all calibres composing them to cover, not just once but several times over, the landing and dropping zones so far used. The heavy and medium AA batteries were sited and arranged so that they could be used both for air defence and for ground fighting.'

That is how, in the first few days of the week, the German blockade grew, the wall against which the British battalions were advancing: the 4th Parachute Brigade and the four battalions which were supposed to reinforce Frost at the bridge. Perhaps there were many who still trusted the optimistic tone of some Intelligence reports.

VI

In the evening of 18 September a member of the Dutch Resistance movement in the neighbourhood of Rhenen made contact with a small group of British paratroopers who were hiding in low undergrowth. He found that they belonged to the 11th Battalion of the 4th Parachute Brigade which had landed that afternoon on Ginkel Heath, a few miles to the east. Their aircraft—and several others—had, however, been shot down near Rhenen by German flak before reaching the target.

The existence of flak at that particular point might have puzzled the RAF slightly. A day before, on Sunday morning, the RAF had silenced the German AA sites round Rhenen (they had previously been located by air reconnaissance). The first wave of troop-carrying aircraft which arrived on Sunday afternoon consequently encountered no opposition over that area. In the night from Sunday to Monday, however, a heavy AA company had been sent under the German Captain Schultz to Rhenen to defend the headquarters of von Tettau, the commander of the German west group. The second lift of airborne troops, which included the 4th Parachute Brigade (the 10th, 11th and 156th Battalions), thus ran into Schultz' defensive fire as they approached the landing and dropping zones.

In one of the aircraft sat Sergeant-Major Gatland of the 11th Battalion. He had not slept much the night before. On Sunday he and his men had watched the first lift fly overhead and seen the white supply-containers slung below the bellies of the Dakotas. And as the aircraft disappeared in the east they had shouted after them: 'Good Luck, we'll be with you tomorrow.' That night Gatland lay on his bunk and smoked one cigarette after another. He talked far into the night with his room-mate, Sergeant George Ashdown, who was to die several days later in a hopeless attempt by his battalion to reach Frost's isolated battalion at the bridge. Next morning the men set off early from their quarters at Melton Mowbray for the airfield. The tension grew, especially as the take-off had to be postponed for several hours on account of ground fog. But finally, flying high in the air, they saw the East Anglian countryside disappear below them. 'Their feelings were mixed', as Gatland says. The shells from the German flak exploded now and again in small black puffs of smoke above the Dutch polders. Soon there came the order—'Action stations.' The men went and stood in a line, waiting for the green light that would mean they had to jump.

The arrival over the fighting area is dismissed in a single sentence of the 11th Battalion's report: 'The fly-in was fairly uneventful, only three 'planes of the Battalion being shot down on the fly-in.'

Aboard one of those aircraft, however, was Sergeant-Major Gatland. In another was his company commander, Captain J. D. King. Captain King's report, naturally enough, takes up more than one line. 'There seemed,' he writes, 'to be many anti-aircraft guns, and of course at 500 feet we were vulnerable even to rifle and MG fire . . . We were now standing and ready to jump as soon as we received the warning-light from the pilot. The plane was occasionally hit by bullets . . . the American crew-chief was killed near the door. My batman, standing near him, lost part of his hand but it was too late to unhook him [from the line in the aircraft to which all parachutes are attached, so that they open automatically after the jump; the open parachute is then released from the aircraft by the breaking of a thin line]. I told him to jump after me. We waited for the light. There was a certain disorder but no panic. Several men were wounded. The plane was losing height. But still no light. When we were very low, perhaps 200 feet, I gave the order to jump. I knew we were several miles from the dropping zone. I also knew that the pilot was in command in the air and had not given us our warning-light. But unless we jumped then, we could not jump at all. When I left the door, I saw I was justified. We had left our formation and both plane engines were blazing . . . I watched other men leave the plane . . . The last one jumped perhaps at eighty feet and his parachute failed to open . . . [After landing] I tried to call my Bn Commander on my wireless set but there was as expected no reply. I was already out of range. Then I collected my men. They were calm and careless, walking about in the open as if Holland already belonged to them . . . We soon established contact with British troops. The plane which had crashed to the west carried men from our own Bn . . . Meanwhile a small German patrol appeared . . . We shot two of them and took their weapons.

'This reinforcement made my total strength some twenty-two men, with one officer (Lt Bell) and my SM Gatland. We soon met up with a Belgian (named, I think Guy[1]), and he offered to guide

[1] whose father had a business in Wageningen.

us. Guy spoke no English. But I gathered in French that Ede was garrisoned and that troops were on and near our dropping zone. Since the country did not lend itself to further movement by day, and as we were relatively weak in all but short-range weapons, I decided to wait in the copse until darkness . . . I asked Guy if he could contact the local underground movement and find how the battle went at Arnhem. He left us and after posting sentries we slept. Nothing much happened. A farmer milked his cows in a neighbouring field and we drank from his milk-can . . . Later a man came from the underground movement. He spoke English and gave me much valuable information and we fixed a rendez-vous for about nine. Everything went smoothly at the rendez-vous. Some . . . [members of the Dutch Resistance] appeared with the Belgian. I gathered the battle was not going well at Arnhem. At the point where our route to the east crossed the main road running south from Ede [to Bennekom] we said goodbye to our guides. They were as sorry as we were to part . . . They had risked much to help us. We knew it then and we know it now, we shall always be grateful. Meanwhile the Belgian had decided to come with us . . . We could easily have managed from there, but he refused to go back.

'We met no trouble until we came near a point where there was evidence of occupation, ie voices, noise and digging, etc and we accordingly proceeded with more caution. This was very desirable as at this stage my men were tired and walked carelessly in absolute pitch blackness. Very near to the south-west corner of the dropping zone, there is a house. When we reached it I realised that it was occupied by troops and its garden too. In fact there were many troops. We lay on a grassy bank and they walked past us . . . I listened to the voices in the garden but they were very soft. I crept nearer but even at a few yards' distance I was unable to say whether they were British or Germans. Nor could the Belgian. He then suggested that he should go to the house and ask for shelter. He would pretend to be a victim of the fighting in Arnhem. If the troops in the house were British, he would call us; if they were Germans he would say nothing.

'I did not like this plan. It was too dangerous for him. But still he went. I heard him talking loudly. The answer was safe, when suddenly he shouted "*Boches*". He was a very brave man, he never came back.'[1]

Captain King then continued his journey in the dark and reached the headquarters of the 4th Parachute Brigade at first light.

VII

Brigadier Hackett's 4th Parachute Brigade experienced little serious difficulty during and immediately after the landing on Ginkel Heath, although, in fact, the landing did not take place in complete quietness. Helle's SS Battalion, which occupied positions on the heath facing the 7th Battalion of the KOSB, had continued to offer some opposition, but the 4th Parachute Battalion landing in their rear and a simultaneous frontal attack by the 7th KOSB soon caused the SS battalion to flee in confusion.

It must have been less encouraging for Brigadier Hackett to hear, as he very soon did, that he would have to hand over his 11th Battalion for the purpose of reinforcing Frost's battalion at the bridge. In exchange for the 11th Battalion, Brigadier Hicks— who took this decision in the absence of General Urquhart, temporarily missing—had attached the 7th KOSB to the 4th Parachute Brigade, but the 7th KOSB had already been in action for twenty-four hours against Helle's SS battalion, while they had also to protect the landing of the Polish Parachute Brigade's equipment at Johannahoeve, further to the east, on Tuesday.

Yet all these setbacks were little compared with what still lay in store for Brigadier Hackett as he set about carrying out his task: to capture the high ground to the north of Arnhem. The eastward advance to his objective was to be halted by the German *Sperrlinie*, whose strength and composition are already partly familiar from the previously-quoted report of the commander of the Hohenstaufen Division, Harzer.

[1] Guy was taken prisoner by the Germans and escorted that same night to another headquarters by two soldiers. On the way there he managed to escape. The Germans fired a few shots after him but to no avail. He emigrated to Johannesburg after the war. It gave me—Boeree—great satisfaction to be able to establish contact between this Belgian and the British captain some years later.

That *Sperrlinie,* under the command of Major Spindler, ran along the Dreyenseweg in approximately a north-south direction, linking the Amsterdam road and the railway, which exactly north of Oosterbeek run almost parallel eastwards towards Arnhem (see map 9). The German line thus blocked off the ground between the Amsterdam road and the railway. *North* of the Amsterdam road a number of other German units were disposed in an east-west direction; these were some naval units and Krafft's SS battalion, which after regrouping near Deelen airfield had been put into the line again here. This east-west German cordon was, of course, inferior in fighting strength to Spindler's *Sperrlinie,* but that was no great disadvantage; the main force of the British attack—as the Germans realised—had to be aimed eastwards in the direction of Arnhem. The German cordon along the Amsterdam road connected at its eastern end with the northern end of Spindler's *Sperrlinie* and was able to harass the British forces on their flank as they marched eastwards, and to prevent them from attempting to outflank the *Sperrlinie* to the north. Hackett, of course, knew nothing of all this. But the three battalions of the 4th Parachute Brigade were soon brought face to face with reality. The battle reports at first show signs of self-confidence and optimism. The 10th Battalion, for instance, states: 'The Battalion was ready to march off within one and a half hours of landing ... The Battalion marched off just before dark in the evening of 18th and all seemed to be going well ... When the transport met up with the Battalion, from the Glider Landing Zone [at Reyerscamp, a mile or two to the east], the Battalion was in a strong position.' On leaving Ginkel Heath the 10th Battalion followed the Amsterdam road in the direction of Arnhem.

In the report of the 156th Battalion which followed a more southerly route, along the railway track, towards Arnhem, we read: '17.00. The Battalion moved off [from Ginkel Heath] ... 20.00. The Battalion met and joined up with the glider lift at the railway-crossing [at Wolfheze Station]. The gliderborne lift [to Reyerscamp LZ] was complete with the exception of one glider, containing two jeeps, which landed in the sea.'

But the report of the 7th KOSB—which was now attached

to the 4th Parachute Brigade but had in the meantime also to protect the landing of the Polish Brigade's equipment—already gives some indication of the coming difficulties: '19.00 the CO moved off the battalion [from Ginkel Heath] . . . The route which led along the railway was being used by 4 Para Brigade, which led to some confusion and delay. When near Wolfheze station the Battalion got clear of the units of 4 Para Brigade, commenced a night advance [Monday night] towards its objective . . .'

That objective was the ground near Johannahoeve Farm, some kilometres further to the east, where the Poles were to land the following day. But this ground lay immediately in front of Spindler's *Sperrlinie* . . . The report of the 7th KOSB lists the positions the various companies had to occupy, and continues: 'It was soon found that these positions were strongly held by the enemy who had permanent and prepared MG posts on them and in the vicinity. As it was impossible to locate and deal with these in the darkness, the Battalion, after suffering several casualties, took up a position before dawn, based on Johannahoeve, with Bn HQ there.'

But in the meantime the 10th and 156th Battalions had also been halted. The reports describe the situation in no uncertain terms. The 10th Battalion, marching along the Amsterdam road was 'held up by light ack-ack fire . . . [and] also came up against self-propelled guns and tanks. The companies dug in either side of the Arnhem-Utrecht road with the intention of holding off any attacks by tanks by day and then might march again by night . . .' But it will be clear to anyone who examined the German position on a map, that any further advance must encounter great difficulties. The battalion had become stuck in the angle made by the east-west disposition of Krafft's battalion and the north-south oriented *Sperrlinie* of Major Spindler. Moreover, the Junghans battalion of the German 908th *Sicherheitsregiment* had been fitted in at that point.

The 156th Battalion, which was advancing along the railway line further to the south, likewise discovered the existence of Spindler's *Sperrlinie*. At eight o'clock in the evening the battalion was joined at Wolfheze Station by its transport which had come down in gliders.

'A report was received from an officer of 7 KOSB that the enemy were holding a strong outpost along road from 702805 to 699791 [ie the Dreyenseweg]. 21.00 C Coy encountered heavy opposition . . . which brought the company to a standstill . . . The CO decided to form a firm base in the wood until first light with the intention of entering Arnhem from the north-west next morning. Communication with Para Brigade HQ had broken down by this time. 03.30 the firm base was completed.'

And so the battalions composing the 4th Parachute Brigade, having landed on Monday afternoon, were brought to a halt in the course of Monday night. The 10th Battalion had been stopped on the Amsterdam road, with the German battalions commanded by Krafft and Junghans on their left, and Spindler's *Sperrlinie* straight ahead. Close to the 156th Battalion, the 7th KOSB had taken up positions near the Johannahoeve dropping zone, where they were to protect the landing of the Poles on Tuesday. But they were occupying unsuitable positions, for the dropping zone lay immediately ahead of Spindler's lines. Further south, along the Utrecht-Arnhem railway line, the 156th Battalion had been forced to dig in for the night; the German line had proved an insuperable barrier for them, too.

Brigadier Hackett was in a very unenviable position: within twelve hours of landing, his brigade was facing an enemy who were superior in tanks, armoured cars and self-propelled guns. Hackett and his headquarters staff followed a route parallel to and north of the railway line until they reached the Buundercamp Hotel. The hotel was close to the Reyerscamp landing zone, where the gliders carrying the 4th Parachute Brigade's motor transport had landed. The proprietor of the Buundercamp Hotel recalls: 'One of the gliders came down low over the wood and landed in my garden. Several injured men jumped out of it. They helped each other and marched to the Reyerscamp field. Only the pilot was left behind in the aircraft. He was dead, behind the joy-stick. Some days later his body was taken away and buried by the Germans.'

When Hackett arrived at the Buundercamp Hotel in the evening of Monday, 18 September, he asked the proprietor to bring all available mattresses downstairs. Most officers on his staff spent the night outside, in the garden. There the glider still lay, with the pilot dead behind the controls.

VIII

Tuesday, 19 September came. While Frost's battalion at the bridge continued their desperate fight against an enemy that was becoming stronger all the time, the German ring closed slowly but surely round the rest of the division. In the east Spindler's *Sperrlinie*, in the north Krafft and some naval units, and in the west von Tettau's group, steadily advancing. And in the south the Neder Rijn, wide, deep and swirling. (See map 9.)

The 10th Battalion—constituting, as we saw, the north wing of Hackett's position—remained under fire from the German mortars, tanks and SP guns throughout Tuesday morning and afternoon. The Germans also mounted infantry attacks but all of these failed. The ferocity of the fighting in this sector is clear from the post-humous award of the Victoria Cross, to Captain L. E. Queripel of A Company. Captain Queripel had assumed command of the company immediately after the landing because the company commander, Major Ashworth, had been mortally wounded before the landing took place. In his book *Arnhem* General Urquhart tells how: 'Captain L. E. Queripel persistently crossed a road which was under enemy fire to position his men. He picked up a wounded NCO and carried him to cover and was hit in the face. Then he moved on a German strongpoint consisting of two machine-guns and a captured British anti-tank gun . . . and killed the crew of three . . . As the Germans closely harassed the withdrawing troops, Queripel and a party of men took up a covering position in a ditch. He was wounded in the face and both arms, and the party were short of weapons and ammunition, although they had a few Mills bombs, rifles and pistols. And as the SS Grenadiers closed in, hurling stick bombs into the ditch, Queripel promptly hurled them back. Soon, most of those who had shared this last stand were dead or badly wounded, and Queripel ordered the survivors to get clear while he covered their exit with a final bout of grenade throwing. He was last seen alone and still fighting in the ditch.'

By about noon the 10th Battalion had dug in and were occupying a relatively good position.

The 7th KOSB—who were further south, near Johannahoeve, awaiting the landing of the Poles—were also under heavy German shell-fire during the morning, and not only some houses in the vicinity but also Johannahoeve Farm itself was set on fire. An attack by German Messerschmitts caused the battalion some casualties.

The 156th Battalion—which formed the southern wing of Hackett's position—made an unsuccessful attack on the *Sperrlinie* along the Dreyenseweg in the early morning. About 07.00 hours C Company, supported by B Company, succeeding in capturing a strong outpost in front of the German line. But then they ran into the line itself, which had been reinforced with tanks and other armoured vehicles. At 08.30 hours A Company went over to the offensive. The German armour and self-propelled guns inflicted heavy losses on them, and finally the battalion was halted. Half an hour later B Company attacked at the same spot; they suffered the same fate, and their commander was mortally wounded. At 09.30 C Company and Headquarters Company commenced an attack; thirty men of the battalion reached the Dreyenseweg. At 11.00 B Company suffered heavy losses in dive-bombing attacks by Me 109s. At 14.00 hours the survivors of the 156th Battalion withdrew to their original positions..

Immediately to the rear of the line formed by these three halted battalions Brigadier Hackett had set up his headquarters in a copse. A farm to the left of it was hit by German shells and went up in flames.

Meanwhile, Urquhart had succeeded in escaping from his enforced hiding-place in the home of a middle-class Arnhem family. He arrived back at his headquarters in the Hartenstein Hotel about eight o'clock on Tuesday morning. It must soon have become obvious to the commander of the British airlanding division that the situation was not exactly rosy. The messages which reached him in the course of the day indicated that the situation was in fact growing worse with every hour that passed. Hackett's 4th Parachute Brigade (the 10th and 156th Battalions of the brigade proper and the 7th KOSB) had, as we have seen, been brought to a standstill by Spindler's *Sperrlinie* along the Dreyenseweg. Its assignment, to occupy the high ground to the north of Arnhem, appeared impossible to carry out.

Frost's battalion at the bridge was surrounded and was fighting stubbornly against stronger and increasing German forces who were, moreover, being reinforced with tanks—including some of the latest Tiger type. By daybreak on Monday A Company of the battalion had evacuated their advanced post on the northern ramp of the bridge. The battalion now occupied a number of houses and other buildings in the immediate vicinity from which the approach could be kept under fire. (The *southern* end, as previously mentioned, was in the hands of the Germans.) A careful examination had shown that there was no demolition charge under the bridge.

Seen from the point of view of the isolated battalion, which was completely out of radio contact with the rest of the division, the situation was difficult but not hopeless. They could shortly, they thought, expect the advancing British Second Army to arrive from the south, while the battalions of their own division would no doubt be trying to break through from the west. This knowledge was a moral comfort for Frost's men, as the 2nd Battalion's battle report shows: 'During the morning [of Monday] German armoured cars and half-tracks tried to cross the bridge from North to South . . . altogether ten armoured cars and half-tracks were accounted for. Throughout the day and following days, the Battalion area was heavily and continually mortared with little effect on the houses . . . During the late afternoon and evening a strong attack developed along the river bank from the east. It was supported by heavy mortar fire and two tanks. One tank was knocked out by six-pounder and one by Piat. Just before dark, houses 1, 11, 9 and 17 [occupied by the battalion] were set on fire by the enemy and burned down.' (See map 10.)

'Throughout the day there had been rumours, and great hopes of 1 and 3 Battalions arriving, but by night it was accepted that they would not get through. Later we heard that South Staffords and 11 Battalion were on their way to join us and hopes were revived.'

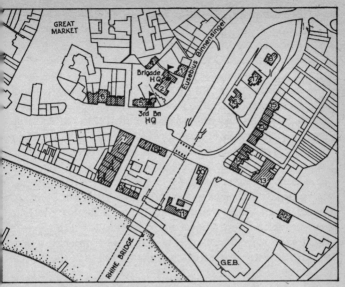

MAP 10 Fighting by Frost's battalion at the Rhine bridge. The numbered blocks of houses are mentioned in the text.

On Tuesday morning 'the attack east of the bridge was resumed with heavy mortaring and attempted infiltration throughout the morning. At midday three tanks got into position near the river and shelled 10 at close range, making it temporarily untenable. McDermont's platoon [occupying 10] suffered some casualties and were evacuated under the bridge. A group armed with two Piats scored three hits on tanks and then observed two more tanks. After obtaining more bombs . . . [their officer] returned to see the tanks pulling out. The enemy had meanwhile occupied 10. McDermont's platoon counter-attacked and reoccupied the house. Grayburn then led an attempt to rescue [12 and] 13 [which had been captured the previous evening by the Germans]. It resulted in more casualties and the attempt was abandoned. Soon after this a heavy gun from south of the river shelled 8 and 9. The top two storeys of the houses were demolished and B Company suffered some casualties. Two armoured cars penetrated along the river bank to 9 where George Murray accounted for one; the other withdrew.

'. . . Pressure continued until dark. Block 8 and house 10 were set on fire, forcing A Company into Area B and the ruins of 11 and B Company into block 7. Just before dark a Tiger tank drove down the road opposite 1, 2, 3, 5 and 6. It kept the six-pounder positions under small-arms fire and pumped shells into each house in turn. Battalion HQ stopped three shells before we could all get out . . . Meanwhile houses 14 and 16 were set on fire . . . Our position was now greatly weakened. We had suffered heavy casualties . . . Ammunition was getting fairly short and we had been burnt out of the key position east of the bridge, house 10. [The] enemy was occupying all houses to the north and west of our positions. Although they did not attempt infiltration from this direction, they were able to keep us under automatic fire—to which we could not afford to reply. The number of wounded was reaching serious proportions. They were all evacuated to the cellars of the Brigade HQ [in house 2].'

IX

The report speaks for itself. What can easily be overlooked as we read it is that this hard fighting took place in the heart of a city whose civil population had not been evacuated. The air-landings had suddenly brought a strange and confusing element into daily life for the people of Arnhem. Four years of German occupation had greatly altered the pattern of life of every Dutch civilian. However unpleasant they were, those alterations had come gradually and people had, up to a point, grown used to them. The black-out, food rationing, the black-market, the terror by the German Security Service—people had, for better or for worse, learned to live with them. But suddenly, without the slightest indication of what was going to happen, they found themselves practically in the front line; the change was for some civilians so great that at first they scarcely realised its cruel seriousness. The close proximity to each other in which they lived their day-to-day life during this time, and the inferno of house-to-house fighting, sometimes led to bitter tragedies. It was the old people in particular who, perhaps even with some resentment, discovered that an unnatural and cruel happening was threatening the confines of their small familiar world.

In one of the houses near Arnhem bridge lived a family consisting of husband and wife, a son and a daughter. There they kept a boarding-house for aged ladies. At the time of the air-landings there were three guests, two of them sisters. All three were very old—one of the sisters was eighty. At the back, on the first floor, the house had a balcony. From the balcony, which was supported by pillars, a stair led to the garden; the entire construction was made of reinforced concrete.

When Frost's 2nd Battalion reached the bridge on the evening of 17 September, and fighting broke out round it, this family fled with the three old ladies to the basement. They spent the night there. At three o'clock in the morning they heard the front door of the house being burst open. It proved to be British soldiers, who reassured the occupants of the house and disappeared. Then all was quiet again. But not for long. At six o'clock on Monday morning a jeep stopped outside the house. From the street came the disquieting sounds of fighting. A group of about fifteen British soldiers led by a lieutenant came into the house. They barricaded the outside doors and set up machine-guns at the windows.

That was just the beginning.

Close to the house the British set up an anti-tank gun. It started firing about six in the morning. The street in which the boarding-house stood was within the gun's field of fire. By noon there was not a single whole pane of glass in the house.

And so the hours passed. The British lieutenant told the people of the house that the position was serious and attempts to get reinforcements to the bridge had failed. The west wing of the block of houses to which the 'pension' belonged was already in German hands. On the street outside the boarding-house a British bren-gun was set up.

At five o'clock on Monday afternoon the boarding-house was hit by a German shell. Roof tiles and lengths of gutter clattered to the ground. Another house to the rear of the boarding-house caught fire but the British troops occupying it managed to put out the flames.

Nightfall on Monday brought no respite. In the darkness bitter fighting took place between the British and Germans for the possession of a wrecked tram-car in the street. On Tuesday morning the occupants of the boarding-house were awakened by the rattle of firearms. The house next door was found to be on fire. The son of the boarding-house keeper went out to scout around. In the vestibule he found a badly wounded soldier. The bren-gun had disappeared from outside the house. A solitary British soldier sat on the edge of the pavement, leaning against a thick tree. The soldier was dead.

In the afternoon the German mortar fire opened up again. The top floor of the boarding-house received a direct hit, while a shell also exploded in the garden. But in the kitchen an unruffled British soldier went on preparing a meal for the others. He said there was nothing to worry about.

But all these happenings proved too much for one of the old ladies. Before anyone could stop her, she had run outside. She wanted to escape from the fighting that was going on all round the house and penning her in, to get away from the fire that was consuming the other houses. She ran on to the street. On her left a German tank was firing at the British positions. From her right came the tracer bullets of a British machine-gun. The fire from the German tank killed her. She fell at the feet of the dead British soldier who was still there, at the edge of the pavement. His dead eyes seemed to hold an astonished look of non-comprehension.

At nine o'clock on that Tuesday evening, the British troops left the house and withdrew to the positions near the bridge. The occupier and his son made a tour of inspection through the house. The house on the left was still on fire and the flames could be expected to spread to the boarding-house. It was becoming too dangerous to stay in the basement. The boarding-house-keeper's family and the two surviving old ladies—the sisters—sought safety under the balcony and the concrete stairway at the rear of the house. The roof began to burn and then the attic. Then the upper storey caught fire. The bath and the cooker fell through the burning floor. The temperature under the balcony was rising.

One of the two sisters, who until that moment had apparently viewed all these happenings without the slightest concern, suddenly said angrily: 'Can't you do anything to stop this din?' The others tried to explain that there was little anyone could do, but their attempts merely brought the snappish reply, 'Then just order me a taxi.'

Meanwhile the heat from the burning house was becoming almost unbearable. The six in their shelter under the balcony kept dipping towels in pails of water to obtain some degree of relief. To leave this shelter and seek refuge against the wall at the bottom of the garden was impossible. Whenever they left the protection of the balcony, German snipers in the houses beyond the garden opened fire upon them. Some time later, however, this fire was silenced by a British bren-gun. When the family and the two old ladies were finally able to run across the garden and shelter behind the high garden wall, the entire house was in flames. About midnight it collapsed in a sea of fire.

And so Tuesday night passed. The six people crouched against the garden wall. They were cold and hungry. But any movement intended to remedy this state of affairs meant almost certain death. The trees at the front of the house concealed German snipers who fire at everything and everyone. The only food within reach was the apples that lay beneath the tree in the garden and they were roasted by the heat of the fire.

At four o'clock on Wednesday afternoon a shell exploded in the garden. The two sisters were killed. The others could do nothing but wait helplessly. Wait perhaps for the shell that would end their lives too. But in the night from Wednesday to Thursday the battle at the bridge ended. At three o'clock in the morning, German voices could be heard near the ruins of the house shouting, 'Heraus!' and 'Hände hoch!' For these four people—father, mother, son and daughter—the nightmare was over. They had lost everything they possessed. And the three old ladies were dead.

X

On 18 September, while Hackett's advancing 4th Parachute Brigade was, as we saw, being brought to a halt by Spindler's *Sperrlinie* to the north of Oosterbeek, and Frost's 2nd Battalion was holding on stubbornly at the bridge in the hope that reinforcements would arrive, the situation on the outskirts of Arnhem was confused. The events that took place there, in the immediate vicinity of St Elisabeth's Hospital, on Monday and Tuesday, form one of the culminating points in this phase of the battle of Arnhem —the dynamic phase in which the British were still trying to carry out as much of the original plan as was possible.

Many of those who have written about the battle of Arnhem have stressed especially the fighting in the immediate neighbourhood of the bridge. Not unrightly—for Frost's battalion and the other smaller units which managed to get through to his position have earned the admiration of both friend and enemy for their conduct. But it is sometimes forgotten that a large part of the battle was fought not at the bridge but outside Arnhem, that not only Frost's battalion but also the other battalions of the same division, the 1st Airlanding Light Regiment of Artillery, the glider pilots who had to bring in reinforcements, and all the other units had to fight hard and often desperate battles. The advance of Hackett's parachute brigade is one example of this, the attempt by four battalions to break through near St Elisabeth's Hospital another.

The first two of these four battalions were the paratroop battalions of Fitch and Dobie which had set out for the bridge immediately after the first lift landed, together with Frost's battalion, but following different routes from him and each other.

Frost reached his objective via the southern route, Fitch and Dobie were brought to a halt by the Germans on the same Sunday evening. When they tried to resume their advance very early on Monday morning, it was soon obvious to them that the objective could not be reached by the routes they had been instructed to follow—the German resistance was too strong. We have seen from the reports of Harzer and Bittrich quoted above that the

armoured vehicles of the Hohenstaufen Division had been despatched westwards along those routes and that, in addition, a
German barrier was being built between the paratroopers and
Arnhem. The 1st and 3rd Parachute Battalions both veered off towards the south and reached the narrow road along the Neder
Rijn which had led Frost to the bridge. Independently of each
other they penetrated into a built-up area of a dozen acres or so
on the outskirts of Arnhem, immediately to the west of St
Elisabeth's Hospital. Fitch's battalion fought for part of the day
in the northern half of this area with the intention of gaining
access to the town via the railway line; Dobie's battalion fought in
the southern half of the built-up area.

The two other battalions which participated in the attempt
to break through near St Elisabeth's Hospital were the 2nd
Battalion of the South Staffordshire Regiment and the 11th Parachute Battalion. Their presence there, as already stated, was the
result of the measures which Hicks had taken after Urquhart
was presumed missing. In view of the urgent need to reinforce
Frost's battalion at the bridge, Hicks had departed from the
existing plan. He had given orders for the 2nd South Staffordshires,
who were guarding the Reyerscamp landing zone in preparation for
the arrival of the second lift at noon on Monday, to proceed towards
Arnhem, leaving the second landing to take place unprotected and
the rest of the battalion to follow them to Arnhem. In addition,
Hicks had decided that the 4th Parachute Brigade, which was also
to land at noon on Monday, would release its 11th Battalion
and allow it, too, to march on Arnhem. The two battalions followed
the narrow road along the river—the route which had first been
used by Frost and then later partly also by Fitch and Dobie—
and reached St Elisabeth's Hospital. Thus four battalions arrived
there in the evening of 18 September, all of them with orders to
break through to the bridge. That is to say, each of them separately,
for at this point there was still no co-ordinated plan; the battalions,
in a manner of speaking, met each other by chance. And the front
on which they could advance was, as a result of the local situation,
not wider than several hundred yards (see map 11).

We have already seen that the situation threatened to create

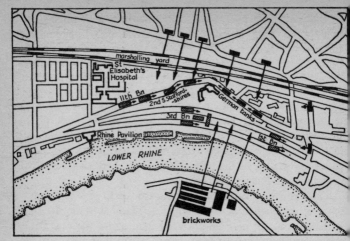

MAP 11 On Tuesday, 19 September, four British battalions (the 1st, 3rd and 11th Parachute Battalions and the 2nd South Staffordshires) tried to break through to Frost's isolated battalion at the bridge. The attack was launched from a line joining St Elisabeth's Hospital and the Rhine Pavilion, which is where the road forks. The 2nd South Staffordshires, followed by the 11th Parachute Battalion, took the higher road to the left; the other two battalions took the lower road along the Neder Rijn. The total width of front between the marshalling yard (which is cut deep into the hilly ground) and the Rhine was very small (see also Map 12). There were German machine-gun nests in houses on the north side of the marshalling yard. German anti-aircraft guns sited at a brickworks on the south bank of the Rhine fired horizontally. Despite heavy casualties the 1st and 3rd Parachute Battalions gained ground. But the 2nd South Staffordshires and the 11th Parachute Battalion met heavy opposition; they advanced more slowly, thus leaving the left flank of the battalions on the low road exposed. Then they were attacked by German tanks; both battalions retreated in confusion. In the meantime, the two battalions on the low road were decimated. The remnants of the four battalions assembled on the St Elisabeth's Hospital—Rhine Pavilion line.

some confusion and uncertainty at divisional headquarters. A clear illustration of that confusion is furnished by the battle situation near St Elisabeth's Hospital. On the afternoon of Monday, for instance, the relatively small network of streets to the west of St Elisabeth's Hospital held within its confines both Urquhart and Lathbury; they had left Fitch's 3rd Battalion and been forced to seek hiding in the attic of a private dwelling; the fact that four battalions were in the immediate vicinity was unknown to them.

174

In that same built-up area, in the northern half, Fitch's battalion was fighting; its purpose was to reach the railway line and force its way along the railway line into Arnhem and then to the bridge; Fitch was unaware that several hundred yards away there were three other British battalions preparing to launch attacks.

Lathbury's headquarters staff were with Frost at the bridge; Lathbury had sent them on behind Frost on Sunday evening but when Lathbury was assumed missing simultaneously with Urquhart, Frost became acting commander of the brigade; it was for this reason that when Dobie, who was in the southern part of the built-up area and whose battalion belonged to the 1st Parachute Brigade, made radio contact with Frost at 6.30 on Monday evening, he was instructed by Frost to break through to the bridge.

At 20.00 hours, however, the 2nd Battalion of the South Staffordshires arrived (ie the first part of the battalion; the other part had landed at Reyerscamp that afternoon and was following on). Dobie and McCardie, the commander of the South Staffordshires, decided to make a joint attack at 21.00 hours. In the meantime they received an unconfirmed message that Frost's battalion at the bridge had been overrun by the Germans; they then decided not to carry out the proposed attack. At 23.00 hours they heard over their wireless an artillery observer at the bridge giving firing instructions. This showed that Frost's battalion was still holding out. Dobie and McCardie sent a dispatch rider to Hicks. At 01.00 in the night of Monday to Tuesday Hicks ordered them to withdraw. But just then the 11th Battalion arrived, which had been dropped on Ginkel Heath with the 4th Parachute Brigade that afternoon and had been sent to the bridge by Hicks himself to reinforce Frost's battalion.

Meanwhile—and all this was still taking place in the area round St Elisabeth's Hospital—General Urquhart had come in contact with a Canadian Lieutenant, L. Heaps, who, with a Dutchman as guide, was trying to get through to the bridge with supplies in a bren carrier. Urquhart heard from Heaps that he, Urquhart, was reported missing at his headquarters. Being unaware of the existence of the other British battalions in his immediate vicinity, Urquhart sent Heaps back to his headquarters at Hartenstein Hotel with a message. Partly on account of the not so happy tidings he had received from Heaps, he gave instructions that everything possible should be done to get reinforcements through to Frost's battalion. Heaps returned to the Hartenstein Hotel, informed Hicks and was instructed by him to return to Arnhem and convey his orders to the battalion commanders that they had to make an attempt to break through. Heaps finally found the house in which Dobie, McCardie and Lieutenant-Colonel Lea (the commander of the 11th Battalion) were studying a map by the light of a candle. It was decided to initiate the attack at 3.30 on Tuesday morning, but when the second lift of South Staffordshires had still not arrived, this time was changed to 04.00 hours. It can hardly occasion surprise to come across the following observation in the 11th Battalion's report on the Arnhem fighting: 'No sooner had one "O" group been held than different instructions would come from Divisional HQ. Consequently there was only about one hour of darkness left when the Battalion followed the South Staffords up towards the Elisabeth Hospital.'

Meanwhile, Fitch with the 3rd Parachute Battalion was still trying to break through to the bridge, unaware that the other three battalions were practically just round the corner. The attack he mounted at four o'clock on Monday afternoon via the railway line to the north of the built-up area and St Elisabeth's Hospital was unsuccessful. The local situation was most unfavourable for an attack; three well-positioned German machine-guns and two mortars made an advance impossible. Very soon the battalion was split into two parts, each occupying a block of houses. Fitch decided to wait until half-past two on Tuesday morning. As a breakthrough in a northerly direction had proved impossible to achieve, he intended, when that time came, to march southwards and to reach the bridge by advancing along the bank of the Neder Rijn. Every officer and NCO had, under cover of the darkness and in complete silence, to get his men to the Rhine Pavilion, a building on the bank of the river almost due south of St Elisabeth's Hospital. From there the battle would try to move eastwards and join Frost's battalion at the Rhine bridge.

The battalion, as we saw, had been split into two parts in the course of the previous attack. When Fitch arrived at the Rhine Pavilion with his half of the battalion, he did not wait for the arrival of the other half, but immediately set off along the road with his men (see maps 11 and 12). Shortly afterwards, however, he ran into such violent opposition that further progress was out of the question.

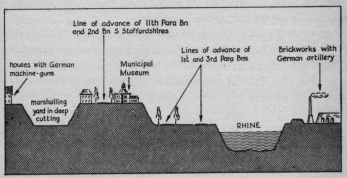

MAP 12 Section through the point where the front on which the four battalions (see also Map 11) tried to break through to Frost's battalion is narrowest, viz about 800 ft.

The German opposition can be explained from the events of the previous day, Monday. On that day, the four British battalions had reached the built-up area to the west of St Elisabeth's Hospital independently of each other. In getting there they had partly followed the route which Frost had taken to the bridge on the Sunday. But at the same time all four battalions had broken through the *Sperrlinie* which the Germans were building up first through the city of Arnhem and later further to the west, to prevent the remainder of the division from linking up with Frost at the bridge. Further to the north-west, Hackett's 4th Parachute Brigade had run into and been halted by this *Sperrlinie* along the Dreyenseweg. But the south-east end of the *Sperrlinie* was apparently still not strong enough on the Monday to be able to stop the British. In addition, the British here were supported in their advance by their artillery which was sited slightly further to the west near the church of Oosterbeek-Laag. The British battalions, however, did not get beyond the system of streets near St Elisabeth's Hospital. The Germans were by now bringing troops into position in the town of Arnhem itself to deny the four British battalions access to the bridge. Moreover, the German artillery at the brickworks on the *south* bank of the Neder Rijn had been instructed to fire on all traffic on the low road along the north bank of the river. And, finally, mobile German units kept up incessant attacks on the four battalions as, for example, in the built-up area.

It is clear that in the early hours of Tuesday, after having at first made some progress with the half of his battalion, Fitch finally came to a halt against the German positions which were built up in Arnhem itself after the *Sperrlinie* had been pierced. Fitch decided to retreat to the Rhine Pavilion and there try to link up with the other half of his battalion. Then they could deliberate about further measures.

All this took place while the commanders of the other three battalions were making preparations for their attack which was to be launched from about the same position as Fitch's advance, a line from St Elisabeth's Hospital to the Rhine Pavilion. About there the road divides into two, running approximately parallel but at different levels. It was now planned that the 2nd South Staffords should advance along the high road, with the 11th Battalion in their rear. Dobie's 1st Battalion would take the low road—between the high road and the Neder Rijn.

For anyone who has been over the terrain or examined a map of it, it will be obvious how desperately little chance of success this undertaking had (see map 11). The British battalions had, so to speak, to be squeezed through a narrow aperture into the town. On their right lay the Neder Rijn; the German artillery on its far bank had practically a free hand against the lightly armed airborne forces. On their left lay the railway line and a marshalling yard. The marshalling yard was a cutting, a huge trench excavated in the ground; and the Germans were in position high on its far side. The width of the front on which the British battalions could advance was thus only several hundred yards. It was impossible to fan out to the left or right, and equally impossible to set up guns to help them force a passage. The enemy, on the other hand, was still receiving a continuous flow of reinforcements, and could cover this narrow corridor from both sides and from practically invulnerable positions. And, of course, the frontal opposition they were able to put up had also to be reckoned with.

At four o'clock on Tuesday morning the three battalions set off. Near the Rhine Pavilion, Dobie, who was to take the low road, ran into an officer of Fitch's 3rd Battalion, which had tried to break through to the bridge just a short time before. The officer told Dobie that Fitch had encountered strong German opposition and had not succeeded in pushing further into the town. Dobie did not allow this news to influence his plans but advanced along the bank of the Neder Rijn. Fitch decided to follow him with what men he still had left; the battalion had suffered heavy casualties in the last few days' fighting.

XI

At first all went well. The fighting was hard but Dobie succeeded in capturing several German guns and taking a few prisoners. By 05.00 hours, according to the battle report of Dobie's 1st Battalion, German opposition was particularly strong. It goes on: '06.00. Our position becomes desperate as enemy were on high ground above us [ie to the north].' At the start of the offensive, when Dobie was following the low road, the 2nd South Stafford (with the 11th Parachute Battalion behind) had set off on the high road. If the advance of the two columns had kept pace with each other, the battalions could have protected each other on one flank. But the advance along the high road was so much slowed down by the German opposition that Dobie's north flank was left exposed. The Germans occupied the houses and gardens along the high road and from there they were able to throw hand-grenades at Dobie's battalions and harass it with all available weapons. When daylight came, the German artillery at the brickworks on the other side of the Rhine also opened fire; this they could do without hitting their own troops on the high road because the steep slope between two roads acted as a stop-butt.

The battle developed into a massacre on that long, unprotected strip of ground, only thirty or forty yards wide. The battle report of Dobie's battalion describes in stark but unambiguous language: 'R Coy six men left. S Coy fifteen men left (approx) . . . T Coy eight men left. Bn HQ about ten left (CO went forward to make recce, position very bad). 06.30 T Coy were cut off and could not disengage. Enemy grenading us from houses [on the higher road] we were trying to get into. Managed to force entry (CO wounded) but only had six men. Enemy in rear also . . . Tanks outside our house. Many civilians in cellar with us. Nothing more to be done. Four wounded in our party . . . 07.30 SS entered house. Party taken.'

For Dobie himself this was still not the end. He takes up the story of his personal experiences as follows: 'I was taken prisoner at 7.30, having been wounded in the eye and the arm. Was taken to hospital . . . after having my wounds dressed . . . I had removed my colonel's pips and crown . . . Shortly after arriving at the hospital, my German guard took my watch, and while he was showing it to a nurse, I managed to make my escape and hid in the bushes on the . . . hospital grounds. After being stopped once by a German soldier and allaying his suspicions by saying "*Guten Morgen*" I decided not to risk crossing the road and spent the rest of the day in hiding. That night [Tuesday evening] I crossed the street into a house, which had been bombed, and managed to find a bed where I slept very soundly indeed until awakened by somebody, trying to get in at the door. It proved to be a [Dutch] doctor . . . He dressed my wounds once more and found me another bed in the house . . .' Later, when the town of Arnhem was evacuated on the order of the Germans, accommodation was found for Dobie with some well-disposed Dutch people at Ede. Dobie's 1st Parachute Battalion no longer existed.

But Fitch's men had been advancing along the road behind Dobie's battalion. Once the latter had received the *coup de grâce*, the German fire—and particularly that of the artillery on the south bank of the Neder Rijn—concentrated its full violence on Fitch's battalion. The result was catastrophic. Slowly but surely the battalion, completely exposed on that flat strip of ground, was mowed down by the German fire. Fitch gave orders for a retreat to the Rhine Pavilion in order to take up positions there. An orderly withdrawal was no longer possible. It was just left to every man—officer, NCO or private—to get back to the Rhine Pavilion, with a whole skin if he could. 'The whole area', says the battalion report, 'seemed covered by fire and the hope of getting out safely was small. The withdrawal began immediately. Casualties were heavy.' Only a handful of men reached the Rhine Pavilion, Fitch was not among them. While his second in command was regrouping the survivors—who included a mixed group of men from other battalions from which they had been cut off earlier—in a defensive position, he found an officer of the battalion in a house near the Rhine Pavilion. '[He] was wounded in the foot', says the battle report, 'and . . . said he had mortar splinters in his foot. He had great difficulty in breathing and speaking. He managed to say that the CO had been killed by mortar fire.' The battle on the *low* road was over. Of Fitch's and Dobie's battalions only a few men still survived. And in the midst of that savage fighting—often man to man—the civilians sat in their basements. They could hear the explosions of hand-grenades and mortar bombs close by on every side. Above their head, in their houses, gunfire rang out. Resignedly they waited and waited until finally relative quiet returned. When a boy of one of these Dutch families whose house had been occupied by Germans went back up to his room, he found that his tin soldiers had been drawn up neatly in battle order by a German soldier.

Also at four o'clock on Tuesday morning two battalions had begun their advance to the bridge via the *high* road; they were the 2nd South Staffords and, in their rear, the 11th Parachute Battalion. The first few moments of the advance were almost ghostly in their unreality. At one instant there was a deathly silence in the dark night, in the next, German fire burst forth on all sides. When it was still, the men of both battalions could hear Frost's battalion still holding out against the attacking Germans at the bridge, less than a mile away in a straight line.

As daylight came, the German opposition increased considerably. The South Staffordshires were particularly harassed by enemy fire from the high ground at the far side of the marshalling yards on their left. Their losses increased but the battalion was slowly gaining ground. At 06.30 hours one of its companies succeeded in occupying a building which has gone down in the regiment's history as 'The Monastery'. It was, in fact, not a monastery but a museum. At 08.00 the attack came to a standstill; any further advance was impossible. By then, however, the South Staffordshires had passed the narrowest point in the corridor—not wider than 275 yards! The battalion was now at a fork in the road. McCardie, the commander of the South Staffordshires, decided to take the road to the right. He asked Lea, commanding the 11th Parachute Battalion, which was following the South Staffordshires, to move from his rearward position and come up on his left flank. That arrangement was agreed upon by the two commanders at 08.30; Lea would now advance not behind but on the northern flank of the South Staffordshires, and in doing so he would follow the southern edge of the low-lying marshalling yards. (Meanwhile, as we have seen, Fitch's 3rd and Dobie's 1st Parachute Battalions, which had mounted an attack along the *low* road at the same time as the 2nd South Staffords and the 11th Parachute Battalion, had already been mauled by German artillery fire from the south bank of the Neder Rijn.)

Lea made this arrangement with McCardie at 8.30 am. But at 11 am he received instructions from divisional headquarters that he was to hold on to the position he had then reached and not to advance. He sent word to the South Staffordshires but for some reason or other (the runner or the receiver of the message was probably killed or captured), the message never reached McCardie. Lea describes these events as follows: '08.30–09.30 CO visited CO 2 South Staffords . . . Attack had petered out. Clear that original plan could be pursued no longer. Arranged that 11 Para Bn would try to get forward on left . . . 10.00. Informed 2 South Staffords that GARBLED message had been received from Div, which appeared to indicate that 11 Bn was to stand fast in present area. Attack therefore off, positions being taken up till Div intention was clear. 10.30–11.00 Div Staff officer with orders to 11 Bn to secure Heyenoord-Diependaal.' As this line was more to the west, further west even than St Elisabeth's Hospital where the offensive had started, the message was equivalent to an order to the 11th Parachute Battalion to withdraw. (Divisional headquarters' reason for issuing this order, can—as we shall see later—be reconstructed with reasonable certainty.)

It is not inconceivable that later events led at first to some difference of opinion between the commanders of the two battalions, so that Lea, whose battalion was in the second line behind McCardie's, received orders from divisional headquarters to withdraw. He passed this news on to McCardie. The latter did not receive the message and assumed that Lea was still in position behind him, ready, as arranged, to move forward and come up on his left flank. But the 11th Parachute Battalion was not in position; it was forming up in a column with all its available weapons to march back to the position assigned to it by divisional headquarters.

So while Lea mistakenly assumed that he could safely draw up his troops in an extremely vulnerable column of march because he was covered by McCardie and his South Staffordshires, McCardie for his part was convinced that he could fall back on positions held by Lea's 11th Battalion if he was forced to give ground before a German counter-attack.

That was when the German tanks did, in fact, counter-attack. From 9 till 11 am A Company of the South Staffordshire had managed to keep the German self-propelled guns at a distance with Piats (the British anti-tank guns had, on Hicks' orders, been left behind at Hartenstein Hotel as reserves), but then they ran out of Piat ammunition. At 12.30 A Company was forced to disengage. The German tanks broke through and 'caused confusion'—as the battle report says—among the unsuspecting 11th Parachute Battalion which was standing ready to march off. Both battalions suffered heavy losses. They were forced to fight their way back to a line west of St Elisabeth's Hospital. There the remnants of both battalions were reorganised and made ready for further action.

That, then, was the situation after General Urquhart had returned to his headquarters on Tuesday morning. Hackett's 4th Parachute Brigade (consisting of the 10th and 156th Parachute Battalions and the 7th KOSB) was being held up to the north of Oosterbeek by Major Spindler's *Sperrlinie* along the Dreyenseweg; it was obviously incapable of carrying out its instructions: to form a bridgehead round the city of Arnhem.

Unless a miracle happened, Frost's battalion was doomed; without reinforcements and supplies they could not possibly hold out much longer against increasing German superiority.

An attempt by four battalions (the 1st, 3rd and 11th Parachute and 2nd South Staffordshire) to break through to the bridge had failed; and in the course of that attempt all four had suffered heavy casualties.

From the west, too, in the rear of the division, so to speak, von Tettau's western group, consisting of several battalions, was approaching; it was an impossible task for the 1st Battalion of the Border Regiment to stop this advance, and the Germans had already occupied Renkum and Heelsum.

Urquhart, realising how critical the situation was, consequently decided upon drastic measures. He would transfer Hackett and his 4th Parachute Brigade to a different position. The brigade would occupy a north–south line running from the Utrecht-Arnhem railway to the Neder Rijn, about halfway between Oosterbeek and Arnhem (see map 13). The 11th Battalion would occupy the Heyenoord-Diependaal area to the north of the railway line. Urquhart's measures probably provide the clue to the misunderstanding between Lea and McCardie during their advance towards the bridge. In *By Air to Battle*, we read: 'Urquhart soon decided that it was quite out of the question to attempt to put it [the 4th Parachute Brigade] north of the railway, in other words, to create that outer perimeter which should include the town within its embrace. On the afternoon of the third day, therefore, the Brigade was ordered to disengage and to move south of the railway so as to occupy, if possible, the high ground between Oosterbeek and the town; but even this task proved impossible.' And in the 11th Battalion's report: '11th Battalion was ordered to do a left flank attack to join up with the remainder of the 4th Brigade . . .' Urquhart's order to Lea was thus a consequence of that plan, but it came at an unfortunate moment—probably because Urquhart lacked accurate information about the position of the British battalions to the east of St Elisabeth's Hospital.

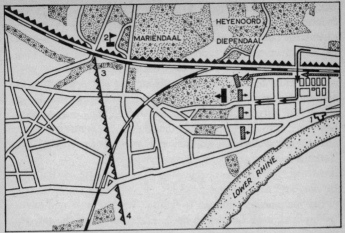

MAP 13   After the unsuccessful attempt by four British battalions to get through to the bridge and the attempt to regroup the remnants (shown diagrammatically, shaded), German tanks and infantry broke through the British positions. Urquhart, unable to form a comprehensive idea of the confused situation in this sector (1 is the Rhine Pavilion), ordered Hackett to march his 4th Parachute Brigade from the north-west (not shown on the map) to the south-east and occupy the line 3–4. From there Urquhart hoped to have the 4th Parachute Brigade march eastwards to the bridge. The 11th Battalion was to occupy the Heyenoord-Diependaal area north of the railway line. Neither order could be carried out. North of the railway line ran the German *Sperrlinie* (the HQ of its commander, Spindler, was at 2); further to the west it bent northwards along the Dreyenseweg, where Hackett's 4th Parachute Brigade had already been brought to a halt. When he withdrew, it was only with the greatest difficulty that he reached divisional HQ at the Hartenstein Hotel; he never made the line assigned to him. Nor would it have been possible for the exhausted men of the 11th Battalion to occupy Heyenoord-Diependaal, which lay behind the strongly held *Sperrlinie*. The remnants of the British battalions withdrew to the west, where, like Hackett's 4th Parachute Brigade, they were later to defend British positions in the perimeter at Oosterbeek.

Speaking about the Arnhem-Nijmegen railway line in his book *Arnhem*, Urquhart says: '. . . it was on this line . . . that I intended Hackett and his 4th Brigade should stop to reorganise before they went for the Bridge.' Urquhart was thus still planning to break through to the bridge, this time with Hackett's 4th Parachute Brigade.

It is clear from this, however, that Urquhart also lacked sufficient information about the German positions, for the Utrecht-Arnhem railway was a part of the German *Sperrlinie*. In the first place the northern end of Hackett's new position would be at right angles to the German line. In the second, Heyenoord-Diependaal, the area it was proposed that the 11th Battalion should occupy, was in fact *behind* the *Sperrlinie*, which was particularly strong at that point. It would be an impossible task for the exhausted men of the 11th Battalion to break through such a strong position. Not only the 11th Battalion and the South Staffordshires were sent to that point, but also the survivors of the 1st and 3rd Battalions.

XII

But the plan was doomed to failure. German tanks and infantry broke through the British lines. The remnants of the 1st, 3rd and 11th Parachute Battalions and of the 2nd South Staffords were forced to retreat in a westerly direction. They were intercepted by Lieutenant-Colonel W. F. K. Thompson, the commander of the 1st Light Artillery Regiment, which was occupying a position along the Neder Rijn, near Oosterbeek-Laag Church. Thompson ordered the retreating troops to take up advanced positions to the east of the church. He later showed Brigadier Hicks round all these units and pointed out the difficulty of commanding them; the troops he had intercepted consisted almost entirely of other ranks without officers—and, moreover, there was no radio contact with the outpost they formed. Hicks sent him a few officers and Thompson arranged for a wireless link. The officers Hicks sent included the deputy commander of the 11th Battalion, Major D. Lonsdale.

Lonsdale had been wounded as early as the Monday before, when the aircraft from which he was about to jump on Ginkel Heath was hit by German fire. At the outpost Lonsdale took command of the 11th Parachute Battalion and the South Staffords—or at any rate what was left of the two battalions.

One of the officers who fought at this advanced post at Oosterbeek was an 11th Battalion Company commander. In a passage already quoted from the personal account of the battle by this officer, Captain J. D. King, we saw how his aircraft had been shot down near Rhenen on Monday afternoon before it could reach the landing zone, and how he and a number of men finally managed, with the aid of Dutch Resistance groups, to reach Hackett's head-quarters. From there he went on Tuesday afternoon to divisional headquarters at the Hartenstein Hotel. He was driven south late that evening in a bren-carrier, in search of his battalion, which by now was under Major Lonsdale's command at the outpost on the Neder Rijn near Oosterbeek.

Captain King continues: 'We headed south, and I fancy took the quickest route from Hartenstein to the Kerk at Oosterbeek [-Laag], then heading east parallel to the river until we reached the second road junction, ie midway between the Kerk and the railway to the east. I remember there was a house or two on fire to the left. We halted at the junction and I soon found what remained of the 11th battalion. It was a remnant of its former self, probably already less than 150 men . . . At dawn [on Wednesday] I awoke and attempted to organise my company. I had NONE. A few men left of the machine-gun platoon had been put under command of the South Staffords. My other men and anti-tank gunners were no more . . . I took over about ten from another company and we organised a defensive position in a house . . . We were attacked here at some strength by infantry, tanks and self-propelled guns . . . Sometime after lunch they managed to set us alight. We put out the fire but three men were killed in one house and an officer and two men next door . . . During the afternoon . . . an attack de-veloped . . . which threatened to cut us off from the area of the church [where the British artillery was sited].

'Major Lonsdale sent me . . . to deal with this attack. We cap-tured five men and a MG but the main trouble seemed to be com-ing from three tanks. By approaching through a house, and from behind a wall, we were near enough to touch the first tank with our hands. We put this out of action by detonating plastic explosive against the tanks. This as you may guess caused a certain trouble. German infantry appeared around us and some of us were wounded. A grenade burst near my legs and a moment later I was shot. The bullet passed under my right arm from the side, bruised a lung, broke my breastbone and came out an inch above the heart. It sounds serious but it wasn't. However, we had to withdraw. But the tanks withdrew first . . . in the confusion I was left behind with two men worse wounded than I was . . . it was late afternoon when I reached Major Lonsdale to report. He was then giving orders to retreat to the Oosterbeek church area. I remember walking to the church, helped along by two of my men, and just by the church I fainted.'

So all that was left of the British battalions in the east was pulled back to Oosterbeek. There the battered and exhausted units occupied the positions that were eventually to form the south-east corner of the British bridgehead in which the last scenes of the battle of Arnhem were to be enacted.

The Canadian lieutenant, Leo Heaps, whom Urquhart had run into after being cut off from his headquarters and forced into hiding in a suburb of Arnhem, says Urquhart, 'was soon to develop a reputation for turning up in the most unlikely places at the most unexpected times. In fact I never really discovered to which unit he belonged'. He wrote a book after the war, *Escape from Arnhem,* in which he recorded, *inter alia,* his impressions of a visit to the British artillery positions near the Oosterbeek-Laag church. 'Inside [the church],' he writes, 'we saw a group of very weary, wet and wounded men. These were the remains of the three battalions who had made the attack on the bridge at Arnhem. There could not have been more than two hundred left, and these had escaped by crawling through ditches half-filled with drainage water. Almost everybody was wounded and wet and covered with mud. By looking out of the big shattered church window toward the open field which ran down to the river, you could see the wounded and the dead lying where they had been struck down by mortar and machine-gun fire while trying to escape. It was a terrible sight in the church. Each man was weary to his bones, and miserable, and most were wounded. Yet they were filled with such great spirit that they could never be defeated. There was only one officer left from my battalion [the 1st Parachute Battalion]. This little band of men was commanded by a man named Lonsdale. He was wounded several times in the face, and when asked if he would go to a house close at hand for treatment, he replied, "I have been hit three times, but I'm still good for several more". He smiled through a blood-caked mouth, and told me they were preparing to take up a position around the church.'

XIII

The co-ordinated attempt by the four battalions to break through had failed. Urquhart's plan to mount a new attack in the direction of the bridge with the support of Hackett's 4th Parachute Brigade remained only a plan; the four battalions which had already suffered such heavy losses at Arnhem (the 1st, 3rd and 11th Parachute Battalion and the 2nd South Staffords) could naturally not stand up to the German tanks, and the remnants were forced to withdraw to Oosterbeek—and Hackett's 4th Parachute Brigade never reached the position which was to have served as the point of departure for a renewed attempt to break through.

Within twenty-four hours of landing on Ginkel Heath at 3 pm on Monday, the 4th Parachute Brigade had—as we have already seen—been stopped by the strong German defence line running along the Dreyenseweg, to the north of Oosterbeek. Its task—to form a bridgehead round the town of Arnhem—had proved impossible to carry out. On returning to his headquarters after being reported missing, Urquhart decided to pull the brigade out from the area north of the Utrecht-Arnhem railway line and to send them to the area south of that line. There was no time to lose; von Tettau's group, slowly approaching from the west, might occupy the railway-crossing at Wolfheze at any moment and this could considerably interfere with and delay the evacuation of the brigade across the railway embankment.

On Tuesday afternoon Urquhart himself drove in a jeep to visit Hackett, whose command post was in a copse near the railway line. After a conference between the two officers it was decided to pull out as quickly as possible, the troops using the railway-crossing at Wolfheze and the vehicles being manhandled over the railway embankment several hundred yards to the east. This last measure, which was carried out by the Royal Engineers, was taken in case the German western group should prevent the withdrawal of the

British transport over the railway-crossing at Wolfheze by their fire.

Hackett duly ordered the 10th and 156th Battalions to withdraw as quickly as possible via the prescribed route. The 7th KOSB were to leave a few units behind to protect the landing of the Poles near Johannahoeve, while the remainder of the battalion would cover the rear of the other battalions at the railway-crossing and the passage of the transport over the embankment. (As we saw, the 7th KOSB had been incorporated in the 4th Parachute Brigade by Hicks—during the time he was replacing the missing Urquhart—in exchange for the 11th Battalion, which Hicks, in view of the critical situation, had sent to the bridge. The 7th KOSB would therefore march off with the 4th Parachute Brigade but on the way they would carry out a task previously assigned to them: to protect the landing zone near Johannahoeve where the equipment of the Polish Parachute Brigade would be landed in gliders; the Polish troops themselves were to land by parachute south of the Neder Rijn.)

Once all the troops had crossed the railway line they would concentrate in the woods near the Wolfheze Hotel. From there they would try to reach the British positions round divisional headquarters in the Hartenstein Hotel at Oosterbeek, a mile or two to the east. This second phase would not be just a retreat since a British line of defence against the Germans advancing from the south-west was already being formed down the west side of Oosterbeek.

The withdrawal of the 4th Parachute Brigade, consisting of the 10th and 156th Parachute Battalion and the 7th KOSB thus began at 4.30 on Tuesday afternoon.

The report of the 10th Battalion has this to say: 'This [retreat] was to prove a dangerous step as the Battalion was in close contact with the enemy and it meant moving back across about one thousand yards of open ground which was well swept by small-arm guns. It had to be carried out, however, and the companies got back to the level-crossing at Wolfheze. Very heavy casualties were suffered crossing the open ground . . . After reaching Wolfheze, the Battalion withdrew towards the Division's perimeter and after laying up during the night pushed through and reached the position of the defence, which was to continue until the 26th.' Brigadier Hackett adds his own personal observations as follows: 'On the following days, manning the eastern and northern edges of the perimeter, the achievements of the remnants of 156 and 10 Battalions were of a sort I have never—personally speaking—seen surpassed . . . By the 23rd, I think it was, when the CO of 10 Bn, Smyth, was fatally wounded and . . . his last remaining company officer was hurt almost as badly . . . the battalion was left at about thirty strong with no officers at all.'

Things were not any easier for the 7th Battalion of the KOSB. The gliders carrying the vehicles of the Polish brigade had meanwhile landed, and the commander of the 7th KOSB, Payton-Reid, had ordered a part of his B Company to assist the Poles to collect their scattered equipment. According to the battalion report, the landing went well, despite heavy German anti-aircraft fire. But the Polish war correspondent, Marck Święcicki, who was on the spot, gives a less rosy—and unfortunately more accurate—account. And he is borne out to some extent by the American General James Gavin, who writes (in his book *Airborne Warfare*) that of the forty-four gliders which left England only thirty-one arrived at Johannahoeve. Święcicki himself says of the landing: 'Cast off from the tugs, they [the gliders] would be landing in a moment. But at that very moment something happened which we had not expected. From the north other tiny dots . . . grew and grew . . . Messerschmitts! Their machine-guns snapped and barked . . . Several gliders caught fire and . . . dived in a mad flight to the ground . . . One of the gliders broke up in the air like a child's toy, and a jeep, an anti-tank gun and people fell out of it . . . When they [the Messerschmitts] stopped, the forest opened up. Skirmishing Germans, looking in the distance like rabbits jumping, or field mice, moved . . . forward. The German infantry fired at the gliders which had escaped the Messerschmitts . . . The bullets tore through the gliders' wooden walls, over the jeeps and guns which had been brought out, and then over the men, throwing more and more of them to the ground. The men who had escaped whole fled. Yes, they fled; for it couldn't be called a retreat or a defence.'

The explanation of the German *Luftwaffe*'s quick reaction is to be found in the report, already quoted above, by Harzer, the commander of the Hohenstaufen Division: 'A liaison officer from the 1st *Jagddivision* also reported. This *Jagddivision* had been released for the battle of Arnhem . . . At that time it still had about 300 operational aircraft consisting of Messerschmitt 109F's and Focke-Wolf 190's. The flying time from the Ruhr to the Arnhem airspace was about ten to twenty minutes after the alert . . . The French fortress town of Dunkirk was still in German hands, and was thus able to signal very quickly to Army Group [B] the exact numbers of hostile transport aircraft, crossing the coast inwards, some of them towing gliders. Army Group was thus informed fully an hour in advance of the arrival of the enemy formations, and so, too, were all our troops right down to the machine-gunners of the divisional group.'

That in all probability accounts for the presence of the Messerschmitts.

The attacks by the German fighter aircraft and infantry had disastrous consequences for the Poles. And, from a tactical point of view, the loss of the transport, guns and other equipment was at least equally catastrophic for the men of the Polish brigade who were to land on the south bank of the Neder Rijn.

The attack by German infantry can also be accounted for from the reports. And the explanation shows once more the great rôle that chance and misunderstanding can play in the unavoidable confusion which occurs in the course of mobile battles such as that at Arnhem. We have already seen how the British 4th Parachute Brigade, advancing from west to east towards Arnhem, had been brought to a standstill by the Hohenstaufen Division's *Sperrlinie*; in addition, the Germans had formed a line which ran from east to west and linked up with the *Sperrlinie* (see map 9). The 4th Parachute Brigade was stopped in the angle formed by the two German lines. Situated in that same corner was the Polish landing zone near Johannahoeve Farm. The battalions in the German east-west line (ie on the north flank of the 4th Parachute Brigade) included Krafft's SS battalion, which has already been referred to in the account of the very first fighting on Sunday, 17 September. Krafft's report states that at twelve noon on Tuesday, 19 September, the *Gefechtsgruppe* Krafft was formed upon orders from Spindler, the commander of the German *Sperrlinie*, out of Krafft's battalion, several naval units and a police regiment. This group was ordered to advance from north to south on a broad front and to make contact on their right wing with the German west group under von Tettau (which was slowly advancing from west to east). The first objective to be attacked by the *Gefechtsgruppe* Krafft was the Ede-Arnhem road, the second the edge of the wood 880 yards south of that road. The report continues: 'Shortly after the start of the attack, about 16.00 [15.00 British time], simultaneously with the dropping of considerable supplies south of the Arnhem-Ede road, new mass air-landings (gliders) took place ahead of the left wing of our *Kampfgruppe*.' (In other words, the Poles landed in front of Krafft's forces while the latter were in the act of attacking.) '. . . For the second time on the same day it proved possible to inflict painful losses on the enemy. This initial success, however, was all that could be obtained, for our advance guards were forced by the concentrated counter-attack of the British (from two sides) to fall back across the Arnhem-Ede road again . . . About 24.00 hours we succeeded in making contact on our right wing with the left wing of von Tettau's division. The encirclement [of the airborne forces] was thus completed . . . 20.9.44—06.00 Battalion moved westwards past our *Kampfgruppe*'s positions into the attack during the night and forced the enemy back southwards over the railway line.'

To sum up, Krafft, who was already on the move southwards, suddenly found the landing Poles in his path. The fact that this was the transport column of the Polish brigade escaped him. When he reached the Ede-Arnhem road and attacked the Poles, he also came in contact with the British 10th Battalion and probably also with companies of the 7th KOSB. The British troops presumably opened fire on Krafft's *Gefechtsgruppe*, who got the impression they were being attacked on several sides. Their advance elements thereupon withdrew. And the battalion which Krafft saw moving along his position from the east next morning at six o'clock, must have been the German battalion commanded by Junghans which had left the *Sperrlinie* on the Dreyenseweg in order to attack the retreating 4th Parachute Brigade. Krafft's impression that this battalion was actually pushing the British southwards across the railway line was quite mistaken. The last British soldier had already left the area north of the railway line many hours earlier.

XIV

So the landing of the Poles was less successful than one might suppose on reading the battle report of the 7th KOSB. This battalion's own withdrawal southwards across the railway line was equally calamitous. The circumstances under which this operation took place were the most difficult imaginable. In the north of the battle area two companies and the headquarters staff were occupied with the attacking Krafft group; a third company had been detailed to protect the transfer of the transport from one side of the railway to the other, and only the fourth company was able to withdraw unopposed to the south with the 156th Battalion.

Payton-Reid, the commander of the 7th KOSB, makes the following comment on this situation: 'That plan [for withdrawal] was, as we now see, forced on our higher command, but its execution had most disastrous consequences. It is against text-book teaching to break off an engagement and withdraw from the battlefield in broad daylight, and that is what we, and the two battalions of 4 Para Bde had to attempt—and without delay. As a result, this fine Scottish Borderer Battalion which at four o'clock in the afternoon was a full-strength unit, with its weapons, transport and organisation complete . . . was reduced, within the hour, to a third of its strength . . .'

The battered battalion, some units of which were prevented by the confused fighting from reporting at the agreed assembly point, remained in position on the railway line until all troops and vehicles were on the southern side. Then the 7th KOSB also moved southwards. As darkness was falling they reached the vicinity of divisional headquarters. There they received orders to take up positions on the northern end of the bridgehead that was being formed round divisional headquarters. At midnight on Tuesday the battalion began to dig in there.

Of the battalion units which failed to reach this position

Payton-Reid writes: 'At the time the fates of "A" and "B" companies were shrouded in mystery but . . . [the two company officers] have since given me some information on this point. Both tell the same tale of being constantly harried by the enemy, during their attempts to withdraw according to the orders, and of confused fighting in the woods. "A" Company at one point came across a party claiming to be Poles, but when they went out to meet them were promptly fired upon. "B" Company actually joined up with 4 Bde HQ, by whom they were directed to Hotel Wolfheze, where they found only some aged inmates and evidence of recent German occupation, including booby-traps. Here they listened on the hotel radio to the BBC news, from which they gathered that our main forces were concentrating near the river—a somewhat unusual way of being "put in the picture". In both companies, after numbers had been greatly reduced by hours of close hand-to-hand fighting, those who still remained next day were overrun before they could reach the Divisional perimeters.'

Thus, during the hurried retreat of the 4th Parachute Brigade, the 10th Parachute Battalion and the 7th Battalion of the KOSB had suffered heavy casualties before reaching the British positions round Oosterbeek. The last battalion in the brigade, the 156th, and the headquarters staff moved off together. They, too, suffered serious losses. Owing to the short time available for the operation and to attacks by enemy patrols a part of the battalion was cut off from the rest. By seven o'clock on Tuesday evening about 200 men had reached a point just south of the railway line. This group, which included brigade headquarters staff, spent the night there. A night that was filled with the din of German mortars and exploding shells, and with skirmishes with German patrols. At seven o'clock on Wednesday morning the move to the British positions round the Hartenstein Hotel was continued, a distance, as the crow flies, of several kilometres. Towards evening, after long and savage fighting in the woods, a group of some seventy men reached the British lines.

More telling than a matter-of-fact report on how this fighting went are the details recalled by Brigadier Hackett, who writes: 'On the 20th, pushing through the woods . . . towards Div HQ, we were really hard pressed. The number of killed in 156 was high, including the Commanding Officer Sir W. R. de B. des Voeux, and several other officers . . . Up to then [several hours after the start of the march] the whole thing, in spite of its losses during the previous two days, had continued to "handle" . . . as a brigade, and I was very proud and pleased at the way in which, after each new blow, the pieces so rapidly fell once more into a recognisable shape.

'But from the time that the enemy's infantry, with a few small tanks, got right in amongst us, it grew increasingly hard to control, and towards the end of the day I could only pull in all I could lay hands on, into a small pocket and command them more or less as a company. What was left of the 10th Battalion had of course got on ahead of us, and managed to rejoin the rest of the Division. [The 156th Battalion had covered the withdrawal of the 10th Battalion about noon on the same day.] The 20th was a difficult day for us, towards the end of which the men, though in admirable heart, were desperately short of water, food and ammunition. Many of us—myself included—were now using German rifles. Much of the fighting was hand to hand . . . I remember . . . using rifle, grenade and bayonet all that afternoon like any infantry private . . . and having to lead a rush or two at close quarters, which is an unusual and stimulating experience for a brigade commander in modern times . . .

'In the evening we made a dash for where we thought the Division would be if it were still functioning. But the interesting thing was that since we had been out of contact ever since mid-morning and only had our own experience of the remainder of the day, by which to judge, we could not be certain that the same thing had not been happening to them too.

'The men, in fact, made no secret of their conviction that the division had been liquidated. They were none the less ready, even after the rough time they had had, to make an effort to rejoin it, and in the event a comparatively short fast dash brought all we had left inside the perimeter. It all seemed wonderfully peaceful by comparison with the day's performance in the woods.'

The evening of Wednesday, 20 September, more than seventy-two hours after the British division's first landings: round divisional headquarters, the Hartenstein Hotel at Oosterbeek, the remnants of what until a day or two before, or even a few hours before, had still been well-equipped battalions at full fighting strength were moving into position for their last grim fight. Of four battalions that had tried to force their way through to the bridge at Arnhem only small groups of exhausted men remained. And Hackett's 4th Parachute Brigade had managed to reach the British lines only at the cost of heavy casualties. A gradually tightening ring of German infantry, tanks, self-propelled guns, mortars and anti-aircraft guns were closing round the small piece of ground into which the remnants of nearly the whole division were pinned along the Neder Rijn. Nearly, because three or four miles to the east, at Arnhem bridge, Frost's 2nd Battalion was still fighting on that Wednesday evening.

The night of Tuesday-Wednesday had been relatively quiet at the bridge over the Rhine. The battalion had sent out patrols but the cordon which the German Major Brinkmann had drawn round the British positions proved impossible to break through. Burning buildings—they included several churches—turned the night into day. It was now quite clear to Frost's men that the rest of the division was also in difficulty. The only hope was that the British XXX Corps could advance quickly enough from the south to relieve the battalion at the northern end of the bridge.

Wednesday morning started with the usual German mortar fire. The airborne defenders were being pushed together into an ever decreasing area. But still they dominated the approach to the bridge. The houses and other buildings in which they had taken shelter were set alight or reduced to ruins by the German fire. Frost and one of his company commanders were wounded by the same mortar bomb. House after house had to be evacuated as fire drove out the troops occupying them. But they dug in in the gardens and waited until the fires in the ruins went out. Then they returned. Access to the bridge had to be prevented at all costs.

In the afternoon five or six German tanks succeeded in crossing the bridge from north to south. The British anti-tank guns were under German rifle fire; it was impossible to man them. A rumour that xxx Corps would assault the southern end of the bridge at 5 pm caused the fighting to flare up again for a time. But ammunition was running short, every shot had to be a hit. By evening all the British troops east of the bridge had been pushed back to the west of it.

Shortly before darkness fell, the last few houses still held by the battalion were attacked by the Germans with phosphor bombs. Brigade headquarters was set on fire. The flames could not be put out. Over 200 wounded lay in the basement of the building. These were transferred to another building but even before the operation was completed that building, too, was on fire. There was now nowhere left where the wounded could be taken. Frost gave orders for the wounded to be handed over to the Germans. That was done but the Germans took advantage of the short truce which it necessitated to infiltrate their infantry into positions which they had previously been unable to reach. It did not make much difference. The British were now surrounded on three sides by burning buildings. Their ammunition was running short. The survivors of the battalion were split up into small units which had to try to get out of the town independently of each other.

Shortly after dawn on Thursday, 21 September, the fight was over. About half of the forces had been killed or wounded; most of the rest were taken prisoner in the course of Thursday morning. Only a few managed, after many vicissitudes and with the assistance of the Dutch Resistance movement, to escape to freedom.

In the original plan it was expected that the British 1st Airborne Division would have to hold the bridge for only twenty-four hours, by which time contact would have been made with the troops advancing from the south. Only twenty-four hours—but of the entire division only the 2nd Battalion, the brigade headquarters staff, C Company of the 3rd Battalion and several other small units reached the objective. And they held it for longer than thrice twenty-four hours.

Not in vain—a much used phrase and one which often refers

rather to a distant, ultimate result attained by common sacrifices than to a direct tangible result. In the case of the struggle at Arnhem bridge the tangible result has been acknowledged by the enemy.

Bittrich, the commander of the two German armoured divisions against which the British fought, declares: 'I am doing no more than my duty of honour when I pay tribute to our adversaries in the battle of Arnhem-Nijmegen. They were typical of the extremely tough and highly trained British soldiers who had fought against us since the beginning of the invasion. A classic example of the indomitable fighting spirit of these troops was the performance of the British forces (Frost's battalion) at the bridge in Arnhem; even after defeat these men left the battle-field with morale unbroken.

'The stubborn defence of the bridge by Frost's battalion was the reason why the measures which the II SS Panzer Corps had initiated in order to force a decision in the Nijmegen area, failed in their original intention. The heroic fighting of this group of British parachutists at the Arnhem bridge made it impossible for the 10th SS Panzer Division to advance quickly along the main Arnhem-Nijmegen road.'

The crossing of the Rhine at Pannerden by the 10th SS Panzer Division (under Harmel) was delayed considerably because there were insufficient pontoons. These forces consequently arrived at Nijmegen too late to reinforce the bridgehead effectively. (The Germans' intention was to form a bridgehead south of the Waal, in order to launch an offensive against the British Second Army at a later date.) Bittrich continues: 'After reconnoitring the bridgehead I suggested to Field-Marshal Model that the Nijmegen bridge, which already had a demolition charge in position, should be blown up. Field-Marshal Model rejected this suggestion . . . arguing that the bridgehead might be the point of departure for future attacks towards the south . . . As was to be expected, the bridge was captured by the enemy.' (Gavin's 82nd US Airborne Division and the British Guards Armoured Division.)

The battle of Arnhem Bridge had been fought.

Not in vain.

CHAPTER FIVE

OOSTERBEEK

(21–26 September 1944)

I

The 1st Airlanding Light Regiment of Artillery, whose guns were sited near the Oosterbeek-Laag church, by the Neder Rijn, was firing in support of the 2nd Parachute Battalion encircled at the Rhine bridge, a mile or two to the east. One of the regiment's officers was with Frost at the bridge, directing the fire of their guns. This man had to be in continuous contact with the artillery positions at Oosterbeek. But late in the afternoon of Wednesday, 20 September, this contact failed and people at Oosterbeek observed that the noise of fighting in Arnhem gradually diminished.

By the afternoon of 20 September it became clear that what everyone had expected was about to happen: the small British force, short of food, water and ammunition, tortured by exhaustion and lack of sleep, fighting an enemy whose strength was increasing all the time and who was using tanks, could not hold out any longer.

For Urquhart this meant that the division's objective, the capture of the road bridge at Arnhem, was unattainable. It also meant that the German units which until now had been tied down by Frost's battalion would be freed to strengthen the German *Sperrlinie*, whose primary task had been to prevent the division from linking up with Frost's battalion at the bridge. And it meant, finally, that this *Sperrlinie*, and in fact all the German troops involved, could now concentrate on their second task: the destruction of the rest of the British airborne division.

It was now up to the British to occupy the most favourable positions they could, pending the coming German attack. For although the road bridge had not been captured, the operations of the 1st British Airborne Division had still to be regarded as part of the entire operation MARKET GARDEN. In other words, the advancing ground forces, the British Second Army, had to be guaranteed a crossing of the Neder Rijn. If that was not possible at the road bridge, the most suitable place for a largely motorised army, an alternative would have to be found. For example, a bridgehead where the division could hold out with the greatest chance of success until the arrival of the Second Army and from which connections with the south bank of the river (and therefore with the troops which would arrive there) would be as good as possible. Several miles west of Arnhem there was a ferry between Driel on the southern bank of the Neder Rijn, and Heveadorp on the northern. That would have been the obvious place for a line of communication across the river, now that the attempt to capture the bridge had failed. It is, of course, theoretically possible for military engineers to build a bridge across a river at any point. But a bridge is only of use if it connects with existing roads on both sides of the river. It is not possible to construct new ramps and roads at the same time—that would take too long. The tactical solution is to build the emergency bridge at a point where approaches and roads already exist—at a ferry, for instance.

In looking for a place at which to await the arrival of the Second Army and at the same time defend himself against the attacking Germans, Urquhart had to take a number of factors into consideration. First, his headquarters, which were already set up in the Hartenstein Hotel at Oosterbeek. Second, the artillery positions near the Oosterbeek-Laag church. And third, the Driel ferry.

The Hartenstein Hotel, surrounded by a wide lawn, is a remarkably easy target not only for artillery and mortar fire, but also for machine-guns and snipers. When the headquarters unit of the division was marching along the Utrecht road to Arnhem on Sunday, 17 September, it was intended that they should find accommodation in the Musis Sacrum building in Arnhem. But German opposition delayed the advance and brought it to a standstill in the evening.

On the right-hand side of their route, the British discovered a fairly large building with a lawn in front, on which garden tables and chairs were set out. They decided to shelter in this hotel for the night of Sunday—Monday, leaving it next day when they resumed their advance. The choice of the Hartenstein Hotel was thus not based on any tactical consideration. But no further advance was possible on the next day, and the Hartenstein was adopted temporarily as headquarters. It was to remain headquarters until the end of the battle.

Here are the opinions of some officers who visited it in 1944 when it was divisional headquarters. Leo Heaps (in *Escape from Arnhem*): '. . . it was not unusual for a stray German to infiltrate to within a few yards of the big house where Divisional Head-quarters proper was located.'

Marck Święcicki (in *With the Red Devils at Arnhem*): 'On Thursday morning the Divisional command moved to the cellars. The ground floor now had no windows . . . and the general impression was far from reassuring.'

Lieutenant Wolters, a Dutch naval officer who was attached to Urquhart's staff as the representative of the Dutch Military Authority: '19 Sept . . . That night I slept in my little room, there was no glass left in the windows . . . 20 Sept: I slept in my room at Hartenstein under the table because a part of the ceiling came already down . . . 21 Sept: I slept in the corridor before my room, because the room was no longer practicable . . . 22 Sept: I slept in a room downstairs, the staff had removed to the cellar. The rest of the hotel was no longer for habitation . . . 23 Sept: I slept in the corridor of the entrance, there was no fit room left.'

Captain King (who spent one night in the Hartenstein): 'It didn't appear to be ideally suitable as a Div HQ. It was too obvious, too good a target.'

None of the writers is enthusiastic. In addition, the hotel was a mile from the river.

The artillery positions were equally far from ideal. The guns had originally been sited at one of the landing zones, to the south of Wolfheze. But when Frost reached the bridge on the evening of 17 September, the 3rd Light Battery had to be moved to an advanced position because it was not possible to support Frost from the Wolfheze position. The British artillery commander, Lieutenant-Colonel W. F. K. Thompson, states that the position at Oosterbeek-Laag was a 'provisional' one. He later ordered the entire regiment to be moved to it. Thompson says: 'Here it was very difficult to find suitable troop positions and those chosen were mortared during its [3rd Light Battery's] preliminary reconnaissance. However, there being no alternative, by evening the whole Regt was dug in in its final position.'

During the whole of the final phase of the battle the Oosterbeek perimeter was based on two positions, the Hartenstein and the artillery site, both of which can be considered anything but suitable. In his book, *The Battle of Arnhem*, Christopher Hibbert states that he brought the criticism concerning Urquhart's choice of this perimeter to the notice of the British airborne division's commander and that Urquhart replied: '. . . our only intention was to get forward to the Arnhem bridge with as many units and as quickly as possible. Circumstances decided otherwise and it was only as a result of them that the perimeter was slowly formed . . . it almost formed itself; at any rate in outline . . . The loss of the high ground at Westerbouwing was a sad blow and it was planned to recapture it . . . It is still a mystery to me how the Germans . . . failed to make use of the high ground at Westerbouwing.'

Before going into this question, let it be stated expressly once again that the aim of this book is to record the historical facts as accurately as possible. That this cannot be done without occasionally uttering adverse criticism will be obvious. This in turn may produce the retort that it is very easy to criticise *a posteriori*, when all the facts are known—when the cards of both players lie face upwards. The men who fought at Arnhem, the officers who had to make decisions there, could not see the opponent's cards; they were often dead tired through lack of sleep; they were sometimes short of food and drink; they had to take their decisions under the most unfavourable circumstances, with staff-maps which were perhaps not quite up to date, on information that was vague and scarce; but they had to take decisions, clearly-defined decisions, because that is what the troops in the front line needed; they knew that in certain conditions any decision, any order, is better than none. Only with those considerations in mind it is permissible, long after the battle has been fought, to sit at a writing-desk and pen views that are critical in tone.

Urquhart, then, argues that as a result of circumstances the British perimeter formed itself and he is astonished that the Germans did not make better use of the high ground at Wester-bouwing. But it is not unreasonable to suggest that on Wednesday, 20 September, when the German opposition was proving too strong and all the British battalions were withdrawing on Ooster-beek, Urquhart might have moved his headquarters. The retreating units had still not occupied their new positions; they could still have been diverted to positions near Westerbouwing. Had this been done, Urquhart could have made profitable use of this height, which—to his own surprise, as he says—the Germans failed to do.

Anyone who stands on the edge of Westerbouwing cannot help thinking that this is where the centre of gravity of Urquhart's position should have lain. Westerbouwing, a hill some 100-feet high, is on the bank of the Neder Rijn. There is a restaurant there, with quite a large terrace. From the terrace a fairly steep slope runs down to the river bank where the Driel ferry has its landing-stage. The slope on the landward side is less steep. Standing on the terrace one can look over the Neder Rijn and the ferry, over the polder on the other side of the river and far into the Betuwe. Eastwards one can look across the narrow base of the perimeter, a strip of meadowland several hundred yards wide, bordering on the river. Further to the east the church tower at Oosterbeek-Laag, where the British artillery positions were centred (see map 14). Urquhart has every right to be surprised that the Germans did not make more use of Westerbouwing. Anyone who holds that height dominates the flat land by the riverside. But on 20 September, Westerbouwing was still in British hands, although the hill was not strongly defended. It lay in the south-west corner of the perimeter; to the east—on the edge of the perimeter as it later became—a company of the 1st Battalion of the Border Regiment was stationed; the only force available for the defence of the hill was a single platoon.

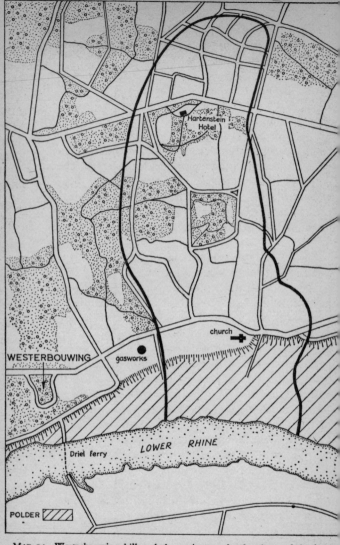

MAP 14 Westerbouwing hill and the perimeter. As the shape of the latter was changing all the time during the fighting, it is shown as it was at an arbitrary moment. Urquhart's HQ was at the Hartenstein Hotel, the centre of the British artillery positions to the left of Oosterbeek-Laag church. Westerbouwing hill communicated with the south bank of the river via the Driel ferry. Once the Germans had captured this wooded hill, which was weakly defended, and with it the ferry, they could enfilade the entire base of the perimeter, which consisted of low-lying polder land (hatched).

On the morning of Thursday, 21 September, Frost's position at the bridge was overrun by superior German forces. Harzer, the commander of the Hohenstaufen Division, now had his hands free to carry out the assignment which Bittrich, the commander of II SS Panzer Corps, had given him: to destroy the remnants of the British airborne division in the bridgehead north of the river as quickly as possible, before the British Second Army could arrive at the south bank. Harzer therefore gave orders for an all-out German attack on 21 September. The situation which existed before that time was, as we have already seen, remarkable. From the east the aggressive Hohenstaufen Division under Harzer was advancing on Oosterbeek. From the west came the relatively passive group of von Tettau, who had placed it under the command of Lippert; the latter did not attack much but moved at a leisurely pace towards Arnhem in pursuit of the British troops who had landed at Renkum Heath and Ginkel Heath. Bittrich made a clear distinction between the two groups: Harzer had an attacking rôle, the western group had merely to block the road to the west.

But on the 20–21 September the western group also came under Harzer's orders, and a new unit, an NCO school of the Hermann Goering Division, was added to the west group. These troops consisted of young, fanatical followers of Hitler and possessed a few tanks. It was this unit that overran the advance platoon of the 1st Border Regiment on 21 September. A counter-attack by the company failed. Westerbouwing was lost to the British, and on that same day the Germans destroyed the ferry-boat.

What remained was the Oosterbeek perimeter: a long, narrow corridor, only a few hundred yards wide at places, with one of its narrow sides on the Neder Rijn; in the north, at the landward end, was Urquhart's headquarters, the Hartenstein Hotel; in the south, the artillery position. This vulnerable corridor, the 'perimeter', was to remain under German gunfire from 21 September until the end of the fighting.

When the parachutists of the Polish brigade landed on the *south* bank of the Neder Rijn several hours after the loss of

Westerbouwing, the way via the Driel ferry to the beleaguered British positions was blocked. Not a single Pole managed to cross the river that night.

III

So the all-round German attacks on the British positions began on Thursday, 21 September, but not until von Tettau's western group, which had until then operated independently, was brought under the same command as the eastern group, namely that of Harzer. This explains why the British battalions as they drew back on Wednesday, 20 September, were allowed to form their perimeter in comparative peace. Until the moment of fusion and the order to attack, the main force of the eastern group remained in the *Sperrlinie*, awaiting reinforcements; not until they arrived would the group start advancing on Oosterbeek. And until that same moment the western group maintained the tactics it had practised for days—dogging the British battalions cautiously but in such a way as to be a great nuisance to them.

Previously, in describing the fighting on Sunday, 17 September, we gave an account of the almost ridiculous operations which this western group—sometimes grandiosely referred to as the 'Von Tettau Division'—conducted in the earliest stage of the battle. It included only a few units of practical fighting value. But although the Hohenstaufen Division on the east side of the perimeter played by far the more important rôle for the further direction of the battle, it is not superfluous to reconstruct the development of the western group from Sunday, 17 September, until Thursday, 21 September. As a fighting force this heterogeneous group was not comparable with Bittrich's experienced (though under-strength) SS divisions. This is clear from, among other things, the statements of several officers who belonged to the western group.

Helle, the commander of the SS surveillance battalion which fought against the 7th KOSB, tells how on Monday afternoon, after the landing of Hackett's 4th Parachute Brigade, he was obliged to withdraw to Ede. This 'withdrawal' was in reality a panic flight: Helle, who had been lying sleeping on a table in the café which he had made his command post, came within a hair's breadth of being taken prisoner. When he arrived in Ede, he heard the rumour that his battalion had been annihilated and he and his entire staff killed. This rumour also reached Amersfoort, where the officer in charge of MT was told that the British had already reached Scherpenzeel. Gussmann promptly departed for Apeldoorn with his vehicles, which included the canteen lorries. 'The consequence', says Helle, 'was that we didn't have a hot meal for several days.'

After his 'withdrawal' Helle tried to reassemble the companies which made up his battalion. He was not very successful. The remnants of the battalion were finally merged with Eberwein's battalion, which also formed part of the western group. And when Helle quotes his casualty figures—forty-two dead, 124 severely wounded and 120 missing—it is safe to assume that the word 'deserted' could be substituted for 'missing' without any loss of accuracy. Helle's adjutant, Naumann, who was sent eastwards on Tuesday morning with the remnants of the battalion (about seventy men, with Naumann as company commander), is equally unable to report great feats of arms. He states, for instance: 'About 11.00 hrs [on Tuesday, 19 September] I had combed out the wood . . . There was no resistance. Our plan was to advance along the [Utrecht-Arnhem] railway line and to cut the landed troops in two parts. It did not succeed because the troops which had landed were marching ahead of us, also in an easterly direction.' In other words Naumann was trailing the 4th Parachute Brigade who had landed on Monday afternoon and were now making for Arnhem north of the railway line via Wolfheze. Naumann also reports that Eberwein's battalion, which was advancing on his southern flank, came across a number of wounded Germans in a wood: 'They had been neatly bandaged by the British before the latter left them.'

Until Wednesday the battalions forming the western group had operated independently. (A result of von Tettau's 'generalship': on Sunday he had sent one battalion after the other to the east from Rhenen, without any further instructions.) On Wednesday, 20 September, the German units approached Wolfheze, where the British 4th Parachute Brigade withdrew southwards across the railway line in the afternoon. 'From that moment onwards', says Naumann, 'all the German units were combined into a single *Kampfgruppe* under the command of Lippert. On 21 September this *Kampfgruppe* started to attack the western flank of the perimeter on orders from Harzer.'

Although it means anticipating the fighting round the perimeter from 21 to 26 September, here are some observations by Naumann and Lippert about the situation in the German west group. Naumann narrates that during the attack on 21 September Helle's battalion tried twice in vain to cross an open stretch of ground; on both occasions the battalion was called back. Then Lippert suddenly appeared on the scene and ordered a third attempt with the object of overrunning the entire northern sector of the perimeter. 'Helle was convinced', says Naumann, 'that this was impossible. He objected, said that his battalion always got the hardest jobs to do, that his men were exhausted and had suffered heavy losses, and that is was impossible to carry out the order. Lippert relieved... Helle of his command.' A more detailed account of this incident it that Lippert complained to von Tettau about Helle's conduct and that von Tettau gave orders for Helle to be sent back to Amersfoort. Lippert then sent for Helle to come to his car and there, in front of the driver, he shouted at the astounded Helle: 'You are dismissed your command, go back to Amersfoort!' And then he drove straight off.

But a few days later Lippert experienced the same fate. Of the other units in the original western group he says: 'It was a hotchpotch. Originally I had no contact with them. Except for my own 2 Coys, the troops had no front experience. My boys [from the school for NCOs] had already fought on the eastern front. Arriving at von Tettau's HQ [on the evening of Sunday, 17 September] I inquired about the enemy's strength, location, etc. But he knew nothing . . . A couple of days before the battle I . . . was dismissed. The reason was that I had a lot of misunderstandings with von Tettau . . .

'. . . Von Tettau's HQ was a nuisance. He never did anything I wanted: reinforcements of men, supplies of food and ammunition, removal of the wounded. Fortunately, General Rauter visited my command post every day and when I asked him to get me out of some scrape, he always helped me. That irritated von Tettau, he looked out for a chance to accuse me. A couple of days after the Helle incident, I was summoned to his HQ. There he snarled at me and asked me how it was possible that Doorwerth Castle behind my front lines was in British hands. I was perplexed. Was it possible that those ninnies of the *Schiffstammabteilung* [one of the unusable detachments of naval personnel which von Tettau had given Lippert] had been taken by surprise? I could scarcely believe it. I drove to the castle where I found all in order. The garrison was resting, the guards were at their posts and watchful. I was furious and returned to von Tettau's HQ. There I shouted: "What idiot said that Doorwerth Castle was in British hands?" Then suddenly General von Tettau appeared and I repeated my question.'

And then von Tettau did what so many senior officers have done on discovering that they have blundered in dealing with a subordinate. He did not apologise for his conduct, he did not even mention Doorwerth Castle again, but he reproached Lippert for his undisciplined behaviour. He worked himself into a rage and dismissed Lippert his command, just as Lippert had dismissed Helle.

I V

To return to Thursday, 21 September, the British battalions, having withdrawn to Oosterbeek, now occupied their defensive positions; a perimeter had been formed which was based on two unfavourable sites: the Hartenstein Hotel, Urquhart's headquarters, in the north and the artillery position in the south, near the bank of the Neder Rijn. The German eastern and western groups had come under a single command, and the commander of the Hohenstaufen Division had ordered an all-round attack on the perimeter: the remnants of the British airborne division had to be destroyed before they could make contact across the river with the British Second Army advancing from the south.

The question arises to what extent the seriousness of the situation was appreciated within the perimeter itself, at Second Army headquarters or in London. One cannot escape the impression that with regard to the final result of the operation the position was still considered to be more rosy than it really was. One of the causes of this was the lack of good communications. In the American *Military Review* of September 1952 Major James A. Huston (Office of the Chief of Military History) writes: 'One of the biggest failings in the operation was that of communications. The British I (Airborne) Corps was not aware of the seriousness of the situation of the 1st Airborne Division at Arnhem until forty-eight hours too late. In response to an offer by the commander of the 52nd (Lowland) Division (Airportable) [which, under the original plan, was to have flown over to the Veluwe in gliders, but not until later] to send a force in gliders to aid the 1st Airborne Division, General Browning had sent (on D plus 5) the following message: "Thanks for your message, but offer not—repeat not—required as situation better than you think." '

Chester Wilmot (in *The Struggle for Europe*) says that radio contact between the besieged forces at Oosterbeek and the British Second Army in the south was first made at 9 am on Thursday, 21 September. According to Wilmot, Urquhart reported over this link that the enemy was making powerful attacks on the British troops holding the bridge, that the general situation was serious, that relief was urgently needed and that he still held the Driel ferry. Thompson, who commanded the British artillery at Oosterbeek-Laag, says in his report that this wireless contact was made with his transmitter; it was the only link between the division and Horrocks' xxx Corps, which formed the spearhead of the British Second Army. From Urquhart's messages to xxx Corps Horrocks deduced that both the bridge and Driel ferry were still in British hands. He therefore issued new instructions to his Guards Armoured Division, which was under orders to break through to the bridge on the main Nijmegen road: if their way to the bridge was blocked, they were to wheel westwards across the Betuwe in the direction of the Driel ferry. The Polish Parachute Brigade (which, according to the original plan, was to land near the southern end of the bridge) would jump that same afternoon near Driel in order to capture the southern approach to the ferry. It was thought that the Poles and the Guards together would be able to set up a strong position from which infantry could be ferried across the river to Urquhart's perimeter. If both banks of the river were firmly in Allied hands an emergency bridge could be built across the river at the ferry.

But at 9 am on Thursday, 21 September, Frost's battalion at the bridge was overrun and the high ground at Westerbouwing fell into German hands—and with it the landing-stage of the Driel ferry. The capture of this valuable position is mentioned in both British and German records although neither side indicates the tactical importance of the event. Hicks, the commander of the 1st Airlanding Brigade, notes: '09.00 Advanced platoon of B Coy 1 Border at Heveadorp attacked by a number of Tiger tanks and overrun.' Remarkably enough, the German source is not the battle report of Harzer, who by that time had all the German troops round the perimeter under his command. Harzer does not even mention Westerbouwing: presumably he concentrated almost exclusively on the operations of the eastern group.

The fight for Westerbouwing is referred to in the personal diary of the German Colonel Fullriede. This diary has already been quoted for Fullriede's opinion of von Tettau's headquarters ('a club for old gentlemen'). Fullriede's name is chiefly known from the fact that several weeks after the battle of Arnhem he set fire to the Dutch village of Putten as a reprisal for Resistance operations and sent almost the entire male population to German concentration camps. Only a few of these men returned after the war. Fullriede was an officer of the Hermann Goering Division. The Worrowski Battalion was formed from the pupils of an NCO training school of this division, and it was this battalion, consisting of very youthful but fanatical Hitlerites, that attacked the Westerbouwing position on the Thursday morning.

Fullriede, who, to judge by his diary was not an admirer of Hitler (he was for years a farmer in South Africa), writes: '21 September. In the attack on Westerbouwing the Worrowski Battalion lost all its officers except a lieutenant, and half of its other ranks. These terrible casualties were due to a certain Colonel Schramm who was in command of this operation and had forbidden the use of heavy weapons because he was afraid his own men would be hit. The idiot preferred to let hundreds of them die. Despite intervention by the OKW I sent about 1,600 recruits back to Germany. To send them into battle would simply have been infanticide.' This incident also furnishes yet another example of how complicated the interrelation of commands was in the German forces. The Hermann Goering Division belonged to the *Luftwaffe* but fought as a ground force. By this and other means Hitler had earlier infiltrated various units with party connections into the army. Fullriede was thus able to by-pass the Army High Command and appeal to Goering's *Luftwaffe* High Command, and the entry in his diary for 24 September contains the sentence: 'Colonel Schramm finally relieved of his command at my insistence . . .'

The 1st Battalion the Border Regiment, which had occupied the most westerly position on the Neder Rijn after the start of the air-landings and then moved slowly eastwards in the Arnhem direction, was thus obliged to give up Westerbouwing. The battalion now occupied a position to the east of Westerbouwing, in the south-east corner of the perimeter.

v

Earlier that morning the British officers had held a council of war at Urquhart's headquarters. It was decided to divide the perimeter into two parts, the western half coming under the command of Hicks, the commander of the 1st Airlanding Brigade, and the eastern under that of Hackett, commanding the 4th Parachute Brigade.

The 1st Border Regiment's activities were thus conducted in Hicks' half of the perimeter. The north-east sector of that half was no quieter on Thursday, 21 September. There, too, the consequences of Harzer's order for an all-round attack were being felt. The 7th KOSB were fighting what has gone down in the regiment's history as the 'battle of the White House'. The 'White House' was the Dreyeroord Private Hotel, situated at the northern extremity of the perimeter.

Payton-Reid, the commander of 7th KOSB, has this to say about it: 'I do not think that any who were there will forget the White House and its surroundings. When I knocked at its door about 9 pm on 19 Sept all was peace and quiet, since we had, temporarily, broken contact. Had I dropped from Mars, I could scarcely have aroused more interest and I was immediately greeted as a liberator by the numerous occupants—it was, I found, a small hotel. Never have I felt such a hypocrite. I had come to announce my intention of placing soldiers in the grounds and vicinity and the delight with which this news was received was most touching—but at the same time most pathetic, as I knew I was bringing them only danger and destruction.

'By the next night the building was reduced to a shell and its inmates were crouching uncomfortably in the cellar. It was then garrisoned by a section of men who were living in the eerie atmosphere of a haunted house. The moon shone through shot-holes in the walls, casting weird shadows, prowling footsteps could be heard on the enemy side and one felt that faces were peering through every window. There was, too, every reason to expect unwelcome visitors, since it was just outside that Major Sherriff and I were joined by a stray Boche . . .' (As they were making a round of the sentry posts Payton-Reid came across someone who spoke German to them. Sherriff was first to recover from his surprise. Although he was wounded, he attacked the German and killed him with his own hands.)

Payton-Reid continues: 'During our second day in this position we suffered heavy casualties through sniper fire . . . It was on this day that the Medical Officer, Captain Devlin, asked me if he could move his Regimental Aid Post with the walking wounded, whom he could not get evacuated, to another house as his present one was becoming distinctly unhealthy. I pointed out that the proposed new location was well outside our Battalion perimeter and that, there-fore, we could give him no protection there.

'He decided, however, to rely on the protection of the Red Cross, so off he set, followed by a limping, bandaged and somewhat bedraggled group shepherded by one or two medical orderlies. That was the last we saw of them. It transpires that they walked straight into a Boche patrol, with whose leader Major Coke, him-self one of the wounded, had a lengthy discussion regarding the ethics of the situation, declaring that as they were proceeding under the Red Cross (and presumably with their fingers crossed!) they could not be touched.

'So eloquent was he in expounding this interpretation of the Rules of Warfare, that he almost persuaded the German subaltern to let them proceed unmolested. Finally, however, the latter said he must consult his CO, to whom Major Coke was invited to repeat his arguments. This time they were met with the derision to be expected, the German major laughing heartily and declaring that the wounded would be much better off under his care, which—as things turned out—they probably were. Alas, Major Coke was killed shortly afterwards when, lion-hearted as ever, he was leading an attempt at mass-escape.

'Our final episode before leaving here was what has come to be known as "The battle of the White House". By this time we had, because of diminishing numbers, evacuated the house itself . . .

'During the afternoon of the 21st [Thursday] the enemy infiltrated close to our position, through the house and woods and under cover of a mortar barrage. When he finally came into the open to attack, the stolid patience with which we had endured his constant pin-pricks gave way to a ferocious lust for revenge, which was reflected in our greeting to him. Everything opened up. Riflemen and bren-gunners vied with each other in production of rapid fire; mortars, their barrels practically vertical, lobbed bombs over our heads at the minimum possible range, anti-tank guns defended our flanks and Vickers MGs belched forth streams of bullets as only a Vickers can. The consequent din was reinforced by a stream of vindictive utterances in a predominantly Scottish accent.

'The German attack was stopped but they went to ground and returned the fire hotly, displaying, in several cases, marked bravery. When it was adjudged that we had won the fire-fight, we went for them with the bayonet in the good old-fashioned style, with more blood-curdling yells, and this was too much for them. I have been told that close on 100 German bodies were found and buried there.

'It had evidently been the intention of the Germans to wipe us out completely on this occasion because they had enlisted the aid of a loudspeaker which kept blaring forth that Montgomery had forgotten us and that, as we were surrounded, we should surrender. In view of the outcome of their attack these remarks were somewhat inappropriate and were treated by the Jocks with the derision they deserved.'

And in the evening and night of 22 September the perimeter shrank and several British positions—including the 7th KOSB's 'White House'—were abandoned.

VI

Yet, despite everything, the all-round German attack on the Oosterbeek perimeter was less successful than might have been expected. This fact is partly explained by the fierce resistance of the airborne troops. The German commander describes it as follows in his battle report: 'But still the British replied with violent rifle and gunfire. They defended bravely, even ferociously, the positions which they had meanwhile consolidated thoroughly.'

Another explanation—also confirmed by statements from the German commanders—of the result of the enemy attack on 21 September is provided by the landing of the Polish parachutists near Driel on the southern bank of the Neder Rijn. The Polish brigade, it should be expressly repeated, had not been sent as eleventh-hour reinforcements for the British airborne division. It had been assigned a task in the original MARKET GARDEN plan, namely to land at the southern end of the bridge over the Neder Rijn at Arnhem. As lack of aircraft meant that the British division could not be transported in a single lift but in three lifts on successive days, it was decided that the Poles would land on Tuesday, 19 September. On the same day, according to plans, their motor-transport detachment would land in gliders *north* of the Neder Rijn, near Johannahoeve, while the men would drop on the *southern* side near the road bridge. Not a very happy arrangement but perhaps an unavoidable one.

Things turned out even more unhappily. The gliders carrying the motor-transport detachment of the Polish brigade did in fact land at Johannahoeve on the afternoon on Tuesday, 19 September. They landed at the very moment that Hackett's 4th Parachute Battalion—as previously described—was moving away from the landing zone. The landing of the Poles was transformed (as their war correspondent, Marck Święcicki, states) into a stampede. The British withdrew, the Germans—Messerschmitts and ground troops—attacked, and practically the whole of the Polish transport was lost.

As a result of the bad weather the troops of the Polish brigade, under the command of General Stanislaw Sosabowski, did not land until two days later. By then the bridge at Arnhem had fallen and the area round it was in German hands, so there was now no point in dropping there. Their transport had been as good as totally destroyed two days before at Johannahoeve. And of the 110 aircraft in which the Polish parachute troops were moved, only a half, approximately, arrived over the target. The others were either forced by the weather to return to England or shot down by German flak. About 750 men jumped near Driel ... 'on the south bank of the river opposite the area still held by the British', writes Major Huston in the article already cited. 'They then could cross the river on the Heveadorp Ferry ... By the time these troops assembled and reached the river bank, however, they found that the ferry had been sunk, and the Germans controlled the north bank at that point.' With their transport unit lost, only half of their aircraft arriving over the dropping zone and the crossing place falling into German hands several hours earlier, the landing of the Polish parachutists seemed set to be a total failure.

VII

Although there is no point in representing the drama of the Poles as a success, the German reports clearly indicate that the landing of the Poles created a critical situation in the enemy camp. Bittrich, the commander of II SS Panzer Corps, says: 'When the fighting power of the 10th SS Panzer [Frundsberg] Division began to wane and the enemy's intention to push northwards supported by strong forces [British XXX Corps] became clear, a critical situation developed. The Polish parachute troops who dropped at Driel a day or two before the surrender had to be regarded at least as moral support for the 1st British Airborne Division (from whom they were separated by only the Rhine). At this stage I gave orders for Knaust's Battalion (Army) to be removed from the Arnhem front and sent to the Elst area via the Arnhem bridge, which was now firmly in our hands again. This battalion, reinforced by a company of Panther tanks from the 9th SS Panzer Division and supported by strong artillery units of the 10th SS Panzer Division, was ordered to defend Elst.' Bittrich also speaks of this as 'one of the most decisive phases of the entire Nijmegen-Arnhem operation.'

And Harzer, who led the German forces at Arnhem, writes: 'Meanwhile the *Kampfgruppe* 9th SS Panzer [Hohenstaufen] Division had formed reserves from the arriving stand-by units . . . Neither the capture of the bridge at Arnhem nor the formation of powerful reserves by the *Kampfgruppe* 9th SS Panzer Div had happened a day or even an hour too soon, as was to be proved in the early afternoon of 21 September . . . That was when new reinforcements for the parachutists landed south of the Neder Rijn near Driel.'

The landing of the Poles thus forced the Germans to remove a valuable battalion (Bittrich is full of praise for its commander, Major Knaust) from Arnhem, so that the German attack round the Oosterbeek perimeter on 21 September was weakened.

The reason why the Germans considered the Polish landing such a serious matter and talked of a 'critical situation' was the possibility that the Poles would not try to cross the Rhine but make a quick dash to the north-east and cut the Frundsberg Division off from the newly recaptured road bridge at Arnhem. The Frundsberg Division was pushing across the Betuwe in a southerly direction towards Nijmegen. A Polish attack aimed at the southern end of the bridge over the Rhine at Arnhem would take the Frundsberg Division in the rear and might cut it off from the important line of communication which had just been opened up after very hard fighting. So it was a matter of urgent importance for the Germans to strengthen this weak point quickly. A *Sperrverband* or 'blocking formation' was therefore formed south of the Rhine, in the Betuwe: the *Sperrverband Harzer*. It occupied positions between the Arnhem-Nijmegen road and the Poles who had dropped at Driel; its assignment was to attack the Poles and keep the road to Arnhem open (see map 15).

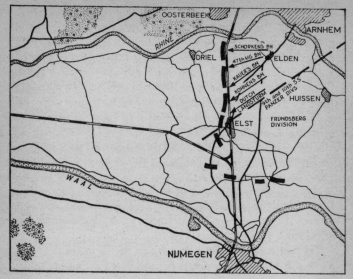

MAP 15 The situation in the Betuwe on 21 September, after a sketch-map by Harzer, the commander of the Hohenstaufen Division. When the Polish para-chutists landed near Driel, Model and Bittrich were convinced that the Frundsberg Division would be unable simultaneously to halt the British Second Army, operating northwards to Arnhem from Nijmegen, and seal off the gap between Elst and Arnhem. This was because the German commanders thought the Poles would move eastwards along the Rhine from Driel to the southern end of the Arnhem road bridge. The dividing line between the Hohenstaufen and Frundsberg Divisions, which first ran immediately south of the Rhine, was therefore shifted further to south, near Elst. The *Sperrverband Harzer*, consisting of Schörken's battalion, MG Battalion 47, Kauer's battalion (Luftwaffe ground staff), Köhnen's battalion (*Marine Kampfgruppe* No 642) and a battalion of Dutch *Landsturm* (territorial reserves raised by the Germans), was positioned along the Arnhem-Elst railway embankment.

Thus the battle of Arnhem took on a new facet: fighting in the Betuwe. While, on the north bank of the river, inside the perimeter, the remnants of the British airborne division were battling stubbornly on, hoping for speedy relief, the Betuwe, south of the river, became the scene of a struggle by the Poles and, later, units of the Second Army to establish communication with the perimeter. A struggle which depended to a large extent on the terrain. The name given to this area by the British—'the Island'—may not be accurate, but it gives an indication of how the British commanders thought about it. They did not make the acquaintance of this low-lying, fertile strip of ground between the Rhine and the Waal in the spring, when its thousands of fruit trees are in blossom; for the officers and men of the Second Army the Betuwe with its meadows, farms and ditches was not a typical example of Dutch countryside, flat and open. In the autumn of 1944, the Poles and British regarded it as, in the words of xxx Corps' report, a 'depressing area'. This polder country with its dykes lends itself perfectly to defence. Even small units can carry out effective defensive actions by occupying the roads, for it is impossible, even for infantry without transport, to make any progress other than on the roads, across this low land criss-crossed by ditches. Tanks, transport and guns have to stick to existing roads. Only the orchards can be used for artillery positions. The narrow secondary roads would subside under the weight of heavy tanks; the small, light bridges would collapse. So it is understandable that the Frundsberg Division was able to withstand the repeated attacks of the Second Army as it tried to advance from Nijmegen towards Arnhem. But the disadvantages of the Betuwe applied equally to the enemy. Harzer comments: 'Unfortunately, the . . . terrain round Driel did not permit the use of tanks, otherwise we would have managed to scatter or destroy this Polish parachute brigade before nightfall [on Thursday, 21 September].'

VIII

'The task assigned by II SS Panzer Corps HQ to the *Kampfgruppe* 9th SS for 22 September', Harzer reports, 'was as follows: "9th SS Panzer Division (*Kampfgruppe*) to continue to attack the remnants of the 1st British Airborne Division from all sides and destroy them as speedily as possible." ' The same report also states: 'By the evening on 21 September the British had been driven into an area of about one-and-a-quarter miles square. They nevertheless continued to defend stubbornly and all our invitations to them to surrender—made by loudspeaker—were answered with violent artillery fire. The street fighting also remained very fierce. House after house had to be cleared out by the infantry, effectively supported by pioneers using flame-throwers.' Tanks, flame-throwers, artillery. German reinforcements had been streaming in from all directions for the last few days. The entire perimeter was now continuously under German artillery fire. Loudspeakers in front of the British lines bellowed appeals to the troops to surrender. The voice gave the numbers of British casualties and prisoners of war and added that captured British officers advised the forces in the perimeter to give up the hopeless struggle. Then came music: 'In the Mood' and 'One More River to Cross' . . . But even in their desperate situation, deprived by the loss of Westerbouwing and the Driel ferry, of their last possible chance of taking the initiative, Urquhart's division proved that it was made up of crack troops. The perimeter slowly shrank—but it remained intact.

On that Friday morning Horrocks, the commander of the British xxx Corps, signalled to Urquhart: '43 Div ordered to take all risks to effect relief today and are directed on ferry. If situation warrants you should withdraw on or across ferry.'

Urquhart replied: 'We shall be glad to see you.'

Horrocks therefore suggested that if Urquhart considered it to be necessary he should retreat to the Westerbouwing, which would enable him to cross the Rhine by the Driel ferry. That was on Friday, 22 September.

It was already too late. The Germans were now in possession of Westerbouwing and would hold it until the action was over. The report of the 1st Airlanding Brigade refers to a plan to recapture Westerbouwing early in the morning of 23 September to enable the Poles and the troops of the Second Army to cross the river at Driel ferry. But the plan was abandoned at 9.45 at night—the poor visibility made it impossible to be sure of support by the artillery of the Second Army south of the Rhine. It did prove possible that night to get several dozen Poles across the river in two small inflatable rubber dinghies. They were assigned to the 1st Battalion of the Border Regiment, which was posted near the gasworks on the eastern edge of Westerbouwing. 'As they were not battle-inoculated,' says the report of the 1st Airlanding Brigade, 'they did not dig satisfactory slit-trenches and were quickly reduced by half by shelling.'

IX

Next morning—Saturday, 23 September—the Germans shifted the main force of their attack to the southern end of the perimeter. Bittrich's order to crush the British resistance north of the Rhine before reinforcements could be brought in from the south was still in force. Harzer, knowing that the Poles were on the other bank and that the divisions of the British xxx Corps would try to break through to the Polish positions in order to reinforce them, decided to cut the perimeter off from the river bank. He ordered the *Kampfgruppe* Spindler to attack from the east along the bank of the Neder Rijn—in other words, an attack on the British artillery positions at Oosterbeek-Laag—in the hope of linking up with von Tettau's group in the west. Throughout Saturday the north bank of the river was under fire from both east and west by the attacking German units.

This did not mean that the rest of the perimeter was left in peace. On Friday and Saturday the *Luftwaffe* had flown a pioneer battalion from Glogau in Germany to Deelen airfield on the Veluwe in transport aircraft. This battalion, supported by flame-throwers, began a house-by-house operation in Oosterbeek on Saturday. 'The British resistance, however,' says Harzer, 'was still so strong that the "Cauldron" [as the Germans called the perimeter] could only be slightly reduced in size but not pierced.'

Some short entries in the report of the 1st Airlanding Brigade on the day's fighting are colourfully illustrated by personal recollections. The official report says: '14.52. A heavy attack developed against 7 KOSB and continued at intervals during the day. Support fire . . . given by [British] heavy guns from the south bank of the river.' The commander of the 7th Battalion of the KOSB, Lieutenant-Colonel Payton-Reid, recalls that the morale of his men that morning was excellent. They were convinced that the troops of the Second Army would soon be there to relieve them. 'Morale', writes Payton-Reid, 'was still further raised by everyone having a shave and a hot breakfast, both rather unique experiences. It was as well that we started off in this spirit because there was no peace during the rest of that day nor the night which followed. All who were there will have many experiences by which to remember this period. My own recollection is of . . . enemy infiltrations here, anti-tank guns knocked out there, houses battered by shelling, and ever-mounting casualties . . . About this time two people who, though not Borderers in fact, had . . . become so in spirit, came very much to the fore. These were Captain Johnny Walker, our fire observation officer from the gunners, and Sergeant R. F. Tilly, a glider pilot.'

In the Allied airborne divisions the employment of glider pilots was a problem. They were not used in the same way by the Americans and the British. After landing they could not, of course, return to base and had to stay with the troops they had brought. In the British view, these pilots belonged to the army rather than the air force, so they were trained in ground fighting and formed separate units after landing. Thus the troops in the perimeter included a glider-pilot battalion fighting as infantry. A detachment of glider pilots was also used to protect the artillery positions of the British airborne division. Shortly before the death sentence was carried out on Rauter, the head of the German SS and police in the Netherlands, he expressed his surprise that of the six British battalions which landed on the first day, three were left behind to protect the landing and dropping zones. Rauter remarked—an observation obviously inspired by conversations on this subject with Model and Bittrich—that all six battalions should have been ordered to make for the bridge, and that the glider pilots (about 1,200 men) could have been used to protect the landing zones. Although this was not done, the reports show that the glider pilots were valuable to Urquhart's division after landing.

American views on glider pilots differed considerably from those held by the British. General Gavin, who commanded the 82nd US Airborne Division which landed at Nijmegen, stated: 'One thing in most urgent need of correction is the method of handling our glider pilots.' Gavin advocated an arrangement whereby pilots would be attached to the airborne divisions and would train simultaneously with them. But others, including General Ridgway, were of the opinion that the glider pilots should remain in the air force, although they might, if necessary, be used for certain tasks normally performed by ground troops.

It is of one of these pilots that Payton-Reid is speaking. 'The latter', he continues, 'had, for no known reason, decided to remain with us instead of rejoining his own unit and had appointed himself my "bodyguard". On one occasion I was going round the front with him and when we arrived near where we expected to find one platoon he shot ahead round some houses to locate it. He shot back even faster, however and, seizing me by the arm, dragged me along with him, whispering: "There's a trench round there cram-full of Boches!" As he thought they could not have failed to see him, we deemed it wise to get out of sight, so leapt through the window of a damaged house nearby. Our leap took us further than we anticipated, because the floor had been demolished with the result that we dropped right down into the cellar. And there we were, caught in a trap, expecting at any moment to see Hun faces peering down on us. Only Tilly's strength and agility saved the situation. By standing on my hands he could just reach ground level . . . A few minutes later we reached the proper platoon position where, now it was safely over, our adventure took on the appearance of a huge joke . . .

'It was a great moment when we realised that we could now call on the support of the Corps artillery of the ground forces [of the Second Army on the far side of the Neder Rijn] . . . The fire itself was most effective and broke up several attempted enemy attacks. It would probably have been considerably more so had not our FOO . . . chosen this precise time to get himself hit on the head by a bullet. Having been born under a lucky star and having, according to himself, a thick skull, his life was undoubtedly saved by his steel helmet. Nevertheless the MO insisted on his being admitted to the RAP so we had perforce to endeavour, in our own amateurish way, to perform his duties. For the Corps artillery [on the other side of the river] this must have been the "Gunners' Nightmare" because our methods were unorthodox in the extreme. As our only wireless set was established in a cellar, the officer observing the shoot had to relay his alterations over a human chain extending from roof to basement, a system hardly to be recommended for either speed or accuracy. The astonishing thing is that it seemed to work, even if the Gun Position Officer must have been startled to receive, in lieu of the prosaic "on target" some such ejaculation as: "Marvellous, you're right among them. We can hear the b——s screaming." '

X

The incessant German attacks on the perimeter were not only rendering the position of the British troops desperate; they were also making critical the situation for several field hospitals. The airborne forces had originally housed a number of wounded in one of the buildings of the mental asylum at Wolfheze, but when they advanced to Arnhem and left Wolfheze, they took the wounded with them. On the Utrechtseweg they found two hotels—the Vreewijk and the Schoonoord—which they converted into emergency hospitals and to which the wounded were transferred from Wolfheze on Monday, 18 September.

In some respects the history of these hospitals was the same as that of the Hartenstein Hotel which had been chosen as headquarters. On the assumption that the original plans would succeed, the hotels were considered as temporary hospitals: once Arnhem was captured, the wounded would be taken to better-equipped hospitals. But the advance came to a halt and the British were pushed back to the perimeter, with the result that the Vreewijk and Schoonoord were now exactly in the front line. This meant that despite the large Red Cross flag on the roof and the small flags in the garden the hospitals came under German artillery fire. And a few days later when the Germans, slowly gaining ground, occupied the Schoonoord and placed armed sentries outside its windows, it became a target for the British machine-guns which had been set up in neighbouring houses. It was a difficult problem: on the one hand, it was forbidden to fire at a hospital, but on the other, it was not permissible to run a hospital in the front line; and the Germans were breaking the Geneva Convention by having armed soldiers entering the building.

At 1 pm on Saturday, 23 September, a German officer under the protection of a large Red Cross flag paid a visit to Brigadier

Hackett and stated that the Germans would blow up the Schoonoord (where a large number of German wounded were also being cared for by British doctors) if the British did not evacuate their positions in nearby houses. Half an hour later he withdrew this threat on condition that the British would not fire from the immediate vicinity of the hospital.

XI

Meanwhile, to the south of the Neder Rijn, contact had been successfully established between the ground forces of the British Second Army and the Polish parachutists who had jumped near Driel. After their landing on Thursday, 21 September, the position of the Poles was far from happy. They possessed no transport, they were separated from Urquhart's division by the Rhine, and the Driel ferry was in German hands. Nevertheless, their landing brought some relief—even if only indirectly—to the British in the perimeter. The Germans, fearing that the Poles would move eastwards along the south bank of the river, were forced to build up a line quickly to prevent this. The troops they used for the purpose were taken from positions round Oosterbeek. Nevertheless, no one could hope that this advantage would be of more than temporary duration: German reinforcements continued to flow in and very soon the Polish forces would be in a position as unpleasant as that of the airborne troops in the perimeter.

In the evening of 22 September, however, some units of the 43rd Division succeeded in breaking through from Nijmegen to the Poles, by executing a westward outflanking movement just north of the town. They thus slipped past the right flank of the Frundsberg Division who were blocking the highway from Nijmegen to Arnhem. The corridor they thus opened up to link the Poles and the Second Army scarcely merited the name. It took in several narrow roads in the flat, low-lying Betuwe. Nonetheless, the river was reached in the evening of 22 September. An attempt to get supplies and ammunition across the river to the perimeter in DUKWs[1] failed: the large, unwieldy vehicles slid off the high embankment and not one of them was launched successfully.

[1] Amphibious vehicles.

Narrow as it was, the corridor across the Betuwe was to remain in British hands until the end of the battle and it was the route by which the remnants of the troops in the perimeter were brought out to Nijmegen and safety. For several days before then the position on the south bank had been of assistance to the troops in the perimeter in various ways such as 'spotting' for the artillery and collecting intelligence. On one of those days the British reported that they had attacked a tow on the Neder Rijn consisting of a tug-boat and four barges and had sunk the tug and three of the barges. They received the laconic reply: 'Congrats on brilliant naval action. Splice the mainbrace.'

While small flashes of humour such as this proved that the morale of the troops was unbroken, they could not alter the deadly seriousness of the situation. Not only in the perimeter, not only south of the Rhine in the Betuwe, but even south of Nijmegen, on the road to Eindhoven, there was little in the situation to justify optimism. It is very significant that the corridor by which the Second Army was supposed, under the original plan MARKET GARDEN, to advance through Eindhoven, Nijmegen and Arnhem to the Zuider Zee, was nicknamed, 'Hell's Highway'. It was along this narrow strip of ground in places only several hundred yards wide, projecting deep into enemy-held territory, on a road which mostly ran across open territory, that a modern, motorised army had to be pushed. The final goal was the Zuider Zee, but for the airborne forces at Oosterbeek this corridor was the artery which might perhaps bring them new life.

The German commanders, too, appreciated the importance and weakness of this corridor. Model realised that the Allies were sending powerful units of the British Second Army to the Nijmegen and Arnhem area with the ultimate aim of entering Germany round the northern end of the Siegfried Line. In addition, the German armies to the west of the corridor were in danger of being cut off if the Allies succeeded in reaching the Zuider Zee. For the entire remaining course of the fighting it was Model's chief aim that the Allied life-artery running straight across Brabant from Eindhoven to Nijmegen should be severed.

Early in the morning of 22 September German troops attacked

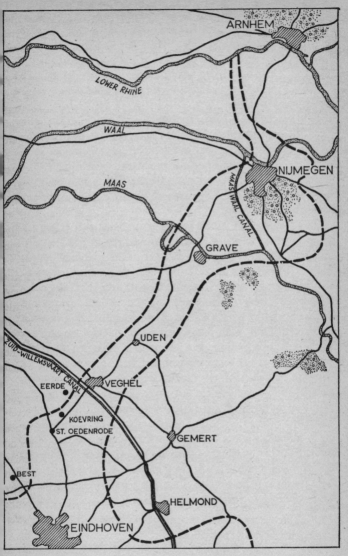

MAP 16 The narrow corridor via which the British Second Army advanced from south to north and which was cut several times by German attacks on its east and west flanks.

from both east and west the very narrow section of the corridor near Veghel. Although they did not quite achieve their objectives, and Allied counter-attacks slowed down the German advance, German units managed to cut the road to the north of Veghel (see map 16). This success did not last long, but the operation as a whole had yielded the Germans a valuable position from which to launch a new operation.

This development had a very adverse effect, from the Allied point of view, on the fighting in the Betuwe. Instead of being able to send troops and supplies to this area, the commander of xxx Corps considered it imperative to order units which had been intended to reinforce the troops in the Betuwe to turn about and move southwards in the direction of Veghel. Dozens of precious hours were thereby lost.

On 23 September Model reorganised a large part of his army group in order to adapt it as advantageously as possible to the situation created by Operation MARKET GARDEN. On that day, too, 'Hell's Highway' was attacked from both the east and the west by German troops. Hard fighting, however, enabled the Allies to keep the narrow artery to Nijmegen and the Betuwe open. In the Betuwe itself the 43rd (Wessex) Division recorded several successes on that cold, rainy Saturday. Units of this division advancing north-westwards from the area just north of Nijmegen forced their way through to the south bank of the Neder Rijn (see map 17). The 5th Battalion of the Dorset Regiment under Lieutenant-Colonel B. A. Coad was cut in two by German artillery fire from Elst, but the forward part of the battalion with the commander reached the village of Driel. Towards evening the rest of the battalion managed, under cover of a smoke-screen and by crawling through ditches, to join the others at Driel. Other units of the 43rd Division had meanwhile advanced in easterly and westerly directions, so that by the evening of Saturday, 23 September, the road from Nijmegen to Driel was reasonably well covered on the flanks.

XII

Hope of reinforcing the perimeter at Oosterbeek, on the north bank of the Neder Rijn, had still not been abandoned. As assign-

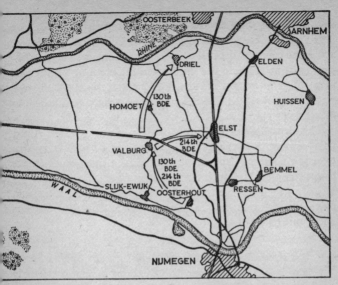

MAP 17 Units of the 43rd (Wessex) Division outflanked the German positions and reached Driel by way of Valburg and Homoet. It was via this corridor that the British airborne forces, later evacuated from Oosterbeek, were taken back to Nijmegen.

ments for the night of 23–24 September Horrocks, the commander of the British xxx Corps, ordered: (a) that the perimeter had to be supplied; (b) that the Polish parachutists who had landed near Driel should be ferried across the river; and (c) that the perimeter must be extended westwards by attacking with two battalions. The last of these commands could not possibly be carried out. It was beyond human power to carry out such a large-scale operation across the wide, fast-flowing Neder Rijn as long as the well-armed Germans on the high north bank completely dominated the south bank. Not only that, but the British units which had pushed across the Betuwe had brought with them enough assault boats for only a single battalion. It was therefore decided to ferry as many of the Poles as possible and several DUKW-loads of supplies across the river that night.

One of the brigadiers of the 43rd Division, H. Essame, has this to say on the subject: 'Enemy shelling and mortaring added to the confusion and the operation did not start until a late hour. The stout-hearted Poles, ferried across in sixteen assault boats by 204 Field Company and 5 Dorsets, and supported by every weapon 130 Brigade could bring to bear, persisted in their efforts despite their heavy losses from the fire of an enemy fully aware of their intentions. They were, however, unfamiliar with this type of operation and by dawn [on Sunday, 24 September] only about 200 had succeeded in reaching the far bank.'

The result of the operation was that some of the landing-craft were sunk and the others left on the north bank, where (according to Essame) they were shot to bits next day by the Germans. There were consequently no boats available for the operation which was to be undertaken in the evening of 24 September.

XIII

The situation was hopeless. Everything went wrong—even the weather, which made it impossible to bring in reinforcements and supplies by air. But there were other reasons. In drawing up its plans, the British 1st Airborne Division had decided upon an area to the north-west of Arnhem as the dropping zone for supplies. As the attack in the first stage of the operation was brought to a standstill, however, and the British were subsequently forced to concentrate in the perimeter, this dropping zone was never in British hands. Once again, the penalty for having poor communications had to be paid. According to the 1st Airborne Division, messages stating that the original dropping zone could not be used and specifying another, nearer Oosterbeek, were repeatedly transmitted. Unfortunately, these messages did not get through in time and the British troops in their positions could only watch the urgently-needed supplies floating down over enemy-occupied territory. Rauter said after the war that the German troops largely lived on British rations which reached them in this way. He also asserts that as early as 17 September a British officer was captured who had on him instructions on how to lay out ground markers and use smoke signals on the dropping zones. The German officer Naumann of Helle's battalion confirms this and states that the instructions were successfully carried out by the SS: British aircraft dropped panniers containing supplies accurately on the zones marked out by the Germans.

In all, only a small percentage of the supplies reached those for whom they were intended; the rest fell into German hands. This was all the more tragic because the British pilots of the supply aircraft carried out their assignment with great devotion to duty. Flying low, straight through the hell created by German anti-aircraft guns which were receiving fresh reinforcements daily, they stayed on their appointed course. When SS General Rauter (during his sojourn in a Dutch prison as a war criminal) read an English account of how two blazing aircraft flew on through German AA fire precisely to their target, dropped their containers and then crashed, he wrote in the margin: 'These airmen were heroes . . .'

On 22 September—as reported by Harzer, the commander of the Hohenstaufen Division—the remnants of the British airborne division were so tightly compressed in the perimeter that it was no longer possible for the RAF to drop them supplies. A day later, on the evening of 23 September, Urquhart signalled to the south: 'Morale still adequate but continued heavy shelling and mortaring is having obvious effects. We shall hold but at the same time hope for a brighter twenty-four hours ahead.'

XIV

Sunday, 24 September. The first units of Tank Battalion 506 —sixty Mark VI Tiger tanks—arrived in Arnhem from Germany. As these heavy tanks could not be used in the narrow streets of Oosterbeek, Bittrich gave forty-five of them to the Frundsberg Division, which was operating towards Nijmegen. With regard to the fighting at Oosterbeek Harzer ordered that renewed attempts should be made from west and east along the north bank of the Neder Rijn to cut the perimeter off from the river. But attack across this low, open terrain was difficult and the German west group was brought to a halt near the gasworks at the eastern foot of Westerbouwing. Throughout Sunday the German artillery concentrated its fire on the vulnerable oblong perimeter.

'The more the perimeter shrank,' writes Harzer, 'the more stubbornly the British troops defended every heap of ruins and every inch of ground.' But the British battle reports leave the reader in no doubt that the end was approaching, slowly but surely. True, the RAF, despite heavy losses, made another attempt to drop supplies in the perimeter, but almost all the containers came down behind the German lines.

Hour by hour new German infiltrations into the British positions were reported. House after house, ruin after ruin, yard after yard was lost. Ammunition, water, food—everything was running short.

The British commanders, south of the river, now also realised how precarious the situation was. From the church tower at Driel, Generals Horrocks and Thomas (commanders of xxx Corps and the 43rd Division respectively) had been able to see with their own eyes that the British position on the north bank had no military value: the most important point, the high ground at Westerbou-wing, was in German hands. The perimeter's only link with the Neder Rijn was a flat strip of ground stretching many hundreds of yards inland from the river to the more wooded and higher ground at its northern end.

The available sources are not completely in agreement about the moment at which the decision to evacuate the perimeter was taken. In his book, *The 43rd Wessex Division at War, 1944–1945*, Major-General H. Essame (who was one of the division's brigadiers at the time) states that a conference attended by, among others, Horrocks and Sosabowski, the commander of the Polish Brigade, took place on the morning of Sunday, 24 September. The meeting was of the opinion that Urquhart's division had such a narrow stretch of the northern river bank under its control that it would be necessary to reinforce the perimeter *before the division could be evacuated*. It would therefore be necessary to ferry the 4th Dorsets and some more Poles across in the night of 24–25 September. If Essame's account is accurate, the decision to evacuate the perimeter must have been taken as early as the morning of 24 September. Chester Wilmot gives a somewhat different version of the facts. According to him, on the afternoon of 24 September, Dempsey (the commander of the British Second Army) and Horrocks met in the town of St Oedenrode in the Dutch province of

234

North Brabant and decided that *a final attempt would be made in the night of 25–26 September to form an Allied bridgehead to the north of the Neder Rijn*. This operation would, however, depend on whether the Allies succeeded or not in keeping 'Hell's Highway' open for the northward movement of ammunition, assault craft and bridge-building material. Horrocks—still according to Wilmot—left St Oedenrode at 4.30 pm. During his drive northwards through Veghel the road was again cut at Koevring by the German Jungwirth Battalion (see map 16). And this time it was to be forty-eight hours before the Allies managed to reestablish their line of communications to the north. This setback, together with the information, obtained by air reconnaissance, that German troops were digging in on the north bank of the Neder Rijn and that German tanks were making for the only point where an Allied crossing of the river was possible, was, says Wilmot, the reason why Dempsey and Horrocks decided 'reluctantly' to evacuate the perimeter.

It is possible that Horrocks in the talk he had with Thomas and Sosabowski (and to which Essame refers) gave orders for *preparations* to be made for evacuation but that he still hoped it would be possible to execute the original plan, namely to establish an Allied bridgehead on the northern side of the Neder Rijn. It may, however, be that when the supply line through Brabant was cut by the Germans, he reluctantly made a definite decision to evacuate the perimeter.

Horrocks himself, finally, states that—if the ferrying operation on the night of 24–25 September had succeeded—he was hoping, by crossing the river further to the west, to be able to attack the German troops besieging the perimeter in the rear. After his conference at Driel, Horrocks went to Dempsey at St Oedenrode. Neither general took an optimistic view of the situation. He returned to the north—he relates in his book, *A Full Life*—but it was only by the barest margin that he got through, the Germans having cut the road at Koevring. Next morning, Monday, 25 September, at ten o'clock he heard that the ferrying operations in the night had not been very successful. He and General Browning, the commander of the British airlanding brigade to which Urquhart's division belonged, thereupon (ie in the morning of 25

235

September) came to the conclusion that there was nothing for it but to evacuate the perimeter.

There had indeed been little success that night, as the Dorsets and Poles would be the first to agree. The Dorsets were to cross at 10 pm on 24 September to the northern end of the Driel ferry, ie slightly to the west of the perimeter. The Poles were to cross on the right flank of the Dorsets. A later departure than 10 pm was undesirable because the river would start flowing faster after midnight. It was a cold, drizzly evening. The Dorsets found their way in the dark to the assembly point, several hundred yards from the river bank, where they were to find their boats. The road was muddy and slippery. Heavy German mortar and artillery fire delayed their progress. Nevertheless, the battalion reached the assembly point by ten o'clock. But the boats weren't there. They were to have been brought across the Betuwe in lorries. Two of the lorries had taken the wrong road in the dark and driven into the German lines at Elst, two others had skidded off the muddy road. The last lorry reached the Poles' position but the boats were minus oars.

The crossing by the Poles was cancelled for the time being, and such boats as were available were assigned to the Dorsets. At one o'clock in the morning the Dorsets took over their boats and carried them through the orchards to the river.

That, too, is war. War is not just full-scale fighting in which there is sometimes not even room for fear, in which men and officers are often compelled by circumstances to act quickly, almost instinctively. There is more to it than that. War also means crawling along muddy roads and ditches on a cold, rainy evening, the din of enemy fire, shells exploding, the knowledge that in several hours, in thirty or forty minutes, a very chancy operation is to start—crossing a wide, swirling river to a dark, unfamiliar shore where the enemy is waiting. War is also learning at the last moment that the operation has to be called off for lack of means to carry it out. And when that happens, it also means mustering the will to win despite everything, waiting for three whole hours in a raw, murky night to see what will happen, or looking round for ways and means to overcome apparently insuperable setbacks.

Even before the Dorsets had boarded them, one of the boats was set alight by enemy mortar bombs and others holed by splinters. There was heavy machine-gun fire from the far side. A number of burning buildings on the northern bank lit up the wooded slope of the high ground at Westerbouwing. The boats were launched. A number were carried away by the current. Nevertheless, several dozen Dorsets reached the north bank of the Neder Rijn, at the foot of Westerbouwing—and the hill was occupied by Germans. The enemy sent hand-grenades rolling slowly down the hill. The Dorsets attacked; that cost them half of their number. A second batch of Dorsets arrived, after a nightmare crossing of the black swirling river. By 3.30 that night several hundred men had been embarked. Only a few dozen reached the other side. The others were killed by bullets from Spandaus or their boats overturned and they were drowned. At 3.30 am (it was the morning of 25 September) an attempt was made to ferry the supplies across. Of the six DUKWs only three could be launched: the Neder Rijn embankment was too steep for these unwieldy craft. The three which reached the far side became hopelessly stuck in the mud. Finally, first light and enemy fire put an end to this desperate attempt to relieve the airborne forces in the perimeter.

Again—that is war. That, too, was the battle of Arnhem. Without detracting in any way from the feats of those who fought in the Oosterbeek perimeter—and upon whom the attention of all historians has, understandably, been directed—it may perhaps for once be permissible to give wider publicity to the men who, whatever their rank, tried to cross a wide, turbulent river in small, vulnerable boats on that raw, dark, rainy night in September to aid their friends. Friends they did not know and had never before seen. Of course, they went because they were ordered to. They grumbled, they swore, and many of them concealed all signs of fear from the others. They were afraid of the rattle of Spandaus, of the deep black water; they did not know what awaited them on the far bank, where wooded slopes were lit by the glow from several burning buildings. They went because they were ordered. Ordered in the name—though it may sound gushing, there is no other word—of freedom. Who will reproach them for grumbling, cursing, choking back their fear? They went through with it; to this day they still have their nightmares. Even they. Even the men who from a feeling of solidarity—though that word is not one they would use, sounding obsolete and sentimental—went to help their friends on the far side of an unknown river.

Harzer, the commander of the Hohenstaufen Division, has little to say about the night of 24–25 September: 'By the evening of 24 September we had succeeded in reducing the British 1st Airborne Division's bridgehead to a width of 1,000 yards at places.'

And Hicks, the commander of the 1st Airlanding Brigade in the perimeter wrote: '*25th September*. 04.45 Liaison officer arrived to find out whether we had made contact with the follow-up troops, who were said to have crossed the river with supplies and ammunition. No contact had been made and it subsequently transpired that the crossing had taken place about 1,000 yards to the west in the Heveadorp area [opposite ground held by the Germans].'

XV

In his report on the battle of Arnhem Harzer writes: 'On 25 September 1944 Field-Marshal Model again insisted on the rapid liquidation of the Arnhem "cauldron" [the perimeter at Oosterbeek] in order to release the German troops engaged there and to ensure that the danger of an enemy bridgehead on the northern bank of the Rhine would be removed for good. At the same time the field-marshal appreciated that a crack British division and a brigade could not be destroyed as quickly and efficiently as would have been the case had he had an armoured division at full fighting strength. To avoid bloodshed, the field-marshal agreed that the British airborne division should be given the *coup de grâce* by heavy artillery fire . . . As a result of this systematic shooting which had now gone on for a week, the enemy's morale quickly sagged . . .'

The critical situation in the perimeter had reached a climax. Even the British battle reports could hardly be clearer about this point. The diary of the British artillery position at Oosterbeek-Laag, for instance, reads: 'The 25th was a day of crisis. A considerable force of enemy penetrated between the gun area and Div HQ cutting the Div area in two.'

South of the Rhine the 43rd Division had been ordered to capture the town of Elst, which was occupied by the Germans, to protect the eastern flank of the Allied corridor across the Betuwe and at the same time to screen its western flank. The fighting for Elst was hard and ferocious. The town had to be taken house by house from the SS men of the Frundsberg Division, which was supported by the Luftwaffe. The battle went on throughout the night of 24–25 September. In the course of the next day units of the 43rd Division succeeded in clearing Elst of Germans. At least one remarkable incident took place during the fighting. The British troops opened fire with an anti-tank gun on a number of railway wagons which they regarded with suspicion. A huge explosion destroyed not only the high railway embankment but also houses in the immediate vicinity in which British troops were sheltering from the rain. The wagons had apparently been loaded with ammunition; in view of the fighting the station-master at Elst had taken the wise precaution of having them shunted away from the town.

The ultimate aim of these various operations by General Thomas' 43rd Division was to strengthen the corridor through the Betuwe in such a way that the British 1st Airborne Division could be evacuated without difficulty from the perimeter. The evacuation was given the code name BERLIN, and it must be admitted that the choice of this name betrays a certain cynicism, for Berlin was the goal that Montgomery had been hoping to reach by way of Operation MARKET GARDEN.

At first there was some uncertainty south of the Neder Rijn as to the fate of the 4th Battalion of the Dorsets which had tried to land on the flank of the perimeter—near the Westerbouwing—in the night of 24–25 September. All communication with the rest of this battalion was cut. Nevertheless, an officer managed to reach Urquhart's headquarters in the course of that night and explain to him General Thomas' plan for the evacuation of the perimeter. At 10.30 am on Monday, 25 September, Urquhart signalled that he agreed to Operation BERLIN and requested that it be carried out.

Brigadier Hicks records in his battle report: '13.30. Order for operation "Berlin" issued, ie for evacuation to the other side of the river during the night [25–26 September].'

At 9 o'clock in the evening of 25 September all the artillery at the 43rd Division's disposal opened fire from the Betuwe on the German positions round the perimeter. The first boats were launched under cover of this deafening barrage. The first one reached the north bank at 9.40 pm and shortly afterwards, favoured by the darkness, the rain and the hard wind, the task of ferrying the airborne troops from the perimeter to the south bank started. Operation MARKET was over, Operation BERLIN had begun.

The Germans at first misinterpreted British intentions. Harzer states: 'Shortly after nightfall on 25 September the [German] troops positioned along the northern bank of the Rhine reported that the British were using heavy mortar fire to interfere with relieving parties. It was further reported that a loud noise of engines could be heard from the south bank . . . The German commanders thought at first that reinforcements were again being brought in for the British still resisting in the position of all-round defence at Oosterbeek. It became clear about midnight that units from the perimeter were crossing in boats to the south and hence that the enemy had decided to evacuate the bridgehead which had cost them such a high price to obtain. About 9 am on Tuesday the noise of fighting at Oosterbeek ceased . . .'

Payton-Reid, the commander of the 7th Battalion of the King's Own Scottish Borderers, writes: 'And then, wonder of wonders, we were on the south bank—safe and sound. Once there it seemed as though a haven had been reached and, despite mud and fatigue, all trudged the four miles to Driel with light hearts if somewhat heavy footsteps. Until now I had always thought exaggerated these scenes on the cinema-screen, depicting the staggering and stumbling of worn-out men, but now I found myself behaving in exactly that manner . . . [Some hours later in Nijmegen] Despite my fatigue I felt as I sat down to the meal they provided . . . and thought back on to the past remembering all the acts of heroism and unselfishness I had seen—I felt as I sat there what a proud and privileged thing it is to be a SOLDIER.'

EPILOGUE

The rest could make up a second book: a book with more detail, more examples of personal courage, more names of men and army units; a book which would show that the part played by many who are not named here was just as important as that of those who are; a book about the hundreds of airborne troops who remained behind on the north bank after the perimeter was evacuated and who later returned to the liberated south with the help of the Dutch Resistance movement; a book about the Germans' fear that the Allies would try again to enter Germany round the north end of the Siegfried Line, a fear which led to the German decision to construct a defence line along the River Yssel as an extension of the Siegfried Line and which meant that shortly after 26 September the entire civil population had to leave Arnhem; a book about the battered and deserted city which was plundered by Germans until the end of the war; a book about the members of the Dutch Resistance groups who saw and, sometimes openly, sometimes in secret, did their job when the air-landings began on 17 September; a book with the tales of those, whether British soldiers or Dutch civilians, who were present at Arnhem; a book, in short, which would record everything that has not been narrated here. And all that has not been told, not because it is unimportant but because it might confuse the picture as a whole, the present book being an attempt to present such a picture—and to put an end, with the aid of facts, to the betrayal myth. This attempted analysis, this reckoning is dedicated to the memory of those who lie buried in the little green cemetery with the 1,500 white headstones at Oosterbeek. They fought, hungered, thirsted and died perhaps without realising fully the purpose of it all. They were only obeying the command of a superior, some cursing, some praying. But it was also with their lives that our freedom was bought. The names of many of them will be known to us as long as those stones in Oosterbeek stand. Others we shall never know. On their head-stones only three words are chiselled: an epitaph which is more than the bare statement, 'unknown soldier', more than the token of a vain attempt to identify their remains. These three words are a comforting reassurance for those who did not see son, husband or father again after Arnhem, and for countless others who have scarcely, if at all, heard of Arnhem. They are: 'Known unto God'.

SOURCES

PUBLISHED

'Albrecht' Telegrams. (An investigation based on the *original telegrams* from the Dutch espionage group with the code name 'Albrecht'; a book about this group, entitled *Albrecht meldt zich* (*Albrecht reporting*), appeared after the war.)

Boeree, Lieutenant-Colonel Th. A., (rtd). *De Slag bij Arnhem*, N. V. Drukkerij en Uitgeverij voorheen J. Frouws, Ede, 1952.

Boeree, Lieutenant-Colonel Th. A., (rtd). *De Slag van Arnhem en het 'verraad' van Lindemans*. Articles in *Ons Leger*, Nov.–Dec. 1955.

Boeree, Lieutenant-Colonel Th. A., (rtd). *Het mysterie van de Hohenstaufendivisie in de slag bij Arnhem*. Articles in *Ons Leger*, 1958.

Bryant, Sir Arthur, *Triumph in the West*. Collins, London, 1959.

By Air to Battle. The official account of the British First and Sixth Airborne Divisions. His Majesty's Stationery Office, London, 1945.

Club Route in Europe. The Story of XXX Corps in the European Campaign. (Limited edition.) Hanover, 1946.

Command Decisions. Twenty crucial command decisions that decided the outcome of World War II, prepared by the Office of the Chief of Military History, Department of the [United States] Army, from official military documents and combat records. Harcourt, Brace and Company, Inc., New York, 1959.

Essame, Major-General H. *The 43rd Wessex Division at War, 1944–1945*. William Clowes and Sons Ltd, London, 1951.

Gavin, Major-General James M. *Airborne Warfare*. Infantry Journal Press, Washington, 1947.

Heaps, Leo. *Escape from Arnhem*. The Macmillan Company of Canada Ltd, Toronto, 1945.

Hibbert, Christopher. *The Battle of Arnhem*. B. T. Batsford Ltd, London, 1962.

History of 2nd Battalion the Parachute Regiment. Gale and Polden Ltd, Aldershot, 1946.

Horrocks, Lieutenant-General Sir Brian, *A Full Life*. Collins, London, 1960.

Huston, Major James A. *The Air Invasion of Holland;* two articles in *Military Review*, Fort Leavenworth, Kansas, Aug–Sept 1952.

Ingersoll, Ralph. *Top Secret*. Partridge Publications Ltd, London, 1946.

Lipman Kessel, A. W. *Surgeon at Arms.* Heinemann, London, 1958.

Mackay, Major E. *The Battle of Arnhem Bridge.* Article in *Blackwood's Magazine*, Edinburgh, October 1945.

Montgomery, Field-Marshal Viscount. *Normandy to the Baltic.* Hutchinson and Co Ltd, London, 1947.

Pogue, Forrest C. *The Supreme Command.* Office of the Chief of Military History, Department of the Army, Washington, 1954.

Sosabowski, Major-General Stanislaw. *Freely I served.* William Kimber and Co Ltd, London, 1960.

Stainforth, Peter. *Wings of the wind.* Viking Press, London, 1952.

Święcicki, Marck. *With the Red Devils at Arnhem.* Max Love Publishing Co Ltd, 1945.

Urquhart, Major-General R. E. *Arnhem.* Cassell, London, 1958.

Wilmot, Chester. *The Struggle for Europe.* Collins, London, 1952.

Your Men in Battle. The Story of the South Staffordshire Regiment— 1939–1945. Express and Star, Wolverhampton, 1945.

UNPUBLISHED

Bittrich, SS *Gruppenführer und Generalleutnant der Waffen-SS* W. *Answers to a questionnaire compiled by Lieutenant-Colonel Th. A. Boeree* (rtd).

Boeree, Lieutenant-Colonel Th. A., (rtd). *Correspondence and conversations with British and German officers and NCOs not named in the present list of sources.*

Harzer, *Obersturmbannführer* Walter. *Battle report and personal correspondence on the part played by the Hohenstaufen Division in the Battle of Arnhem.*

Krafft, SS Sturmbannführer Sepp, *Report addressed to Himmler personally.*

Oberkommando der Luftwaffe. *Secret reports on the Allied air-landings, September–October 1944.*

Payton-Reid, Lieutenant-Colonel R. *Supplementary notes to an account by Lieutenant-Colonel Th. A. Boeree (rtd). of the fighting at Arnhem by the 7th Battalion of the KOSB.*

Rauter, *Höherer SS- und Polizeiführer und General der Waffen-SS* Hans Albin. *Report compiled by Lieutenant-Colonel Th. A. Boeree, who also had personal talks with Rauter in the latter's cell after the war.*

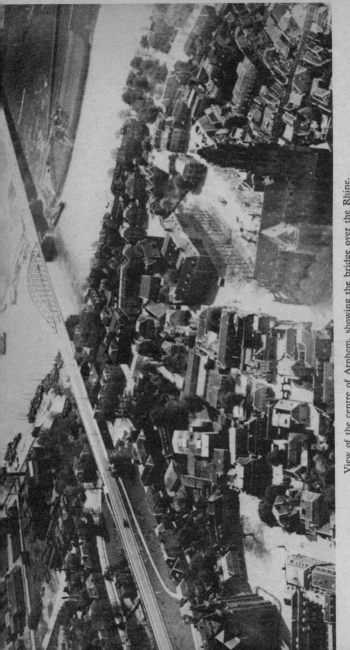

View of the centre of Arnhem, showing the bridge over the Rhine.

Field artillery and machine-guns near the bridge over the Waal at Nijmegen, where American parachute troops had jumped simultaneously with the Arnhem landings.

Below: A composite aerial photograph of the Polish landing zone taken on 20 October 1944, when all positions had long been abandoned (cf Map 9). The numbers refer to positions occupied by units of the 4th Parachute Brigade in the period of 18–20 September 1944. 1. A Coy., 7th KOSB; 2. B Coy., 7th KOSB first position; 3. Do., second position; 4. C Coy., 7th KOSB; 5. D Coy., 7th KOSB; 6. HQ and HQ Coy., 7th KOSB; 7 and 8: parachutes and gliders, respectively (see also inset); 9. Arnhem–Amsterdam road on which 10th Parachute Btn had taken up position; 10. Ede–Arnhem railway line; A: wood where Lt-Col Dobie's battalion took up position for the night 17–18 September 1944; B: German AA gun positions.

Aerial photograph, taken by the RAF after the battle, of the outskirts of Arnhem where the four parachute battalions made a vain attempt to break through to Frost's battalion at the bridge (see also maps 11 and 12).

A six-pounder in action in the vicinity of Arnhem.

Street fighting scene in Oosterbeek.

Street fighting scene in Oosterbeek.

INDEX